Billy Scarlet

An Odyssey

Written by

Savannah J. Parker and Zeke Parker

Ink Smith Publishing

www.ink-smith.com

ISBN: 978-1-939156-14-3

Ink Smith Publishing

P.O Box 1086

Glendora CA

"For everyone who helped us get this far. Also for Terry "Perk" Perkins who was always there to help work out the kinks."

Billy Scarlet

An Odyssey

Chapter
One

Of all the people that fate could have chosen for this story it chose me, the bastard child of a pirate and a governor's daughter.

You see, my father was a pirate named Billy Scarlet. His rightful surname is unknown, I guess. He took on the name Scarlet for one reason and one reason only. Sometimes I think that the reason he did it was to mess up my life, but no, he took on the name Scarlet long before I was born. He's called Scarlet because that is the color of his eyes, and I was scarred by that in two ways. For starters I got the name, which meant that everyone knew he was my father, but worst of all, I got the eyes. I was told that my mother couldn't keep me after she saw me. I betrayed everything she had worked so hard to hide. If I had've gotten blue eyes like her then she would have kept me, but when all was said and done I was too much of a giveaway to who my father was and heaven forbid she get disgraced for it all.

Before she gave me away to a church on an island in the Barbados that took on orphans, she gave me a name. That name was Sabilla or well, Billy Scarlet, then she left me to deal. The head mistress of the church, Mistress Lora, told me that my mother said that she hoped that we would meet again someday. Personally, I never cared to see someone who birthed me, but didn't care enough about me to raise me.

At the church there were about thirty other kids. The people that worked at the church tried to teach all of us things like manners and how to be ladies and gentlemen. Most of the kids did pretty good, but there were some exceptions. Among them were me, a boy named Davy Mitchems and a girl named Clara Honeycut.

None of us could stay out of trouble. We could never keep our minds on what we were doing. No matter what we did or how hard we tried, we always had our heads in the clouds, as Mistress Lora would say.

It wasn't our fault really. There were enough distractions to feed our imaginations was all. You see, the church was in a harbor and there were men coming off of warships all the time, and they would tell us stories of their adventures and their lives at sea. After hearing the stories all we could do was sit and daydream about living as sailors.

All the three of us could think about was a life at sea. Though, it wasn't normal for women to be on board a ship. However, me and Clara wanted to see what life on a ship was like, and we were always getting in trouble for it. As a matter of fact, the way that the three of us became friends was we met in the room that the church ladies would put us in if we got in trouble. They said that young ladies had no business thinking about living on ship full of men. It was improper for women to live among men in such a way. Women were supposed to be mothers and keepers of the house, not sailors. It was not at all how ladies should act and we needed to get it out of our heads, as we were told daily by Mistress Lora. We tried for a while to act like proper young ladies, but that didn't work for us at all, so it was off to the room with us, more often than not.

I spent about half of my childhood in that room and the other half I spent doing things to get put into that room. I couldn't believe that they kept putting me in there, because such a punishment never stopped me from getting in trouble. It's not that I meant to get in trouble, it was just that I would sit and stare into the harbor while I was supposed to be in class or doing chores and I was never alone at doing this. Either Clara or Davy would be with me every time, but a lot of the time it was all three of us.

The room was nothing but a dark little closet. There was one window and one door and nothing else but a few long forgotten spider webs that hung limply from the ceiling. The window gave us a good view of the harbor which kind of defeated the purpose of putting us in the room in the first place. Mistress Lora put us in the room to keep us from thinking up crazy ideas about going to sea, but all we could do in the room was stare down into the harbor below.

Me, Clara and Davy spent at least two hours a day, four to six days a week in that room. But I didn't mind being in the room with them because they were two of the three people that would look me in the eye for more than a few seconds. The fact that I was so different never bothered them in the slightest way. Even when we first started getting to know each other it didn't startle them at all, like it did with just about everybody else, but we had been very young and it seems that children accept things better when they are younger than they do as they grow up.

The third person that never seemed to be bothered by my eyes, was an old man that worked for the church, named Garth McHale. He was a Scottish man and he was like a father to me. As a matter of fact he was the closest thing to a father that the three of us ever had. He was an older man who was slick bald and he had a crescent shaped scar on his left cheek. I had asked him about the scar once and he told me that it was a long story that even he could not fully explain and all he could tell me was the he had not been hurt when he got it. This confused me, but I pushed no further.

As I said before, I didn't mind spending time with any of them, but there was one person that I couldn't spend more than ten seconds with without getting into a fight with. Whether it was a fist fight or a word fight, we would go at each other every time we were around each other. This person was a girl named

3

Lartha Caine. She seemed to have been put onto this earth to make my life miserable, but then again she probably thought the same thing about me. I know that mistress Lora did. She actually told me that once. I have learned to take insults without being bothered. That was just something that I had to do to survive. One thing that I learned was that in such an age, if one was the child of a pirate, they had to grow up tough, otherwise growing up was not an option.

Now I suppose that I'll let the story begin. I would say that I'll begin telling the story, but for a story such as this it will have to begin itself. It's not something that can be told in such a way as other stories, because no one ever told it. The story told itself long before this beginning. You'll see what I mean if you care to continue.

Chapter
Two

"Get up Billy," Came the always perky voice of Clara Honeycut.

"No." I moaned and pulled the covers over my head.

"Come on Billy," Came the slightly changing voice of Davy Mitchems. "Mistress Lora is going to be making the morning sweep soon, and if you're not up you'll get in trouble."

I sat up. "And if you're in here we'll get in trouble anyway. Besides, all that she would do is throw me in the room."

"Yea," Davy walked over to the door. "But today is Wednesday and you haven't got in any trouble yet this week, and I don't think that you should start off the day by getting put into the room."

"Well, I can't very well get dressed with you in here," I told him.

"I'm going," He opened the door and looked out to make sure that the coast was clear, then looked back at us and smiled before disappearing down the hall.

Now I'll take a minute to tell you what Davy and Clara looked like. Davy had big brown eyes, thick, wavy, light brown hair, a dimple in his chin and his lips always reminded me of a baby doll's.

I always thought that Clara was very pretty. She had curly, dark blond hair, honey, gold eyes, fair skin, and a light sprinkle of freckles across her nose. She was the daughter of a lady of the night, who didn't want to keep her. I never was able to see why someone wouldn't want to have Clara around. Though, her mother didn't want her and she had no idea who her father was, she was always trying to look on the bright side of things, even when me and Davy were sitting around feeling sorry for ourselves.

"Billy, get up." Clara pulled the covers off of me causing them to flutter to the floor. They just laid there as if by pulling them off of me, she had awakened them for a moment, then they fell back into a deep slumber.

"Fine." I got up out of bed, stepped over the slumbering heap of covers, and went over to the mirror. Mistress Lora said that it was vane to stare at oneself in the mirror, as I did every morning, but for some reason I would look at myself to see if I had changed in the night.

People told me that I was pretty, but I never would believe them. I had blondish red hair, full, but small lips and fair skin. Now that may sound like I was pretty, but then I add the red eyes, and not just regular red, but scarlet red. It scared a lot of people when they looked me in the eye, so a lot of the ladies at the church would avoid my gaze. I knew my eyes made me a misfit, but it did help me to know who I could trust. I always knew I could trust someone if they would look me in the eye for more than a few seconds, but that didn't help the fact that I was different from everyone else and different meant dangerous.

I would wish on things like stars and dandelions, and every wish would be for my eyes to change colors. Sometimes I would even sneak off to the altar in the church and pray that I would someday be pretty, but I never saw any changes in my appearance. I so badly wanted to look like everyone else. I wanted to have green, blue, or brown eyes like all the other girls, but alas it was not to be.

I quickly got dressed, washed my face and pulled my hair back, then I turned to Clara. "Am I presentable?"

"Well enough," she answered.

Just then, Mistress Lora burst through the door.

"Sabilla, why isn't your bed made?" she asked.

I winced and looked down at the floor. Mistress Lora always had a way of making anyone feel small and powerless. She towered above me in an, almost queen like manner, and I knew there was no way that I could reason my way out of getting in trouble. "I have no excuse."

"Very well," she said. "I'll have mercy on you since you haven't gotten into any trouble all week, so far. Make it up, now."

I breathed a sigh of relief, swept my covers up off the floor, and made it up as fast as I could. Once I was done, I turned back to face Mistress Lora, feeling grateful and yet, very surprised. She had never been merciful on me in such a situation, but I wasn't going to mention it.

"Very good," she nodded and proceeded to scan the room as if it might have some offending dust speck hiding somewhere in one of the corners.

Mistress Lora was a tall, thin lady with fair skin, and silvery hair that she always kept in a bun on top of her head. Not one hair ever seemed to be out of place. She didn't seem to be the kind of lady that would run a place like the church. She seemed more like she would belong in a royal court somewhere, giving people orders and constantly making everyone around her nervous, though she did the last bit anyway. I always wondered what had made her want to take care of children like us, but I never would have been brave enough to ask such a bold question.

"Come along girls," she said. "Go ahead and get your breakfast, then get to your studies and chores."

The two of us walked out of the room and down the narrow, stone hallway.

The whole church was built out of these huge, gray stones. At times I would pretend that it was a castle. Sometimes Clara would join me, but most of the time she would just laugh and shake her head. Davy on the other hand would pretend with me almost all the time. One time he called me princess, but

I told him not to. I know that he was just being nice, but I didn't like the idea of being a princess. I didn't like the idea of having all sorts of fancy things and getting everything that I ever wanted. I never wanted to be a princess or to have a perfect life and that's a good thing, because that's not what I would ever get. I had always thought that it would be much more fun to be a knight, or shield maiden, in my case. I never wanted to be the damsel in distress who needed the knight to come save her. I wanted to be the one to fight a battle and save a kingdom from certain death. Clara said that I had read to many books, but I could tell that she liked the idea too. If she hadn't liked the idea she would not have added to the stories that I would come up with, as often as she had.

It seemed odd to me, but sometimes when I would pretend, I could swear that I had done what I was playing like I was doing, at some point before. Davy and Clara would tell me that it sounded a lot like a book that we had read, or something, but neither of them could ever name the book, or say when we read it. I just tried to brush it off, on most occasions, but there was an overwhelming feeling in me at those times that made me sure that I had done that. To make it even more odd, I would have dreams of such battles and there was always a man there with me. Most of the time I would not be able to see his face, other times I would forget it right after I woke up. I had even spoke his name once in the dream, but no matter how long and hard I tried to remember it, I never could. I could only remember that it was similar to James, but that wasn't quite it.

I was brought out of my thoughts by Clara speaking.

"I wonder if Mistress Lora is okay today," Clara said.

"Why?" I asked.

"Well for starters, she didn't punish you for not having your bed made."

"Maybe she knew it was you who pulled the covers off of me and threw them in the floor."

She gave me a cold, yet slightly amused, stare. "Still, you have to admit, it's strange."

"I'm fine with it," I told her. "If it keeps me from getting put into the room, then I'm perfectly happy with it. Besides, don't you think we're a bit older for that now?"

She shook her head. "Maybe that's it."

We continued down the hall, until we came to the dining hall. It was a room full of tables and chairs. Neither were polished very well, so it was an art form to sit down without getting splinters in your behind, but it was an effective way of teaching us to keep our elbows off the table while we ate.

There were three stained glass windows on each wall and at the front of the room there was the door to the kitchen, which is where we went to get our food.

No matter what we had for breakfast there were always eggs to go with it. There were about eighty laying hens that roamed around the church yard. Each of the hens would lay at least one egg a day, sometimes two. I knew because picking up eggs was one of the many chores that me and Davy had to do every day. If we didn't do it, we would be up to our elbows in eggs in a day or two.

Me and Clara walked over to the kitchen and got our plates. It was always really warm in the kitchen and in the winter time we would go in there to warm up, though on a day like that one, it was hard to stand in the kitchen for more than a few minutes. It was a wonder that the ladies who cooked could stand it.

We walked out of the kitchen, having broken a sweat in the few minutes we had been in there, and headed over to the table that we always sat at. In the far left corner of the room sat the smallest table in the dining hall. That was our table.

We picked our way through the jumbled tables. Some of them were pretty close together, so we had to turn at odd angles to be able to get in between them. That was not bad though. The worst part was that to get to our table we had to walk past the table that Lartha Caine sat at. As we passed I noticed that she stuck her foot out to trip me. Her flat out rudeness always annoyed me. I so badly just wanted to yell at her to act her age after all we were fifteen, but it would do no good and I knew that better than anyone. I wasn't just upset because she was trying to get on my nerves or hurt me. Honestly I would have been much less angry had she tried to be a little better at being what she was doing. She could have at least been a bit more sneaky. I just stepped right over her outstretched foot. That made her so mad that she kicked me in the back of the knee. I nearly fell, but Clara caught my arm with her free hand. I stood back up, fighting mad, and was about to swing around and break my plate over her head when I heard mistress Lora say, "I saw that Lartha. That's two hours in the room for you."

Lartha scoffed, crossed her arms across her chest and scowled.

I just gave her a mocking smile and walked over to our table. Davy was waiting for us. He just laughed when we sat down.

"What are you laughing about?" I asked.

"Nothing," He shook his head. "I was just wondering what it would've looked like if you had've actually broke your plate over her head."

Davy knew me well enough to know that was what I wanted to do especially since I had said day after day that if she messed with me in the dining hall again I was going to break my plate over her head. I wanted to do it and had many chances, but every time, either Mistress Lora, Clara, or Davy would stop me and most of the time it was because they knew what I was doing.

We ate our food then got to our chores. Me and Davy had to go pick up eggs, and Clara had to help out with the laundry, so we wouldn't see her again until we were in class together.

Me and Davy each got us a bushel basket and started picking up eggs, alongside of a beaten path. The hens always laid their eggs beside the path as if they wanted to make our job easier.

The closer we got to the back of the church, the stronger the smell of the ocean got. We rounded the corner of the church and there it was. The harbor was spread out before us like a painting that had come to life. There were navy ships, merchant ships, fishing boats, and all other kinds of ships that we weren't sure what they were used for. Salt air blew across us, and every story that I had been told, about the ocean, flew through my mind. The good, the bad, and the enchanting alike, came to my mind. It was completely dazzling.

"Imagine the adventures that we could have on a ship like that," Davy pointed to one of the navy ships that had *H.M.S. Victory* written on the back of it.

"Ships are fun, but all the same, very dangerous," Mr. McHale had walked up behind us without us knowing.

"Were you ever a sailor?" I asked him.

"Yes my dear, I was," he answered.

"You never told us that," Davy said.

"Well lad, you never asked." He laughed a little.

"Did you have a lot of adventures?" I asked.

He looked off into the distance, as if he could see all the things that he had done at sea, playing out on the horizon. "Yes I had many adventures. They were the kind that most people would never believe, even if I told them about it."

"You know that we would believe you," I told him.

"Yes my dear, I know," he nodded, then said in a voice that was so quiet that I could hardly hear him, "You would, because you were there."

I looked over at Davy, but it was obvious that he had not heard what Mr. McHale had said.

"I have a feeling that you, Clara and Davy here are going to have adventures of your own, pretty soon and if you do you'll need help on that adventure." He looked down at me and smiled as if he knew I had heard him.

"What do you mean?" Davy asked.

"I wrote a book about my time at sea," Mr. McHale answered. "It has answers to the questions that you might ask when on such an adventure. I'll probably give you that book someday."

I suddenly remembered what we were supposed to be doing.

"Oh my goodness," I gasped. "We have to finish picking up these eggs and get to class."

"Well in that case you best hurry along," Mr. McHale laughed. "Them chickens are going to get ahead of you."

Davy moved on along, but I lingered there for a moment.

Mr. McHale looked at me. I could tell that he wanted to say something, but he stopped himself.

"What is it?" I asked.

"You better hurry along. You don't want to get in trouble with the mistress, do you?"

"No sir," I walked on, all the while wondering what he had been about to say.

We hurried up with picking up the eggs headed back inside. As we got to the back door of the kitchen I noticed a dandelion growing next to the path and I picked it. The light, fluffy seed quivered slightly in the breeze. I watched them for a moment, then I made a wish.

Any other time that I wished on a dandelion, I would've wished that my eyes would change colors, but for some reason, that time was different. I whispered my wish, blew all the seeds away, and went inside.

My fate had already been chosen long before, and the path of my life was already set, but I will, for the rest of my life, wonder if it was the wish that caused all that happened next. No matter how long, or how much I wonder, I'll never know if it was the wish or if it was just part of God's plan.

Somewhere in the breeze floated a bunch of dandelion seeds and my words. "I wish that I could have an adventure like Mr. McHale's."

Chapter

Three

The rest of the day went on, as usual. We went to our classes and did our chores, like we always did, and I had almost completely forgotten that I even made the wish.

Late in the evening, we went and had our prayers. I walked slowly down the hall to the sanctuary carrying a small white candle that was lighting the way. I walked down the isle of the church with Davy to my right and Clara to my left. The only light was coming from the candles that we carried. We walked very slowly, but it was no because anybody had told us we had to. No matter how many times we walked through the church in the dark, it was still scary. The ceiling would creek above us as if someone was walking in the attic.

There was the sound of footsteps at the front of the church and we all froze.

"Did you hear that?" I asked.

"It was just one of the other children," Clara said. "We're not the only ones that come in here this time of night."

As we reached the front of the church we noticed that there wasn't anyone else there.

"It's okay," Davy said. "Let's just say our prayers and get to bed."

I sat my candle on the floor and knelt down to pray. "Our Father who art in Heaven," I began. I went on through as I always did. "Forgive us our sin as...." I stopped. I had heard the footsteps again. I looked around and saw nothing, so I got back to my prayers. "As we forgive those who have sinned against us. Lead us not unto temptation, but deliver us from evil. For thine is the kingdom, the power, and the glory, forever. Amen." I nodded and stood up. Clara and Davy did as well. We started to walk out, when I was certain that I saw someone at the window.

"Did you see that?" I asked.

"See what?" Davy cast me an odd glance.

"There was something at the window."

"Don't get so jittery." He laughed. "It's always strange in here at night. Why are you letting it get to you now?"

I just shook my head and walked over to the window. It was open, that in itself was odd enough. I looked out and saw nothing but darkness. I slowly lifted my candle, terrified of what it might reveal. I always had a tendency to panic really bad when I got scared of something in the dark. I didn't mind darkness, but it just seemed that being afraid was intensified when there wasn't enough light.

Clara and Davy stood frozen, watching me. When my candle was high enough I saw a large, dark figure standing not too far away. I screamed, dropped my candle, and fell backwards. The candle went out as soon as it hit the floor.

Clara and Davy ran over to me.

"What was it?" Clara asked.

I looked up at the window and saw the figure, which turned out to be Mr. McHale. I fell back and just laid there.

"What's wrong, Billy?" he asked.

My voice was shaking beyond my control. "Why on earth were you at the window like that?"

"I'm just checking things before lights out. Did I scare you?"

I stood up and nodded. I could not speak, I was shaking all over.

At seeing how frightened I was, Mr. McHale climbed through the window and hugged me. "I'm sorry, dear one." He laughed a little. "I know it's scary in here sometimes in the dark. I thought everyone was already in bed."

He sat down on a bench and pulled me into his lap. I was a little old to sit on anyone's lap, but at the time I had been so scared that I didn't care.

He held me tight and rocked me like he had done when I was little. "There, there now," He whispered. "It's going to be okay." He knew how I got sometimes at night. "You don't have to worry about things in the darkness. It's just like in the day time only without light. I'm not going to let anything hurt you."

I finally stopped shaking and he set me back down. "Are you going to be okay now?"

"Yes sir," I nodded feeling embarrassed. "I'm sorry about that."

"Don't be." He kissed me on the forehead.

Just then, Mistress Lora walked in. "Why are the three of you not in bed yet?"

"We're on our way," Clara said.

Her and Davy started to walk on, but I didn't. "Is it alright if I stay here with Mr. McHale for a while?" I asked the mistress.

She looked at me sternly for a moment, then sighed. "I guess, but don't stay up too late. I don't want you falling asleep during lessons in the morning."

"Yes ma'am."

Mistress Lora led Clara and Davy on down the hall and the room was empty, save for me and Mr. McHale.

He just sat there for a long moment, staring at me and the wall, in turn.

"What is it?" I sat down next to him.

"I was just thinking." He smiled slightly. "Thinking of long ago, of times that you would not remember."

"From before I was born?"

He nodded. It seemed as though he wanted to speak, but even if he was to try, words would not come out.

I wanted to ask questions, but I wasn't sure what to say. Just as I was about to speak he spoke again.

"I was thinking about....... about how much you remind me of someone I once knew."

He had once told me that I reminded him of his daughter, but I didn't want to bring up his family at the time. He had often told me of his wife, Lilliana. He had never told me how or when she had died, but when he did tell me about her he had come so close to tears that I felt bad for having asked him about her. His children lived in several different places and sometimes came to see him at the orphanage. I had met his one of his sons, but had never seen this daughter that I reminded him of.

I watched him stare out the window and somehow I got the feeling that it wasn't his daughter that I was reminding him of that night. Then again, maybe it was, I couldn't really be sure.

"I can feel it in the wind," he whispered.

"What?" I scooted up next to him. It always made the hair on my arm prickle when he talked like that.

"Twelve and fifteen," he muttered. "That's twenty-seven."

I nodded, but I was terribly confused as to what he meant.

"It's about to begin."

"What is?" I asked.

He turned to me and smiled as if he had forgotten that I was in the room with him. "Just another step towards forever." He smiled. That was an answer he often gave when he wasn't sure how else things could be explained, but it

16

was a good enough answer as any. "Don't worry about it." He stood up. "I think it's time you got to bed, don't you?"

"Yes, sir." I nodded.

We walked down the hallway using a lamp that Mr. McHale would keep with him when he was working at night.

We got to the door and he hugged me tight. "You sleep well, little one."

"You too," I told him.

He kissed me on the forehead and walked on down the hall. I watched until I could no longer see the light from his lamp, then I went into to our room, climbed into bed, and pulled the covers over me tight, still feeling his strong embrace.

I fell into a deep sleep. I dreamed of a field of thick green grass, with rolling green hills and there was a boy there that looked like an older version of Davy. We were standing at the top of one of the hills, looking down into a harbor. The harbor looked like our harbor, only there was no church there.

He turned and looked at me. "I heard someone in town say that they were going to build a church here," he said.

"What do you mean?" I asked. "We grew up here."

"This is the first time I've ever been here." He laughed. "And it's the same for you. How can you say we grew up here? You grew up in the courts, with your father."

"Davy, you know I've never met my father," I said.

"Billy, we need to get back to the ship." He took my arm. "This heat must be getting to you."

"The ship?" I looked down into the harbor and saw a large ship with light blue sails. "I'm not going anywhere, Davy, until you tell me what's going on."

All of a sudden, there was a loud blast and the sound of people screaming. It took me a moment, but I soon realized that the blast and the screaming were not in my dream. The screaming was coming from somewhere inside the church.

I sat up and looked around. Clara was already up.

"Billy, get up," she said. "The church is being attacked."

I got out of bed just in time for Mistress Lora to burst through the door.

"Billy, Clara, come with me quickly," she urged.

We didn't argue we just followed her into the hall. She had most of the other kids with her, but I didn't see Davy anywhere.

"What's going on?" someone asked.

"Pirates are attacking the town," Mistress Lora answered. "The church has taken some very bad hits in its support beams. The place is on fire. We have to get out of here. The pirates are invading the town, so we must stay together once we get outside. If something happens to me, all of you need to hide in the woods until things settle down."

She was being surprisingly calm, but I knew that she was only being that way to keep all of the children from panicking.

Despite her efforts to keep us calm, I was very scared. I didn't want anyone to get hurt, I didn't want to think about anything happening to Mistress Lora, and I certainly didn't want to get killed by pirates.

Walking outside was like walking into a nightmare. Everywhere you turned there were houses and fields on fire and people were screaming. The worst part was that you couldn't tell where the screaming was coming from, because the smoke was too thick and the cannon blasts were much too loud.

I looked down the hillside, into the town and I could see the pirates coming ashore. I would hear the cannons blasts coming from down in the harbor. Each blast was followed by some part of the town being engulfed by smoke and flames.

"Do you see Davy anywhere?" Clara asked.

"No," I answered and ran over to Mistress Lora. "Where's Davy?" I asked.

"He went to help Garth get the girls out of the kitchen," she answered. "I guess they're not out yet."

I felt a sudden rush of panic. If they weren't out yet, they may not be coming out. The thought of losing Davy and Mr. McHale was too much for me to handle. I ran over to the back door of the kitchen.

"Billy, no!" Mistress Lora called, but I wasn't going back.

I felt the door. It was warm, but not very hot, so I opened it. Smoke billowed out of the room and into my face, burning my eyes and lungs, but I went in anyway.

"Davy! Mr. McHale!" I called.

"Billy!" Mr. McHale's voice came out of all the smoke. "Where are you?"

"I'm at the back door," I answered.

"Can you see through the smoke?" he asked.

I squinted really hard and I was barely able to see him. "Yes sir," I went over to him and took his hand. I saw that all the kitchen girls were with him and Davy was behind them. "Everybody join hands. Don't get lost."

When we got outside, we saw that the pirates had found the others. Most of the kids had run to the woods, but there were two men dragging Clara and Mistress Lora away.

Mr. McHale pulled a knife from his belt and ran towards the men, followed by me and Davy. Though I had heard many stories, I had never seen Mr. McHale fight before. In all of my life I will never forget how horrible the sight was. He swung the dagger around and stabbed the first man through the heart. He pulled the knife out of the first man and threw it at the second. The blade hit its mark. The man fell to the ground with the knife in his back.

I had never seen anyone get killed, but Mr. McHale killed both of the men and saved both Mistress Lora and Clara, then something terrible happened. I heard the gun fire, but there was only a second between then and the moment that changed my life forever. The stray musket fire struck him in the back and he fell to the ground.

Me, Clara and Davy ran over to him.

"It's going to be okay," I whispered. "Come on let's get him to the doctor."

"No, Billy," he said. "Not this time."

"You'll make it," I cried. "You're going to be just fine."

"Don't cry, Sabilla." He smiled, reached into his jacket pocket, and pulled out a book. "The three of you are going to need this. There is so much that I wish I could tell you, but you will find those things out soon enough. Go and live my children. Your adventure has begun." A smile spread across his face as he breathed has last breath.

Tears poured down my cheeks and through a blur of tears I whispered a prayer. "God receive our beloved Mr. McHale into your kingdom, if for no other reason for the kindness that he's shown to us." That was all that I could say.

Davy patted me on the back. "It's okay," he whispered, but I could tell that he was crying as well and no matter what we tried to tell ourselves we knew that it wasn't okay. Nothing was okay anymore. A part of me died with Mr. McHale. He was the only father any of us had ever known and he was gone. I closed my eyes and tried to think of how he had held me to calm me down only hours before, but all that did was make things more painful.

I cried unstoppable tears for the next hour. The thought of never seeing Mr. McHale again, of never hearing his voice, or having him comfort me after a bad dream, made my heart feel like it had been crushed by the stones of the, now falling in orphanage. When I did stop, I felt like I would never be able to cry again, and I hoped I would never feel like doing so.

We sat outside with Mistress Lora until the sun came up, which wasn't long. By then, the pirates were long gone, but the mark that they left on the town and on our lives, would last for years to come. Houses and roads were destroyed, and the church was crumbling. Mistress Lora was right when she said that the supports had taken some bad hits.

Some men from town helped us dig a grave that was overlooking the harbor, for Mr. McHale. They also made him a head stone with his name carved on it. We had not been the only ones that loved him. He had been very well known across the whole island.

Standing next to his grave made me feel like my life was over, even though he had told us that things were only just beginning. I stood there alone. There was nothing I could say or do. I couldn't cry or smile, so I stood there. I felt like I had aged greatly. Like I was far older than my age could account for.

"I don't know what you meant when you told us that our adventure was just beginning," I whispered. "But I promise, I will do everything I can to live it in a way that would make you proud." In my hand I held a dandelion. "It's just another step towards forever," I whispered and let it fall from my hand and land softly, on his grave. I don't know why I did this, but it just seemed right.

As I walked away, I noticed that Mistress Lora was standing over beside the church. I went over to her and she rubbed her cheeks. Her face was streaked with soot and tears. I don't know why, but I had never thought of Mistress Lora even being able to cry.

"We're going to have to get a new place," she said. "This won't do anymore."

"Are you okay?" I asked.

She didn't bother to answer my question. "Thank you for doing what you did to save the girls last night."

I just nodded and walked over to where Clara and Davy were. The two of them seemed to be discussing something.

"We have to get out of here," Davy said.

Neither me or Clara disagreed. We knew there was nothing left for us, and we felt that we had an obligation to fulfill whatever adventure it was that Mr. McHale had spoken of. Not one of us felt like we could make our way down the hillside, much less on some sort of adventure, but we had to try. Mr. McHale would not have wanted us to sit and do nothing, so we pulled ourselves up and got to work.

The three of us went into the church to see if we could find some clothes, that weren't night clothes. We found each of us a shirt and a pair of pants. Plus, we gathered some things that we might need which wasn't much. All we had was about three feet of rope, a scorched blanket, one silver piece and the book that Mr. McHale had given us. We took our things and headed down to the harbor. The walk was silent except for the sounds of our feet hitting the ground.

"Okay," Davy said, once we were down on the docks. "We make an oath here and now that it's only forward from here. We'll never look back."

"Yes," me and Clara nodded. "Never."

Davy then walked over to a man that was signing people in on a passenger ship that had arrived that morning.

"How much would it cost for us three to get passage on this ship sir?" he asked.

The man looked up at the three of us then said, "There is a ship down that way that's taking on crew members. That would probably be the best bet for you boys."

"Thank you, sir," Davy nodded and we walked down the way that the man had pointed.

"He thought we were boys," Clara said, once we were far enough away that the man couldn't hear us.

"Do we look like boys to you?" I asked Davy.

"Do you really want me to answer that question?" He bit his lip.

I crossed my arms across my chest.

"Fine." He shrugged. "Neither of you look much like girls, when you're dressed like that. As a matter of fact, neither of you look much like girls when you're dressed in normal clothes," He took a few steps backwards as if he were scared that I was going to hit him or something.

"Good," I smiled.

"Good?" Clara asked. "How is that good?"

"It's good that we can pass for boys, so that we can become members of one of these crews," I answered.

"Oh wonderful," Clara smiled. "I'll just be a boy named Clara then?"

"No," I shook my head. "You could be called Clark Honeycut."

We walked over to where there was a crowd of men.

"Get lost," one of the men said to us. "They're taking on deckhands, not ships boys."

Just then, a man in uniform walked over and looked the three of us over, then asked, "Do any of you know anything about life on a ship?"

"We've never been on a ship before, if that's what you mean," I said. "But we have been told about life at sea from some sailors that have come to town."

He never once looked me in the eye, but I could tell that he was listening. "What did these sailors teach you?"

"Mostly how to tie a bunch of different kinds of knots," Davy answered.

"Is that all?" the man asked.

"The three of us know how to read, write and do a little bit of math," Clara told him.

"Well, well," he laughed. "The three of you are just perfect then, aren't you? You are no doubt orphans that think that a life at sea would be really good, but I will tell you this, it isn't as easy as you may think."

"We don't think it's easy at all, sir," I told him. "As a matter of fact, we have very little idea what to expect."

"Very well." He nodded. "I'm in need of three ships boys, as we lost two in our last battle and one was promoted. Come and get signed in."

"I thought you were supposed to ask the captain first," I said.

"Do you see my hat and jacket?" he asked.

The three of us nodded.

"Get used to me giving orders," he said. "You may call me captain Hector."

"Aye, captain." We all saluted.

He just laughed and shook his head.

We walked over to the man that was signing people into the log book. He had been watching us ever since the captain had started talking to us.

Davy told the man his name first, then Clara, but when it came to my turn I got very nervous. With a name like Billy Scarlet I was sure to be the first one thrown off if something were to go wrong. I no longer felt the age that I did earlier. I felt like a frightened child.

"Your name, lad?" the man asked.

I looked over at Clara and Davy. They both looked happy, but I could tell that they were just as worried as I was.

"What is your name lad?" he asked again.

I bit my lip. The noises of the crowd seemed to get louder. I could hear my heart beat in my ears. I didn't want to say my name when I was in a room by myself much, less in front of a crowd of men that I was going to have to sail with.

"What is your name lad?" the man almost yelled. "What are you, a deaf mute?"

With that, I looked the man in the eye and held his gaze, even if he didn't want me to.

"Billy," I told him. "Billy Scarlet."

He coughed, rubbed his forehead, and wrote my name down, all the while mumbling something about how the captain should ask more questions about the men that he lets on board his ship.

I walked over and joined Clara and Davy, at the foot of the gangplank. Had I not been pretending to be a boy I would have taken each of their hands as we walked onto the ship, but as a boy, that wasn't going to work.

I slapped each of them on the back and said, "All aboard you sea rats. We've got a job to do here. We're ships boys now. Come on let's move."

They both laughed a little.

With that the three of us boarded our first ship. All our lives we had been dreaming of having lives at sea, but that first time we got on a ship was more terrifying than we could have imagined.

Even with how nervous I was, I fell in love with the ship right away. And that ship just happened to be the *H.M.S Victory*, the ship that we had looked down at from the church hill with Mr. McHale the day before, so somehow I knew that we had done the right thing, by getting on board this ship. I just knew that it was the right one for us.

I stood there for a minute just staring into the riggings. Just then, three boys came over to us. One on them, kind of, snickered at the way I was just staring, which embarrassed me only slightly. I felt redness creep up my cheeks, but I did my best to suppress my blush.

The one that laughed at me was really small, with a stern face and mousey, shoulder length hair. The second one was tall and thin with big, brown eyes, a pointy nose and long, curly black hair. The third one was a little taller than Davy. He had broad shoulders, a round face, green eyes, long red hair and a dimple in his chin.

"Hey," the tall, thin one said. "My name's Simon. This here," he motioned toward the small boy. "Is Danny and this," he motioned to the broad one. "Is Henry."

"I'm Billy," I told him. "And this is Davy and Clark."

"Have y'all ever sailed before?" Henry asked. He had a thick Irish accent.

"No," Davy answered.

"Just stick close to us then," Simon said. "We'll help y'all out and teach ya everything ya need ta know."

They seemed to be really nice, but I was still nervous. I couldn't help but notice the looks that the crewmen kept giving me. That let me know that I should watch my step because by their looks, they knew who my father was and they didn't like him one bit. I knew that if they ever came up with an excuse to throw me over board they would do it without a second thought.

It wasn't long before we set sail and for the first hour or so, I just stood holding into the rail. The sway of the ship was just too strange. I wasn't sick, but I couldn't walk straight.

"Are you okay?" A man came over to me and asked.

I looked up at him. He was wearing a uniform, but he wasn't the captain. He had blue eyes, blond hair and a rather pleasant face. He was over all a very good looking young man.

When our eyes met he just shook his head. "You're the Scarlet boy aren't you?"

"Yes, sir," I nodded. "I'm Billy Scarlet."

"I'm midshipman, Patrick Arthur," he said. "Watch your step around here young Scarlet. We're on this venture going after pirates. Most of the men on this ship won't trust you. Some of them won't care either way, but most of them won't trust you until you prove yourself. As I said, watch your step. A lot of these men have met your father and, I don't think that I really have to tell you this, but your father is not exactly the best man in the world." With that, he walked away.

I knew that none of this would be easy. The last thing that I needed was midshipman, Patrick Arthur discouraging me. I knew that he was only telling me what to expect, but that didn't make me feel any better about it all. It was then that I decided that I would prove to all of them that I was a good sailor, that I, Billy Scarlet, was a good man. (In a sense.) So I took to watching how things were done and memorizing it. I even paid close attention at meals to see how the other men ate and drank. I even hit my biscuit on the table, like they did.

"Why do they hit their biscuits on the table like that?" Clara asked Simon.

"Bugs," he answered with a mouth full of food. "They do it to get the weevils out of it."

Clara bit her lip and swallowed hard.

"Oh come on, Clark." Henry laughed. "It ain't all that bad. Just be glad ya got a meal."

I looked over at Davy. He looked like he felt just as out of place as me and Clara did. The three of us had been taught manners ever since we were old enough to learn them, and now we were supposed to fit in here and let's just say that our manners would seem strange on a ship full of salty sailors like these men.

I just acted like all the other men, and tried my best to stay out of everyone's way when it came to most things.

That night, the other boys showed us where we were supposed to sleep. There were three hammocks. Me and Clara shared a hammock and Davy shared a hammock with Danny. We were assigned that way because of the times that we would be going on watch. The first watch was Simon and Henry, the second watch was me and Clara, and the third watch was Davy and Danny.

As I slept that first night, I dreamed of the night before, the night that Mr. McHale had died. It all played out the same, for the most part. The only thing that was different was that right after he died I heard a man behind me laughing. I turned around and saw a man blow the smoke from the barrel of his pistol. He was a pirate. I could that just by looking at him. He had dark hair that was pulled back in a braid. He had a dark tan and he wore a black pants and a scarlet jacket.

"Don't cry my child," he said. It was then that I noticed his scarlet eyes. He was my father.

I tried to do something, anything, but no matter what I tried I could not move. I tried, with all my might, to wake up, but I was stuck there in that dream, at that moment. There was nothing I could do.

"Billy," came Simon's voice. "Billy, wake up."

I sat up quickly.

"You all right?" he asked.

"Yea," I nodded.

"It y'all's watch now." He climbed into his hammock.

Me and Clara got up and went on deck. The night was calm and cool. A soft breeze was blowing causing the riggings to make an eerie clinking noise. I could also hear the sound of the flag and the sails flapping.

I breathed in a deep breath of salt air. I had heard so many stories of horrible battles at sea, so many bloody tales of men dying, but that night made many of them hard to believe.

I stood there trying to forget my nightmare, wishing that I had Mr. McHale there to tell me that everything was going to be okay. I sighed and looked around the deck. It was then that I noticed a man walking around, talking to each of the other men. I watched him until he got to me, then I stood up as straight as I could.

"Name and rank?" he said, in a low tone.

"Billy Scarlet, ships boy, sir," I answered.

He looked me over. "Age?"

"Fifteen, sir," I answered, but I knew that it was a mistake to say that I was a fifteen year old boy. If I were a boy, my looks would say that I was about twelve.

He nodded. "Carry on." With that, he walked away.

He was a quite dashing man. He wasn't a very tall or broad man, but he had an air about him that made him seem like the very definition of the word confidence. He was around six feet tall with long, dark, curly hair and best that I could tell his eyes were honey gold. None of that really struck me as strange, but there was something about the way he smiled and the way that he walked that reminded me of Mr. McHale. I spent the rest of my watch, wondering who he was.

Despite my curiosity and fear of more nightmares, I was very glad to get back to my hammock, but it seemed that right as I laid down and closed my eyes, it was time to get up again.

We got up and went to breakfast. I just followed the other boys because I still hadn't gotten used to the ship yet and I didn't know my way around very well.

As we came into the dining room (I was sure that it had a different name on a ship) I looked around to see if I could find the man that I had seen on deck the night before. I didn't see him until I sat down. He was sitting at a table across the room from us. He sat next to Patrick Arthur.

"That man over there," I said to Simon. "Who is he?"

"That man?" he nodded in the man's direction.

I nodded.

"He's one of the middies," Simon answered. "The captain's been talkin' about promotin' him ta lieutenant. His name's Apollo McHale. Why you wonderin'?"

"I just saw him on deck during my watch last night is all," I told him.

"Yea, he always patrols the deck at night."

I scooped some food into my mouth. It was some sort of meat stew. It tasted pretty good, but I had tasted much better things before.

Clara did the same and then said, "This stuff is pretty good."

"Aye," Apollo said in a way that made him look more arrogant than he was tall. "The old dog didn't die in vain did he?"

"Oh God," Clara put her hand over her mouth and I was sure that she was fixing to throw up.

Apollo just laughed.

I glared at him from my seat, but it was no use. He just smiled as if he knew some deep dark secret about me. Something about him made me so angry, but I didn't say anything. I just sat there.

I knew that he knew that I was the child of a pirate. That was no secret to anyone on this ship, or anywhere I went. The only other secret that I had was the fact that I was a girl and I was almost certain that besides me, only Clara and Davy knew that, but then again, I said almost.

Chapter
Four

Later on that day, we were all on deck doing our jobs. Us ships boys were mostly watching all the other men doing their jobs, so we could learn how to do them.

The captain was walking across the deck with a man that I guessed was the first mate. He was a tall skinny man, wearing black pants and a blue coat. He had dark hair that was pulled back into a braid. He had rather defined jaw bones, a pointy nose and green eyes that stared at the world from behind thick gold rimmed glasses.

"We need more lookouts in the foretop," the skinny man said with a surprisingly deep voice.

"How many do we have up there now?" Captain Hector asked.

"One, sir," the man answered.

"You," Captain Hector pointed to me. "What's your name, lad?"

"Ships boy Billy Scarlet, sir," I told him.

"Well, ships boy Scarlet," he said. "Go to the foretop and assist the lookout."

"Aye sir," I nodded, then looked over at Danny who pointed to the main mast. I nodded, went over and began to climb up the rope ladder.

I had known what a foretop was, I just wasn't rightfully sure where it was, and I was very glad that Danny had shown me.

I reached the top and went pull myself up onto the platform, when my grip slipped. For a moment I was sure that I was fixing to die, but someone grabbed my arm and pulled me up.

"I've never done it before, but I'm quite certain that a fall from this height could be quite fatal, no matter how tough you are," came the unmistakable voice of Apollo McHale.

"I was told to come up here and assist you," I said.

"Good," he nodded. "But I don't think you'd be much good if you fell and became nothing but a greasy spot on the deck, down there."

I sat down and for the next while we sat in silence. When Apollo spoke it gave me a little bit of a start.

"No one can hear us from up here so I believe that it's safe for me to go ahead and tell you that I know your secret."

"About my father?" I asked, trying to be calm, but in truth I was as jittery as a frightened bird.

"Not about your father," he scoffed. "Everybody on this bloody ship knows who your father is. Matter of fact, he's one of the men we're hunting, but that's beside the point. The point is, I know about your....how would I put it...........femaleness."

I jumped to my feet and stepped away from him. "How? How could you know anything about me?"

"I had been in your town for a few days," he answered. "I was looking for....well......family I'd suppose you'd say. Anyway, I had seen you at that church orphanage. I saw both you and your friend Davy. The two of you were picking up eggs. Now, I don't know where you got Clark from because, I don't remember seeing him there, but I do know that you're not the son of a pirate, but in fact, the daughter of one."

"So, now you're going to report me to the captain and get me thrown off, aren't you?" I crossed my arms across my chest, mostly glad that he didn't know that Clara was a girl.

"No." He shook his head. "Though I may get in trouble for it I'm not going to turn you in. I want to give you lessons."

"On what, how to be a blooming idiot?"

"No, I think you've got that down pretty well."

I just shook my head. "On what then?"

"On being a boy," he answered.

So, for the next hour or so he taught me how to walk and talk, like a man. He kept saying things like, "No, not quick steps, but long strides,", "No, no stop. Do it again," and "Well one thing you got going for you is you don't wiggle your ass when you walk."

At that, I blushed and bit my lip.

"One more thing," he said. "If you hear a comment like that don't bite your lip that way. I know that for the first while you're going to blush about it, but don't go overboard with it. If you do you'll get teased unmercifully by the other boys."

"Well, won't they be the same way?"

He looked skeptical. "Not the ones that have been here for a long time. They're used to that kind of thing."

After a little while, Apollo was called back down to the deck and the ships boys were sent up with me. All of them were laughing and joking. Even Clara was making jokes about weird, boy things.

"Ya know, I heard that we're gonna get liberty in Puerto Rico in a couple o' weeks," Henry said.

"What's liberty?" Clara asked.

"It's where the whole crew gets ta go ashore and do whatever they want," Simon answered.

"I'm sure we'll have plenty o' men in the bars an' whore houses." Henry laughed.

"And where do you plan ta go?" Danny asked.

"I'm gonna get decked out like a true sailor," Henry answered. "I'm gonna get an earring and a tattoo."

"A tattoo of what?" Danny asked.

"A topless mermaid, like Arnold's got." Henry smiled all boyish like.

"He ain't got no mermaid." Simon laughed. "It's just a naked woman. Besides, the day that you get a tattoo's gone be the day I sprout wings."

"Then ya better learn ta fly pretty soon," Henry told him. "And laugh all ya want now, but I'm gone get one no matter what you say."

"I'll get one too," I couldn't believe the words came out of my mouth. "The same kind."

Davy and Clara looked at me with a look of panic on each of their faces. At first I thought that they were going to say that if I was getting one they would too, but them and the other boys said no, so I was stuck with getting an earring and a tattoo of a naked mermaid.

"Do what ya want," Henry said. "Me an' Billy'll be the real men."

'Oh joy,' I thought. 'I'll be a real man after this. Apollo should be proud.'

All the others just shook their heads, as if we were stupid and I couldn't argue with them. I guess that I was trying so hard to fit in that I got a little carried away on that point.

I was going to do it, though. I had made a point of telling them about and it seemed that something deep inside of me thought getting a tattoo was a good idea. The heat must have been getting to me that day, because in any normal frame of mind I would not have agreed to something so stupid, but I certainly wasn't going to back out at that point.

'I must remember that I'm going to have to act like a girl again someday,' I thought. 'This may be a good thing for pretending to be a boy, but girls don't get tattooed.' I pushed it out of my mind and just figured that I would get the tattoo in a place that I could easily hide it.

"Well, I'm gonna go see what goes on in one of those whore houses," Simon told us. "All these men are always talkin' about goin' ta them places and I wanna find out why."

That got me wondering about it, as well. I suppose that it's normal for a kid to think about that kind of thing, but I had never been told about that kind of thing. Of course I had wondered about it before. I thought for a moment about asking someone, but then I just figured it was best not to worry about it. I was fifteen and quite old enough, for a girl, to know about it, but something stopped me from asking.

"You're crazy." Davy laughed.

"Do you know what goes on in one of 'em?" Danny asked.

Davy shook his head.

"Then come with me," Simon said.

"Okay," Davy shrugged. "I mean, it can't be that bad."

"I ain't doin' it," Clara wrinkled her nose and something made me think that she knew what happened, but wasn't going to tell.

"Why?" Simon asked.

"I know more than you do about that kind of thing and I really don't want to get into it."

"What do you know about it?" Danny asked, seeming a little too happy about the idea of learning about anything on the subject.

"I'm not about to tell you. If you want to learn then you have to find out yourselves. I'm not going to tell you and I'm not going to go there with any of you."

"Where you gone go then?" Danny asked.

"I'll go watch Billy and Henry get tattooed," She gave me an odd look.

'Ha ha ha,' I thought. 'Laugh it up all you want. I just might make you get one too if you come with us, so you better watch it.'

"Won't the captain get mad if you get all tattooed up like that?" Danny asked.

"Look 'round the ship an' ask that question again," Simon said.

"Yeah," Henry nodded. "Just 'bout every man on the ship has at least one tattoo."

"They are grown men though," I added, hoping that might sway them.

Henry cast me an odd glance. "Yer close enough ta bein' a man that he won't care. Yeah, yer old ta be a ships boy, but that can work ta be good for ya. If ya come with me ta do it, he won't care near as much 'cause yer older. Ya ain't thinkin' 'bout backin' out are ya?"

"No," I said defensively.

"Good," he nodded.

It wasn't long after that that the supper bell rang. We raced down the mast and went to the galley. (As I found out it was called.)

That evening I sat next to a large man who spoke with an odd accent. Something about him was very creepy to me.

"'Ello, laddy," he said. "Wot's yer nem, there?"

"Billy," I answered. "And yours?"

"Ya can just call me Averett, laddy," he said. "Yer new 'ere ain't cha?"

I nodded.

"Yer gone get plenty 'o 'elp 'round 'ere, don't ya worry 'bout that." He nudged the man that was sitting next to him and they laughed in a way that I didn't like.

Just then Apollo walked up behind Averett. "Hey, lay off, Averett. These boys ain't interested in the likes of you and your gang of draggin' ass bastards." I noticed the way that Apollo's accent slipped into what almost sounded like a country Scottish, when he was angry.

"Wot's it ta you, middy?" Averett asked. "We's just pokin' fun at 'em, and you's just pokin' yer nose in stuff that's none of yer business."

"You ain't got no business pokin' nothin'," Apollo told him, his accent getting stronger the farther he went. "And unless you want me reportin' ya to the captain ya best lay off the boys."

Averett stood up. He was a good head taller than Apollo, but Apollo wasn't about to back down. He looked over and gave Patrick a small nod, and Patrick left the room.

"Well if it means so much to ya then I'm sorry," Averett said in a mocking way.

"I'm serious, Averett," Apollo growled. "If ya lay a hand on any one of those boys I'll see to it that you get as many lashes as the lad feels like ya should."

"Will ya then, middy?" Averett laughed. "Wot 'bout if I lay a hand on you?" He swung his bulky fist and caught Apollo in the jaw.

Before any more punches could be thrown Patrick came back in with captain Hector.

"What's this?" Captain Hector roared. "Are you stirring up trouble again, Averett?"

"No, sir." Averett huffed. "It was that piece o' shit, McHale."

"Oh really?" Captain Hector asked. "I only see one man here who has taken a blow and it's not you."

"It's only self-defense sir," Averett whined.

"Against what?" Apollo rubbed his jaw, his accent now back sounding more British. "Words? Captain, all I did was tell him to leave the ships boys alone."

I wondered why, when he was mad his accent changed, but when he was speaking to the captain, his accent went back to normal.

At that comment, I could have sworn that I saw steam come out of the captain's ears. "Messing with the ships boys again, are you, Averett?"

"No sir," Averett stammered. "I was.......well.......I was simply......."

"Save your strength!" the captain yelled. "You'll need it after fifteen lashes and getting put in the brig for a week on a diet of bread and water. Somebody get this piece of trash out of my sight."

Some men that were with the captain drug Averett out and the rest of the men got back to eating. I did as well, but it was hard to eat and listen to the sound of Averett screaming from his beating.

I wasn't sure what the whole big outburst had been about, but it seemed that Averett must have hurt some ships boys before.

I looked over at Apollo. He sat back down in his usual seat. His jaw was bruised, but he didn't seem too bothered by the pain. He just sighed and started talking to Patrick about something. I couldn't hear what they were saying, but he glanced my way more than once. I felt bad that he had gotten hurt because of me, but he didn't say anything to me about it, so I figured it was best to just to not mention what had happened. Apollo knew what he was doing, and it wouldn't help him if I got in the way. I had not been the only ships boy that he was protecting, so I didn't say anything.

After that day, I was very cautious about who I sat next to in the galley. Most of the time I would sit with the midshipmen at dinner. Sometimes they would eat in the midshipman's berth, so I would just not talk to anybody that seemed creepy.

    ***

Over the next week, I learned some new things. I learned how to act like a boy in some ways, how to fire the cannons, how fire a musket pistol, and that I sunburned very easy.

The surgeon gave me this odd smelling ointment that was supposed to help my sunburn. He said that it was made from some sort of oil and the sap from an aloe plant. Such treatment worked fairly well, even though it made my clothes stick to me.

One evening I stood out on the deck with the other ships boys, my sleeves were rolled as high as they would go to keep them from sticking to me. I was staring out to sea when I felt a finger poke my arm. I turned and saw Simon watching my arm intently. The then poked it again and giggled.

"What the hell is wrong with you?" I asked pulling my arm away from him, my sunburn still stinging from his poking.

"Watch," he reached over and poked my arm again. The place where he touched turned white then slowly faded back to red.

"And that's supposed to be funny?" I asked just as Davy walked up and decided to poke me on the other arm.

"Perhaps it shouldn't be funny." Davy winked at me. "But that doesn't make it any less amusing."

So I had become the amusement as every time they walked by one of the ships boys, even including Clara would poke me just to watch my sunburn change colors so I began to make it a habit to let my sleeves down even if they did stick to me.

One other thing I did that week was I met a man named Arnold Macanally. He was an Irishman and he had been on working ships since he was seven. He started off as a ships boy, and had worked his way all the way up to captain of the top. He was a good man, but he could cuss a navy blue streak.

One evening, we were sitting in the foretop together, talking.

"What're you gonna do when we get liberty next week?" he asked.

"I'm going to get an earring and a tattoo," I answered. "Me and Henry are going to do that together."

"Damn," he laughed. "You boys are out right sailors ain't ya? I got a couple of 'em myself. It hurts like hell, but it'll show the others that ya ain't a little puss."

"What're you gone do when we're on liberty?" I asked.

"It's all bars and them, damn brothels fer me," he laughed.

"Brothels?" I asked.

"Whore houses," he answered.

I nodded, and the curiosity about brothels and what went on in them suddenly came back into my mind. I knew that Arnold would tell me about it if I asked him, but I just felt strange about asking him. He didn't really seem to be the kind that would be very good at explaining things, he did, however, seem to be the kind who would know a lot about brothels and women in general for that matter.

I decided to change the subject instead. "What kind of tattoos do you have?"

"Here." He unbuttoned his shirt. "Let me show ya." He opened his shirt and showed me a tattoo of a naked lady on his chest. She was sitting on a rock with the water splashing over her. The water wasn't splashing enough to cover her, but all the same, it seemed to be trying. She sat with some sort of cloth in her hand that she didn't seem to be holding onto very well, because the water was washing it away. She had her head cocked back, smiling with her hair blowing in the wind. This was obviously, the tattoo that the boys had mentioned earlier.

I must have blushed, because he laughed and patted me on the back.

"I got this here lovely lady in the same port that we're takin' liberty in," he told me.

"What was the place called?" I asked.

"I'm not sure," he shrugged. "But I know that it was right next to a bar called, the Tin Cup."

I made sure that I would remember that name. The Tin Cup. That would be the place where me and Henry got our tattoos.

The next few days went pretty good. We had drills that would last for hours. We were taught how to broad side a ship and how things go in battles.

I was assigned to gunnery division two as a powder monkey. That meant that I would wait for the leader of the division (in this case it was Patrick Arthur) to give the order and I would run to the powder magazine and get the powder that we needed. They put me as powder monkey because I was fast and it didn't take me long at all to get the powder magazine and back. Me and Patrick got teased by the others because I was older than the other ships boys and unlike Clara, I did look older. I didn't look like a fifteen year old boy, but I did look older than Henry, who was the oldest of the other ships boys. Clara was smaller than both me and Davy and we would have a hard time of it because we were older than the others. They weren't quite as hard on Davy, because he wouldn't let them be, but I wasn't much for knowing how to fight back when I was teased in such a way. Patrick, on the other hand, took up for me saying that he was glad to have a powder monkey who was "well sized" as well as fast. By the end of every day I was retaliating to the insults quite well.

My lessons on how to be a boy continued, and at any chance that I got I would pass my knowledge on to Clara, because she had been having trouble with some of the boys calling her prissy. Even Apollo didn't know about her being a girl and if I had my way he wasn't going to find out. Most girls wouldn't mind if a man knew about their more feminine side, but we were not like most girls. That was quite obvious, because most girls wouldn't have to pretend to be boys.

"Why are we doing this?" Clara asked one day as I instructed her in how to walk like a boy.

"It's like Apollo told me, your ass wiggles when you walk and you don't need that."

"I don't care," she stared at me for a long moment before she started back walking. "It's not like any man on this ship is going to be paying attention to my ass anyway."

I scoffed and shook my head. "You'd be surprised."

"That's disgusting, Billy."

"It's the God's honest truth and if you don't want anyone finding out that you are a girl you'll listen to me."

She walked across the room then turned back to face me. "Was that better?"

"Yes," I nodded. "Much better."

"Good." She started to walk away.

"You do realize that you're going to have to start talking like a sailor too, don't you?"

"Damn right," she said without even turning around.

So our lessons continued in that way, but we made sure to keep it out of sight.

Us ships boys sat around a lot. We mostly stayed in the foretop talking about what we wanted to do when we got older.

"I want to be the captain of a ship, in the king's navy," Danny mused. "That way, I'll be able to just sail around all the time."

"I'm gone work my way all the way up to being a commodore." Simon stood up and puffed his chest out and strutted around.

We all jokingly saluted him.

"I want to have adventures," Davy said dreamily. "I want to travel around the whole world and see everything that my sight can take in, and learn everything that I can. When I can afford it I want to buy me a ship." (He was doing fine at that point, but then he began to go overboard with it. I kind of, wondered if he was doing it just to see what the other boys would say.) "If I could marry the sea I would do it, so that nothing could come between us and once my life was over I would want my body committed to the sea, that way my spirit would remain with hers forever."

"Dang," Danny laughed. "What're you a flippin' poet."

"What?" Davy asked.

"Oh nothin'," Danny shook his head.

"Heck, I'd settle fer bein' an officer," Henry said.

"I want to have a farm," Clara said. "Once I'm done sailing, I want to go get married and have a big family and a farm with all kinds of animals."

They all then turned to me. I thought for a moment and the only thing that I could think of was what Mr. McHale had told me to do.

Finally I answered, "I want to live. I want to make the most of the adventure that has been placed before me and I want to do it one day at a time. I want to make a name for myself. My life so far has been spent rotting in an orphanage, merely existing and avoiding the eyes of anyone that wanted a child, because I was afraid that they wouldn't like me. I tell you this now, I'm no longer going to care what people think. I'm me and if people don't like it, then I don't care. I'm me. I'm not my mother, my father or anyone else, but me and that's what I want to be."

They all just stared at me. I wasn't sure whether their staring was good thing or a bad thing that they were staring at me, but I didn't care. I was pleased with what I had told them and I was always a bit of a show off.

I went to the far side of the foretop and sat down. I stared out to sea, trying my hardest not to let tears fall. I may have been a show off, but some things did hurt. I didn't want them to see me cry. What I had really meant by saying what I had was that I wanted to make Mr. McHale proud. I wanted to live in a way that would make me feel like he was smiling down on me. That was all I really wanted. If I could not have him back, I at least wanted to fulfill my last promise to him. I just wanted to live in a way that would make him proud of me.

***

That night when I was on watch Apollo came over to me as he always did.

"That was a pretty speech that you gave up in the foretop today," he said, propping against the rail.

"You were listening?"

He nodded, and when he spoke again his voice was hardly more than a whisper. "You don't like posing like this do you?"

"Why should I?" I asked.

"If you don't like it, then why are you doing it?" he asked.

"You've never done anything that you didn't like doing, but you had to do it anyway?"

"It just doesn't make sense to me." He scratched his forehead. "The reason that most people would leave their home is if they were running from something. That doesn't seem to be the case for you. So tell me Billy Scarlet, what is it that has you to scared to stay home? Is it some form of danger that you can't face?"

I shook my head. "Danger doesn't scare me."

"What does then?" he asked. "What are you running from if not danger?"

I clenched my jaw and tried to make my face seem like a closed book. I just stared straight ahead. "I fear things that neither of us can see. Things that can't be named and I'll leave it at that."

"I've never met anyone like you before," he laughed a little. "You see, I have a thing for sizing people up, but you're one that I haven't quite figured out yet. You're very strong, don't mind taking orders. You're calm, not easily broken, and light tempered, yet you could get hot tempered in a second if you wanted to be. You're quiet and shy with most people, but you don't mind showing off and you don't really seem to be the kind to cry very much."

I had never told anyone, but at the age of eleven I had taken a secret vow that I would not cry unless it was over something that was really worth crying about. In my point of view crying was pointless, though I had done my fair share on occasion. It got you nowhere and it certainly didn't change anything.

I just shook my head. There were some of my feelings that I didn't trust people with. I didn't want to tell the real reason why I had left the orphanage, nor any of my fears, nor why I didn't cry.

Apollo didn't try to get me to press the matter. He just stood with me, and I was glad.

I looked up at him for a moment then said jokingly, "You asked me why I pose to be something that I am not, now I ask you the same thing."

"What do you mean?" He gave me an odd look.

"Why is it that when you get angry you talk like a Scotsman, but when you are fine or you are talking to the captain, you sound British?"

He laughed. "There are many reasons for things such as this Billy. It is no great mystery to anyone, especially when you hear my last name, that I'm Scottish. I was raised in Scotland, but moved to England when I was nine. I picked up the British accent there, but sometimes things get carried away and I go back to my native tongue."

"Ah," I smiled. "Sounds quite savage to me."

"You should hear me when I'm drunk," he paused and laughed as if remembering. "Well, then again, maybe you shouldn't."

After a few minutes he sighed and patted me on the back. "Carry on." At that moment, the glint in his eye reminded me so much of Mr. McHale that it was almost unreal.

After he had walked off I took out Mr. McHale's book and began reading it by the light of the lamp that hung not too far away from me. It started off:

My name is Garth A. McHale.
I'm seventeen years old and I
am soon going to begin a life at
sea. I have seen how ship's logs
are kept and I have decided to
keep a log of my own. On this

journey I hope find adventure for
my life here in Scotland is quite
boring and I would really like
some excitement. I should really
get some sleep. I have to leave at
dawn and it is already past mid
night, I am not sure how far past,
but I do know that if I am to look
like anything that the captain wants
on his ship then I must get some sleep.
Good night.

I turned the page and began reading the next entry:

I have not written in four days. My
first days I spent sick, clinging to the
rail of the ship for dear life. I have finally
gained my sea legs and I pray that
I never lose them. Being sick that
way had to be about the worst feeling that
I have had in all my life. I feel sorry
for those who have not yet gained their
sea legs. I have made a few friends on
the ship as well as a few enemies.
Life at sea is not as good as I thought
that it would be. What we are doing is
charting out new islands. I've been told
that we are going to sail all the way around
the world. I hope that things pick up around

here. So far things have been quite boring.
Some of the men say that now that I am
over my sea sickness that things will start
to seem better. I hope they are right.

After that I closed the book and just stared out to sea. That night was almost the same as every other night. I wondered if Mr. McHale had been through many nights like that. I was sure that he had. He had probably been through every kind of night that the sea had to offer. There were so many things that I wanted to ask him, so much I wanted to tell him that had been going on. I hoped that he would be proud of me for becoming a sailor and I wondered what he meant when he had said that there was so much that he wished that he could tell us, but we would find out soon enough. I also wondered if Apollo was related to him in any way. None of my questions could be answered, though. I hoped that someday I would find something or someone that could answer my questions, but at the time I guessed that I would just settle for what I knew.

I was glad when my watch was over. I slept like a rock until morning. I hardly ever slept before I went out on watch, even though it wasn't until midnight. I would always lay there feeling like the second I closed my eyes would be when Simon came in and woke me up to go out on watch. It was kind of stupid to be that way, but I couldn't help being that way. It was like my mind did that on its own.

I settled myself into my hammock and went to sleep almost right away. Morning came quick, but when the sun did rise I had gotten plenty of rest and was ready to face the new day.

Chapter
Five

Not much happened in the next few days. We did our drills and practiced sword which was fun, but I didn't really enjoy gun fighting though I knew it could save my life one day. Shooting wasn't bad, but after a while of doing the same things over and over again got boring. I was a good shot and could hit my mark almost every time, though.

The days passed on, some slow and some quick, and soon it was time to go on liberty in Puerto Rico. I had won three copper pieces and a silver piece, in a dice game that I had played so I was ready to go see what all I could buy with it.

When captain Hector gave the liberty call, all of us ships boys headed off to do what we said that we were going to do. Me, Henry, and Clara went off to find a place that we could get a tattoo. We found the place called the *Tin Cup* and went the building that was right next to it. It also was a tavern, but it didn't seem as lively as the other places. A man was sitting on the porch of the place. He had tattoos all the way up his arms and I was sure that if his shirt was off, then his chest would have been covered in them too.

"Can I help you boys?" He had strong, Puerto Rican accent.

"Yes sir," Henry nodded. "We would each like to get a tattoo."

A sudden look of panic flashed across Clara's face. She had not been planning to get a tattoo. She had just wanted to watch.

"What kind?" the man asked.

"A mermaid," Henry answered.

"Like this?" The man showed us a tattoo of a naked mermaid that was on his forearm. It was sitting on a rock just like the woman that was on Arnold's chest. As a matter of fact everything about the picture was the same except for the fact that this one had a tail instead of legs.

Henry nodded and smiled all boyish like. "Yes sir. Just like that."

'Lovely," I thought. 'I will be scorned as a woman where ever I go for having something like that on me.'

"Okay," the man nodded. "That'll be a penny each."

We each paid, even Clara, and he got started. It seemed odd to me that after all of Clara's making a point of not getting a tattoo, she would have said no to it, but in the end she must have felt that it was better to go ahead and get one. That or she didn't want to look stupid for just standing there and watching. Either way, she had changed her mind.

I volunteered to go first, so that I could go ahead and get it over with. Arnold had not been lying when he had told me that it would hurt like hell. Getting poked that many times over and over again with a needle hurt so bad that the whole time I was fighting the urge to flat out faint. I got mine on my left arm right above my elbow and I was glad that I did, so I could roll up my sleeves to keep them from rubbing on the now quite sensitive skin.

Henry went next. He got his on his chest. I figured he did that because Arnold's was on his chest and for some reason Henry wanted to do everything like Arnold. I had a feeling that might become a problem later in life. Clara went last and she got hers on her left arm, just like mine.

After the man got done giving us tattoos, we found out that he would pierce our ears for us so we each got an earring in our left ear, as well. Once we were done paying to get hurt we walked around to see if there was anything else that we wanted to do.

We went to a market where there were a bunch of people selling things. I went over to a place where a woman was selling goods. The lady was kind of small. She had auburn colored hair and she spoke with an English accent. A boy was working with her. He looked to be about my age and he was most definitely Spanish.

I noticed a medallion that was on their table. It was a gold medallion with a red eye in the center. The eye looked to be made of jade, but I had never seen red jade before. I didn't know what it was, but something about the medallion seemed so familiar to me. It was almost as if I had seen it somewhere before. The craftsmanship was quite amazing, but I must say that the medallion was somewhat odd and much different from any other jewelry that I had ever seen. The feeling that I got when I looked at it reminded me of when me and Davy would play like knights, saving a castle.

"I'll buy this," I told the boy.

"Most men shy away from that thing," he said. "Most sea faring ones anyway."

"Why?" I asked.

"Because it's different," he answered.

I laughed, thinking that he was trying to scare, or confuse me. "Is that all? I'll take it, anyway it reminds me of something."

"Okay," he nodded. "Father said only to sell it to someone who did not fear its power or had recognized it. You seem to have both going for you." He picked it up and handed it to me.

I took it and right away, I knew that I had seen it before. Its weight in my hands seemed very familiar and after I put it on, I felt like I had worn this piece of jewelry all my life, like this medallion was a part of me.

I paid for the medallion and a small knife then went to join Henry and Clara. They were standing in front of one of the bars talking to Apollo and

Patrick. Clara kept blowing on her tattoo, trying to make it feel better, but all of her efforts didn't seem to be working. When Apollo saw me, I was afraid that he was going to have a fit.

Patrick just laughed. "You boys have been having fun, haven't you?"

About that time Danny, and Simon came running out of one of the brothels, screaming.

Clara nudged my shoulder. "I thought Davy was going with them."

"Well," I propped my hands on my hips. "It seems like they're the ones that that have been having too much fun, if you ask me."

***

Night soon came and we had to head back to the ship. Some of the men had overnight liberty, but us ships boys had to be back to the ship once night fell. It made me a little angry because the youngest of the middies was fifteen and he got to stay out all night, but I knew the reason for that was not age but instead about rank, so I didn't argue about having to return to the ship at sun down.

We all sat up in the foretop that night talking about what we had done that day.

"See." Henry showed his tattoo to all the other boys. It was still red and swollen, but he was very proud of it. "You ain't got any wings yet."

"You're flat out crazy," Simon laughed. "All three o' y'all are."

"We're crazy?" I asked. "Y'all are the ones that came running out of that whore house like there was a pack of wild dogs after ya."

"We ain't the ones that's gone get infections from some stupid picture bein' put on us," Danny piped up.

"Well, we ain't either," Clara huffed. "We know how ta keep 'em clean."

"Well, at least we only hafta deal with what we saw," Simon laughed. "You three hafta deal with those things the rest of your lives."

"What exactly did you guys see?" Clara asked smiling in a way that said, 'I told you so'.

"A lot of interesting stuff." Davy winked.

"Well I'll never tell," Simon answered. "If ya wanna find out what happened you can go into one next time we're on liberty."

That was all that we could get out of any of them. It seemed that they must have seen something that was pretty rough. No matter what they saw, it was enough to make them not want to say anything about it, and I wasn't going to press them at the moment. I knew that I would, eventually get Davy to tell. He seemed to be the only one who came out of the whole ordeal unharmed.

That next day I got to thinking about the subject of brothels more, and I decided that I would ask one of the men what happened in the whore houses. I thought about asking Apollo, but then I figured that would just be too odd, and asking Patrick would have been even worse, because I didn't know him very well, and asking Clara would have implied to the others that I was curious because it was rare that I would ever get to be alone with Clara to ask her about it and I didn't want the other boys to treat me like an idiot because I was older than they were and didn't know about such things. In the end I decided that I would ask Arnold about it while me and him sat in the foretop.

The first thing I did was show him my earring and tattoo.

"Nice," he smiled inspecting them both. "I knew you had it in ya. Now ya look like a good sailor ta me, lad."

"I got them at the place by the *Tin Cup*. The same place that you got yours."

He nodded and looked back out to sea.

I knew that it was now or never. I wasn't sure why I was so nervous about asking. 'It can't be that bad at all. I'm just worrying too much.' I took a deep breath and turned to him.

He gave me an odd look. I could tell that he knew I had something to ask him.

"Can I talk to you about something?"

He came over and sat down next to me. "What's on yer mind, Billy?"

"I was just wondering about a few things," I answered.

"Like what?" he asked, in a, sort of fatherly tone. "Has anybody been messing with you?"

"No, I shook my head and tried to think of the right way to ask the question, but in the end I just decided to be straight forward with it."What do men and women do in whore houses?"

He sighed. "I can't believe that you've been put on a ship full o' grown men and nobody's even told ya 'bout that kinda thing. I mean, yer, how old, fifteen?"

I nodded.

"Yer old 'nough fer learnin' it, so I guess it's best that I go ahead an' tell ya. Otherwise some o' these dumb ass bastards'll be teasin' ya 'bout the fact that ya don't know." With that he began and all the while I was truly regretting the fact that I asked. By the time that he was done, I was gagging and begging him to stop. I didn't care if he thought that I was old enough to hear this kind of a story or lesson, or whatever he thought the horror he was telling me to be. I felt like no one was old enough to hear anything of the like.

"Oh, dear God," I muttered. "Please don't say another word about it."

"You asked." He held his hands up as if to show that he wasn't the reason that I felt sick to my stomach.

I just sat there, quietly. I didn't want to look at him. I didn't want to look at another man ever again. As a matter of fact, I didn't want to look at any person man or woman.

"So all the men on this ship have probably done......" I swallowed hard. "That?"

"Most likely." He nodded. "Look Billy, one day it won't seem that bad to ya. Ya just gotta get over the shock of learnin' 'bout it, is all. I wouldn't have thought a fifteen year old would take it so bad, but I guess we ain't all born sailors."

"MaCanally!" a voice called from the deck. "We need you on the quarter deck."

"Coming!" he hollered, then turned to me. "Later, man."

To tell the truth I was rather glad that he got called down to the deck after that, but then they sent Apollo up there with me.

"How ya doin'?" he asked.

I didn't answer. I couldn't answer. The trauma that had been bestowed upon me was too much for me to handle at the moment, and I certainly didn't want to talk to Apollo about it.

"You all right?" he asked.

I nodded. It was the only response that I could muster.

"What's wrong?"

"I can't talk to you right now." I shook my head as if that would make all the thoughts that found themselves floating through my head, to go away. I didn't want any thoughts of Apollo doing anything I had just been told of, creeping into my mind. "I can't talk to anyone. I can't look at anyone. I can't take it. I don't want to think."

"Billy, what in the bloody hell is wrong with you?"

I just looked at him and he read the look in my eyes.

"Shit," he muttered. "Who did you ask?"

"How did you know?" I asked.

"I heard you and the other boys talking about whore houses and besides, there are very few things in the world that could make you act this way," he answered. "Who did you ask?"

"Arnold," I answered.

"Are you mad?" he huffed. "He probably explained it in a way that would have even made me sick. Why didn't you just ask me?"

"How in the bloody hell was I going to ask you?" I almost yelled. "It would've been too strange. I just felt like it would've been different talking to Arnold about it. I don't know."

There he cut me off. "Calm down Billy, just calm down. You were going to find out about all that stuff one way or another. At least now you know. I still don't see why you asked Arnold."

"You don't?" I huffed. "Arnold is my ship's dad and you're my...." There I paused and my voice drifted off. What was Apollo to me? He was my friend, yes, but I couldn't tell if there was anything more between us.

He waited for a moment as if he was waiting for me to finish, but when I said nothing more, he did not push for me to. We just sat in silence for the rest of our time up there.

I was sort of creeped out for the rest of the day, but I got over it. It was like Apollo had said. I was going to learn about it one way or another. Either way, what could I do about it? It wouldn't make any sense to act all creeped out for the rest of my life, so I just pushed past it and thought about other things.

A few days later, was yet another turning point in our lives.

Me, Clara and Davy were up in the foretop. He teased us about our tattoos and earrings and we teased him what he may have done in the whore house.

"I'll never tell." The glint in his eyes told me that he had done exactly what Arnold had told me the other men on the ship had done.

"I'd take it that means you know everything now." Clara teased.

"I never said that I didn't know any of it before."

Just then the lookout yelled, "Ship off starboard bow!"

"Colors!?" the helmsman hollered back.

"Jolly Roger!" the lookout answered.

"Rouse the captain!" the helmsman yelled.

The three of us quickly climbed down from the foretop. The deck was swarming with activity by the time we reached it.

It was not long before captain Hector emerged from his cabin and gave the order to give chase.

I stood and waited for my signal then ran below deck and got the gun powder.

"Fire!" Captain Hector yelled.

There was a loud drum beat and then we began firing. Everything was going well until the pirates began firing back at us. Not only were they shooting at us with cannons, but they also rained down on us with pepper shot of all sizes. They were about fifteen yards off and their fire was hammering on us pretty hard, but we were meeting their attacks with a doubled effort.

There was a loud blast. I covered my face to keep from getting anything in my eyes. When I uncovered my eyes I saw that Patrick had been shot in the shoulder and he was knocked out. The men in the gun division had stopped firing. They looked around at each other as if they were at a loss for what to do. It then hit me that they didn't know what to do if Patrick wasn't giving them orders.

I had learned the orders by heart so I began giving orders the same way that Patrick had done. I knew that I wasn't high enough of a rank to give orders to able bodied seamen or even deckhands, but I wasn't about to let them just freeze up and do nothing. To my surprise, the men listened to me.

"Swab, the barrel! Wad! Ball! Fire!" I yelled and turned to one of the other men. "Fetch more powder, man!"

He nodded and took off to the powder magazine. I took his place loading the gun, all the while, shouting orders. My voice grew hoarse, but I was not going to stop, even if it meant losing my voice completely. I would not let these men die because they did not know their orders well enough. It made me mad to know that even through all of the training we had been through in the past few weeks, I, a ship's boy, had learned the firing orders, while these men had not, but then again practice was never quite enough like facing a real fight to know what you would do in such a situation.

The pirate ship drew closer and closer. I could see the boarding party that they had ready standing at the rail with their grappling hooks at the ready. Within minutes they threw their grappling hooks across and began pulling the ships together. I knelt down beside Patrick and got his sword and pistol. He was alive, but he wasn't awake. I hoped that he would stay that way until we could overtake the pirates, because as long as he lay there, no one was going to mess with him.

When I stood up a pirate swung his sword at me. He hit me with the flat and it cut my left shoulder. I knew that the next swing would be the death blow, so using Patrick's gun, I shot the man. It was kind of a surreal feeling, to see the man fall to the deck clenching his chest from which blood was pouring, and knowing that I had been the one to take his life. My hands began to shake, but there was no time for me to stop fighting.

There came another blast and something hit me in the back of the leg. I fell to my knees and, without even meaning to, cried out in pain. I grabbed the rail and pulled myself back to my feet. Staying on my feet began to get harder as the time slowly passed. Blow after blow came and I dodged or parried each one. I had heard so many stories of sea battles and wondered what it would be like to be in one, but now that I was there in the thick of such turmoil and destruction, all I wanted was to be somewhere else.

I stood in a way that I could fight off the pirates and protect Patrick at the same time. Pepper shot whizzed past my head and I tried my best not to notice it, but instead to pay attention to what I was doing. Men came at me and I killed them. Staying alive was that simple, but it really wasn't. I tried not to look at any of the men. They were pirates, but any one of them could have been my father, or someone he knew. Any one of these men had a mother and father of their own somewhere and that was all I could think of to start off with. I took a deep breath to clear my head. Then I just fought as hard as I could.

The fact that I was very skilled with my fighting came across as odd to me. It was almost as if something inside of me took over. I had fought like this before, I knew I had. I knew every move to make and was able to out fight the greatest of any of the men that came at me. I could not explain how or why, but I fought like I had been trained to do so from the time I was old enough to walk.

A man came at me, his sword swinging wildly, his eyes blazing with fury. He came at me with such speed and force that I had no time to think. His sword slashed right past my face. I felt the wind from it. It missed me by mere inches. I ducked, swung back around, and slashed the man across the throat.

Finally, after what seemed like hours of fighting, the pirate captain and his men gave up.

Our men went onto the other ship and checked the hold. It was full, to the bursting point with gold, silver, wine, fine silks and precious stones, of all kinds. The first mate took down how much treasure there was, how much it was worth, and what each man's share would be. As a ships boy I would only get half a share, but that was still a good bit of money.

In the middle of getting everything together, Patrick came over to me. He didn't look very good. His skin was very pale. He was shaking slightly and there was blood all over his right side.

"Are you okay?" I asked.

"Thanks to you." He smiled weakly.

"Come on," I said. "You need to get to the doctor."

"It looks like you do too," he nodded toward my shoulder.

"I'll be fine," I told him. "You look like you're just shy of death." I took him by the arm and led him below deck.

The doctor went straight to work on Patrick and his assistant got to work on me. It turned out that I had a large splinter in the back of my leg and a very deep cut on my shoulder, but I was more concerned about Patrick. The good news was that the bullet was no longer in him. The bad news was that he was hurt pretty bad and it would take him a long time to heal.

Just as I was done getting stitched up, a man came in and said that the captain wanted to see me. I looked over at Patrick.

"I'll be fine." He smiled. "Go on ahead. If the captain gets mad about you taking over like that then I'll take up for you. Don't worry. I think he's going to be very proud of what you did."

His encouragement didn't help me much, but I followed the man all the same. I knew that I had done the right thing, but I still had this sinking feeling inside of me that made me sure that the captain was going to be mad and would punish me for giving orders to men that were above my rank.

As I walked across the deck, I looked at all the men. The happiness of our victory had worn off a good bit and now they were seeing all the destruction that had taken place. A lot of the men were hurt and some were dead. All of the ships boys were shaken up. Clara had a black eye, Davy had blood running down the side of his neck, Danny and Henry both had blood on their faces, whether it was theirs or someone else's I wasn't sure, and Simon's left pants leg looked like it had been dipped in red dye. Arnold sat beside one of the cannons with his face in his hands and Apollo was going around making sure that all the men were okay. When he saw me I could tell that it worried him to see the way that I was covered in blood, but he didn't come check on me. I was up and walking around and there were others who weren't doing near as good I was. He had his work cut out for him, helping the other injured men and I didn't feel bad toward him at all, for not checking on me.

As I entered the captain's quarters, I felt a chill of panic run down my back all the way to my toes. Captain Hector was sitting at a table watching me as I came in. I would have saluted him, but I knew not to salute in doors, so I just stood there at attention.

"Sit," he said.

I sat down in the chair that was across the table from him.

"You are a ships boy, is that correct?"

"Aye, sir."

"Today during the battle, young midshipman, Patrick Arthur got injured and you took over command. As a powder monkey you had no right to do that."

"I know, sir." I sighed.

"You gave orders to men that were in ranks above you. Did you not?" He glared at me.

"Aye, sir," I nodded.

"Tell me something, ships boy, Scarlet," The title made me feel small and insignificant. "Why did you do it?"

"Because they stopped fighting, sir," I answered. "They didn't know what to do when someone wasn't giving orders. I felt that since I knew the orders by heart then I would go ahead and help the men, sir. With all due respect, captain, I believe there is a problem with how these men are being trained." For a second I was afraid that I was going too far, but I continued on anyway. "If these men are to be sailors they need to be trained that way. Now I have been here for only a few weeks and I have learned the firing orders while men have been on here for much longer and they have not."

"You are wrong there, Scarlet," he said. "The men in that particular gun division have been here as long as you have. We picked them up the same day that you came on board."

"Then why did you put them all in the same division when none of them knew what they were doing? You could have teamed them with other groups of men so they would have been able to learn quicker."

He stared at me for a long moment. I knew then that I had crossed the line. I had told him that he was not running his ship properly. He gave me another curious look, then nodded to the man that had brought me in. "Bring in midshipman, McHale."

That confused me. Why did captain Hector want to see Apollo? Then something else crossed my mind. Apollo was the only one of the men that knew I was a girl. What if the captain had somehow gotten wind of it and he was fixing to confront Apollo about it? I would have made even worse on myself by talking to the captain the way that I just had. I sat there, hoping he would have a little mercy on me, but something made me doubt it.

The man then brought Apollo in.

"Hello, Mr. McHale." Captain Hector nodded. "Please sit."

Apollo sat down next to me.

"You fought gallantly today, McHale," the captain continued. "I told you, not too long ago, that if you could prove yourself worthy of the position, then I would promote you to acting lieutenant. I do believe you proved that you are worthy of it today."

"Thank you, sir," Apollo said.

"As for you," Captain Hector turned back to me.

'Oh no,' I thought. 'What are they going to do with me? The brig? Marooned on a dessert island? Hung from the mast head? Keel hauled?'

"You are a little old to be a ship's boy, Scarlet," he said which confused me greatly. "Now that McHale has been promoted to lieutenant, we are in need of one more midshipman. You would have to take up a good bit of slack, seeing as how midshipman, Arthur will be out of commission for a little while. Then again we might need two new midshipmen." He looked over at the man who was waiting by the door. "Bring in ship's boy Mitchems."

The captain turned back to me. "Though you haven't been here long, I think you would be good in the position. What do you think?"

"I cannot say, sir," I answered. "I am as low a rank as there is and you are captain. I will do as you tell me."

"Well said, Scarlet." The captain smiled.

***

That evening me and Davy said goodbye to the ships boys and the two of us moved into the midshipman's berth. It was strange, but I kind of liked it. I would miss being in the same place as Clara, but I was sure that she would be promoted soon.

We each got a uniform that someone had out grown and I was assigned to Apollo's old bunk. A new hammock was hung for Davy. The three other midshipmen were named Will Jackson, Stewart Bismark, and Roger Phillis. They were good guys and they told me how I would be running gun division three and that meant that I had to exercise them, teach them to learn firing orders by heart, and anything else that the captain wanted them to learn. They also told me that my watch would now be from midnight until five in the morning, and instead of just standing around watching all the other men I was supposed to stand at attention behind the helmsman and wait for his orders.

Needless to say, I was a little bit worried about it. I had only been on the ship for a week and a half and already I had moved up a rank, and I was going to be giving orders that I was going to be learning as I gave them. All I had done was save the gun division. The captain could have just patted me on the back and said good job, but instead he promoted me. I couldn't even imagine what had gone through Davy's head when the captain promoted him. It was probably similar to what I had thought. At least I had been given a bit of a head's up about it. I was glad that he had been promoted as well. That would make it easier on both of us. We would be able to learn things together.

"It isn't that hard," Will told us. He was tall and broad, but in the face I could tell that he was only about fifteen. "You'll get used to it and besides, me and the boys here'll be watchin' out for ya."

"Thanks," I nodded.

Another problem about being promoted to midshipman was that I was going to have to bathe and get dressed in the berth with all the other boys. I was going to have to be extra careful to keep them from finding out about me being a girl. At least I had Davy there to help me in that area.

My first night on watch went okay. I went out on deck and stood at attention behind the helmsman, just like I was told.

"Ah, so you're one of the new middies?" he asked.

"Aye, sir," I answered.

"What's your name?" he asked.

"Midshipman, Billy Scarlet, sir," I answered.

"Well middie Scarlet, check how many knots we are."

At that moment I felt so stupid. I knew that I had been told about that before.

He sighed. "Check the water depth," He nodded toward a rope that had a bunch of knots tied in it and an anchor at the bottom.

"Aye sir," I said sort of weakly. I went over and tossed it over the side.

"How many?" he asked.

"Forty seven, sir," I answered.

He nodded. "On patrol. In case you don't know what that means, it means to walk around the deck in either a clockwise or counter clockwise motion checking things as you go."

I knew that he was saying that just to mock me, but I kept my head high and went down to patrol the deck. The first person that I came to was Davy. He was on watch at the quarter deck.

"All clear here?" I asked.

"Aye, sir." He laughed a little. "It's weird that we are midshipmen."

"Yea," I nodded. "I think that it's gone take me a while to get used to it. Things are so different this way."

"You'll be fine," he smiled.

"I know," I nodded. "Carry on," I walked on down the deck toward the bow where Patrick was on watch.

"Hello, Billy." He smiled. "I saw you up there at the helm."

"Yes, I'm making a wonderful midshipman. I don't even know what a knot is."

"You'll learn." He laughed. "I'll help teach you and I'm sure that if Apollo has time he'll teach you as well. There are all the other middies too. We won't let you mess up."

"Thank you," I nodded. "I have to keep moving. Carry on."

I walked along the deck. It was very quiet night and in a way I was glad. I didn't want for my first night as a midshipman to make me seem as if I had gone completely mad or anything of the sort. I wanted to get used to the job first.

***

Things went good for the next week and a half. I learned a lot of new fighting skills. I taught my men the firing orders by heart, because I knew that there was always the risk of me getting hurt and I didn't want the same thing to happen as had happened in the last battle.

I had a good bit of time to myself, so I would read Mr. McHale's book. One thing that I did was I sewed a sheath inside my left boot for the knife that I bought in Puerto Rico, but the rest of the time I was pretty busy.

One night, I was standing behind the helmsman.

"How ya doin', Scarlet?"

"Fairly well, sir," I nodded. "And yourself?"

He laughed. "Happy as a pig in the sunshine. You gettin' used to yer job yet?"

"Yes, sir," I mutter, hoping he wasn't trying to mock me.

He obviously picked up on my feelings because he smiled and said, "We all have to take time to get used to it, lad. Yer not born knowin' it. If ya were there'd be no point in learnin' anything."

I nodded.

"An' don't take it so hard when me an' the others tease ya a bit. We jus' want ya ta toughen up some. Ya can't be so tender 'bout things."

"I'm not tender," I protested. "If I was, do you think I would even be here?"

"There ya go gettin' all tender again." He laughed. "I know yer tough, lad. Ya just need ta learn not ta get so offended at small stuff. You'll do fine in time."

"I'll do my best."

"That you will," he nodded. "On patrol, Scarlet."

"Aye, sir," I nodded and started across the deck.

In the middle of my patrol, I heard something below deck. I wasn't sure if it was someone talking, or if something had fallen over. I went down in the hold, which was where I had heard the noise from. I walked around.

"Hello," I called. "Who's down here?"

Suddenly, someone grabbed me from behind. "Ello lady." I recognized the voice right away. It was Averett. I had completely forgotten about him. It had been so long since I had met him, and after he got put in the brig I had not worried about him anymore.

"Yer gone get it, ya little snot nosed bastard." He threw me onto the floor.

"What do you want?" I got back to my feet.

"Yer gonna pay fer what I went through," he growled. "I went through hell 'cause o' you. Now it's yer turn." He punched me hard across the face.

"Help me!" I yelled just in time for him to kick me in the ribs.

I got back to my feet and swung at him, but it was no use. He was a lot bigger than me. "Somebody help!" I yelled at the top of my lungs.

He threw me against the wall and punched me in the stomach. I fell to the floor. It took me a minute, but I came back up with my knife in my hand. I swung it at him and the blade caught him on the right arm.

"You little bastard," he scoffed and grabbed my hand in attempt to keep me from cutting him. Instead of going for him straight on, I stabbed him in the wrist. He screamed and let go of me. I fell to the floor, gasping for breath, praying that my ribs were not broken, and tasting blood in my mouth.

Tears were pouring out of my eyes when he snatched me up off the floor. I tried to fight back, but there was really no fight left in me. My body had gone limp and my strength was spent. I closed my eyes and resigned myself to whatever terrible fate I had in store.

Averret laughed. "Now yer seein' how I do things."

He pushed me back, pinning me against the wall and squeezed my throat. I looked down at the floor and saw my knife. I wished, for all the life of me that I had been able to hold onto it.

Just then, someone came running down below deck. Averett threw me on the floor. "I'll finish you later." With that, he ran off.

I laid there gasping for air, yet trying not to move because I couldn't move without hurting. I was certain that I was just going to die.

"Billy," the voice belonged to Apollo. "Oh dear God, Billy what happened to you?"

"Averett." It was the only word I could utter seeing as how I had not yet caught my breath.

He helped me up. I could still walk, but it hurt pretty bad.

He put his hands on my shoulders and looked me straight in the eyes. The look that he had in his eyes was the same look that Mr. McHale had when he had killed the men that were dragging off Clara and Mistress Lora. "Where did he go?"

"I don't know," I answered, finally able to speak again. "Besides, I don't want you getting in trouble for fighting."

"Don't worry about me, Billy," he told me. "Captain Hector will understand. Did you see which way he went?"

I shook my head.

"Can you walk?"

I nodded. I wasn't rightfully sure if I could walk very well or not, but I didn't want him to have to carry me, so I decided to at least try my hand at it.

"Come with me." He walked with me back up on deck. Off and on, I had to lean on him for support, but I managed to walk the entire way.

We walked across the deck and to the captain's cabin. He knocked on the door.

"Come in," came the captain's voice from the other side.

The two of us walked in. When Captain Hector saw me, he just stopped and stared for a moment. He looked horrified. "What happened to him?"

"Averett," Apollo answered and then took the captain to the side. He spoke to him in a whisper, but I could still hear him. "That man has been hurting the boys for way too long and I plan to do something about it and I plan to do it here tonight."

"Apollo," the captain winced. "Be careful about this."

"Careful?" Apollo said in a tone that did not make him sound at all like he was addressing his captain. He then caught himself, took a deep breath and looked the other man in the eye. "Do you think that vile beast was being careful when he did this to Billy? Do you think he was careful with any of the boys he's hurt? You may punish me for it sir, but to tell the God's honest truth, I don't care if you do. I can't stand for this anymore."

"Do what you must, Apollo," the captain said. "Just try not to arouse any of the other men. You don't want to cause a big fuss over all of it."

"Honestly I believe that most of the men would help me if I told them." Apollo said.

The captain gave him a warning look. "Don't start a riot, McHale."

"Can you keep him in here while I do this?" Apollo asked.

Captain Hector nodded.

"Stay here with the captain," Apollo told me as he walked past me. "I'll be back in a few minutes."

I sat there staring down at my hands.

"Are you okay?" Captain Hector asked.

"Yes sir." Saying it made me realize that my bottom lip was very swollen.

Things were very quiet for what seemed like hours. I began to wonder if everything was okay. I felt a tear run down my cheek, and I wasn't sure whether it was from pain, worry, or both. I quickly wiped it away before the captain could see.

I sat there hoping and praying that Apollo would be okay. The one time that him and Averrett had fought in the galley, Averrett had been the only one to get a hit off.

Suddenly, someone yelled, "Man overboard!" and I knew what had happened. I only hoped that it was the right man that went over.

Once again, all was quiet for a long time. I just sat there wishing that I knew what had happened, yet glad that I did not.

I was very relieved a few minutes later, when Apollo came back in. He looked tired, as if the last hour had lasted days. There was blood on the front of his shirt. There were signs of struggle but there was no question of who has won.

"What just happened?" the captain asked, as if he had no idea what was going on.

"The crewman Averett fell overboard sir," Apollo answered. "And much to our regret, he could not swim and in these shark infested waters I don't believe there's really any hope. It is the loss of a sailor, but one that I believe we can make it through."

Captain Hector smiled and nodded. "May he sink to hell," he said then he turned to me. "Well midshipman Scarlet, I believe you're safe now. Lieutenant, take this young man to the doctor. He looks like he needs to be patched up."

He took me to the doctor and I got my bangs and bruises treated. I had no broken bones, but I was still beat up pretty bad, so I was confided to my bunk for the next three days.

While I was in my bunk I was going to read some of Mr. McHale's book, but it sort of fell open to a certain spot that said:

It was that day that I
received a letter telling me
that my grandson had been
born. His name was Apollo
McHale. My son named him
after one of those Greek gods.
Either of war or love or something
like that.

I closed the book. My heart was beating about five hundred beats a minute. Apollo was Mr. McHale's grandson. It sort of fit together. Apollo had been in the Barbados, looking for relatives and he had been around the orphanage. All of it seemed to be falling in place. It was like a puzzle that was starting to come together. Little did I know, this was hardly the beginning. My new found puzzle had more pieces than any man, woman, or child could count.

***

The day that I was able to get around again, I went and showed the book to Apollo.

"Yes," he nodded after he read the first few pages. "That sounds just like my grandfather. So, you knew him?"

"He helped raise me," I told him. "He was the closest thing to a father that I ever had."

"And you said that he died the night before you came to the ship?" he asked.

I nodded.

He looked as if he was going to cry. He rubbed his eyes and nodded. "One thing that he told me the day that I left was that he wanted me to watch after you. That's how I knew you were a girl. I don't know how he knew something was going to happen to him, but he told me that I needed to watch out for you because there was something very important about you."

"Just before he died, he told me that there was a lot of things that he wanted to tell me, but I would find out in due time. I don't know what he meant by that. Do you?"

He shook his head and smiled. "No. He had told me that about many things and only now am I starting to understand. I don't know what he meant when he told you that, but if he said that you'll find out soon enough, then you will."

***

After that day, time seemed to pass so fast. Things changed faster than I could keep up with. Days became weeks. Weeks became months. Months became years, and before I knew it five years had passed and I was a twenty-year-old salty officer. I helped train the new midshipmen and often times would stand in for the ones who had been hurt, or had not learned their orders just yet, but that was only during battles.

Davy had been promoted to able bodied seaman. He was a quick witted sailor. He was good with a sword and was great with any form of gun. From pistols to cannons, he could call his shots and hit the spot that he said he would.

Prim and proper Clara had become a hot tempered, strong willed, hard headed, sailor that could cuss with the best of them. She had been promoted to head officer of gun division two. Me and her were like sisters, even though we had to act like brothers.

Even as we got older, Clara had no trouble hiding the fact that she was a girl. She was tall, thin and flat chested for the most part. I, on the other hand, was a few inches shorter than her. I was broad and not at all flat chested. I wore shirts that were too big and I kept a band tied around my chest. I even used a corset that I had cut in half so that the top part would hold down my breasts, and I wrapped canvas around my waist so as to balance out the size of my chest, but I knew that wasn't going to work for me for very much longer. Besides the fact that it may not keep things hidden much longer it would also serve to give me a heat stroke in the hot Caribbean waters that we had been sailing. I had grown a lot and no matter what I tried I wasn't going to be able to hide it forever and I knew that I wasn't the only one that noticed it. Apollo, Clara, and Davy noticed, but they had all known in the first place. My biggest problem was that I was beginning to believe that others were starting to notice as well and that made me jumpy. I knew that we more I worried about being discovered the more likely it would be for me to actually cause a problem.

One Sunday evening, when I was sitting at the table in the midshipman's berth by myself waiting for one of the new midshipmen to get there, Apollo came in and sat down across from me.

It had been a while since we had time to talk.

He smiled at me the, same way that he had when we first met, that cocky grin that made it where I couldn't help but smile back. He had changed a lot, and it was almost as if I were looking at him for the first time all over again.

"Good morning, Billy," he said. "I've been needing to talk to you for a while now."

"About what?" I asked.

"I'm not the only one that's been noticing the fact that you're starting to look more like a girl," he answered. "Captain Hector has been asking questions about you. He's not stupid. I think that he knows."

"What should I do?" I asked.

"Don't worry about it. Just keep up your act I'll find a way to keep you from getting disgraced. There's only one problem."

"What's that?" I asked.

"You're going to have to get put off the ship," he answered. "I know you're not going to like it, but the captain won't stand for having a woman on board. The only reason that he hasn't thrown you off yet is because he doesn't know for sure, that you're a girl."

"Where will I go?" I felt helpless. "This ship is my life. It's my home. I have nowhere else to go."

"I know, Billy," he sighed. "Is that your real name?"

"Yes," I laughed a little. "It's funny that you've known me this long, but you don't even know my real name. Billy is short for Sabilla."

He smiled. "No matter what you're real name is I'll always think of you as Billy."

"We have to tell the captain who I am before he finds out some other way," I said.

Just then a man came in. "Lieutenant we have a ship off port bow."

"Colors?" Apollo asked.

The man looked at me. I couldn't be quite sure whether I was seeing right or not, but it was almost as if he had regret in his eyes.

My suspicions were confirmed by Apollo. He cast a glance then looked back at the other man. "I see," he nodded and we headed up on deck.

Clara and Davy came over to me when I got on deck.

"You're going to want to see this." Davy handed me a scope.

I went to the rail and looked out at the ship. I had been told of the ship with the scarlet jolly roger many times, but never had I seen it with my own two eyes, and then as I stood there staring at it I felt terrified. My hands began to sweat and my knees began to shake.

I took the scope from my eye. I felt this sinking feeling inside of me. Yes, I had been in many battles and I had killed men before. I had grown accustomed to fighting to save the people that I cared about and it rarely ever bothered me anymore, but I knew, from the depths of my soul, that the battle that had then been placed before me was going to be different from all the others that I had been in. It was going to be hard to fight against the man who had given the eyes that were scarlet red. The man for whom I was named. The man who was my father.

I thought for a moment, trying to come up with something to do to stop the fight, but there was no way out of it.

I looked at the gun division. They had begun to assemble. My midshipman was not yet up to fighting in a battle such as this. He had only been promoted the day before and he had not been in any rank of the gun division before. With him at my side, I took my place with division three. My men were ready. I nodded to the boy at my side. He nodded back, but I could tell that he was even more nervous than I was.

"Load the guns!" I yelled. They knew the rest of the drill well enough that I didn't have to tell them. I had made sure that every man in my division knew the firing orders well enough that they could do it in their sleep. I didn't want anything to happen like it had when I had first become a midshipman.

They loaded the guns faster than the rest of the men.

"Fire one!" the captain yelled.

There was a loud drum beat and gun division one fired. My men looked at me. They had loaded the guns, but they noticed that I was sort of distant.

"Fire two!"

There came the loud drum beat, followed by the cannon blasts of division two.

I gritted my teeth and waited for the order that would soon be coming.

"Fire three!" the captain yelled.

I paused for about two seconds, then yelled, "Fire!"

Captain Hector looked at me with admiration, though I didn't feel very admirable. As a matter of fact, I felt very strange. I didn't even think, I just shouted orders, because I knew that I didn't want my men to get hurt. I wasn't going to let my personal feelings to get in the way.

The other ship was firing on us as well. They had at least three nine pound guns, and they weren't afraid to use them. The ship was a few yards off when I noticed some of the men load a chain shot into the cannon.

"Chain shot!" I yelled, but it was too late. They had already fired. The shot hit our front mast. After that the pirates took our ship pretty quickly. They threw their grappling hooks across and began pulling us in. At that moment, I realized how a fish felt. We had bit the bait and now we were being pulled in. My stomach lurched as my eyes scanned the group of men who were crowded at the rail.

The two ships came together and they put a gang plank across. It seemed odd to me that the pirates had stopped fighting. They just came across to our ship and did not fire another shot.

I kept my face turned away from all the pirates as they boarded us. I knew that if I were to show my eyes, the peace that had suddenly found its way to us would simply fade away and all hell would break loose.

I stood in between Clara and Davy. The two of them were just as tense as I was, but suddenly, they tensed even more and I could tell that they were staring intently at something, or someone. I looked up just in time for my eyes to lock with the intense red eyes of the pirate, Billy Scarlet.

We held each other's gaze until I was afraid that I was going to just flat out lose my mind. Finally, he walked away and I felt like I was going to fall over. Davy grabbed my hand and squeezed it. That helped a little bit, but there was nothing in the world that could have prepared me for meeting my father.

Billy wasn't a very tall man. As a matter of fact, he wasn't much taller than me. He had long, wavy, dark blond hair, sort of fair skin, and his eyes were much more fierce than mine, but somehow they were very kind. He wore a white shirt that was tucked in, but wasn't buttoned. He wore black pants and

74

boots, and had three pistols strapped across his chest and a sword at his hip.

Despite all his fierceness, there was something about him that I could only describe as whimsical. I couldn't explain why and I didn't understand it, but there was something about him that wasn't like a pirate at all or a sailor even. He seemed like he was from somewhere else entirely.

He walked up to the helm and stood in front of captain Hector and in a surprisingly calm voice said, "If you back off and let us go I won't destroy your ship. If you do as I say no one will get hurt."

"Don't take me for a fool, sir. I have dealt with pirates before," Captain Hector said.

"The boy." Billy motioned toward me as if he had not even heard the other captain's blatantly calling him a liar. "Where did you pick him up?"

"That is none of your damn business," Captain Hector huffed.

With all the calmness in the world, Billy pulled one of his guns and walked over to me. "Forgive me," he said and pointed to gun to my head. "I take the boy or you no longer have to deal with him."

I suddenly felt very faint.

"Leave him alone," Davy said.

Billy paid him no mind. "I will not leave him on this deck alive."

"You will not dare hurt him," Clara growled.

"Not if you let me take him." Billy gave her a cold stare then turned back to me. "What's your name, sailor?"

I knew then that it was the end. There was no way around it; I had to tell him my name. I couldn't tell him my girl name, and I wasn't going to make up any other boy name, though I doubt that any of the crew would have thought less of me for it. So I did the only thing I could do and feel honorable about. I summoned up all the courage that I could, and said, "Billy Scarlet."

"I know what my name is," he huffed. "What's *your* name?"

"That is *my* name, you jackass." I pushed his pistol away. "My name is

Billy Scarlet."

I was quite certain that I had made him mad. His face didn't show it, as a matter of fact he looked a little more than slightly amused, but the way that he jabbed his pistol into my ribs showed that he meant business.

"The boy comes with me and nobody gets hurt," he told them.

"Why do you want the boy?" Apollo asked. "And don't say that's it's none of my business. He's part of this crew therefore it is my business where he does and doesn't go."

Billy gave him a sarcastic look as if to say, 'Take a wild guess,' then said, "Why?" he asked, his voice as full of sarcasm as his stare. "You want to write it down in the log book, lieutenant?"

I could feel Apollo's temper on the verge of exploding, but he did not say anything. It seemed that Billy had a way of making anyone feel stupid just by using the simplest phrase.

"You, my good man are in no position to ask questions. I have overtaken your ship and have offered you a deal in which you have two choices. I take the boy and no one gets hurt, or the opposite. Choose quickly." He cocked the pistol.

I looked from Apollo, to Clara, then to Davy. All three of them looked as if they could kill Billy, but no one moved or said a word, so I decided to take my fate into my own hands.

"I'll go with him," I said.

"What?" Davy and Apollo asked, at the same time.

"It doesn't seem that any of you are going to choose my fate so I have chosen for myself. I don't want any of you to get hurt so I'm going with him." With that I walked toward Billy's ship.

"Billy," Davy called to me.

I looked back at him.

"Be careful."

I laughed a little. "You worry too much." And once again I sailed away from the life that I was used to.

As the two ships parted ways I looked back and saw Clara and Davy standing at the rail and even though captain Hector was talking to him, Apollo was watching the ship sail away. That was some comfort. At least they cared about me.

***

Within the hour, the two ships were completely out of sight of each other.

I was very surprised at how organized Billy's ship was. It was almost as organized as a navy vessel.

All the men were rough and cursed a lot, but I was used to that. All of them had tattoos and earrings and most of them looked (and smelled) like they had never bathed in their lives. So I guess that as far as pirates go, they were all pretty normal. They didn't seem as crude as the pirates that we had taken prisoner on *the Victory*. As a matter of fact they seemed rather decent in comparison. I couldn't even be sure that they really were pirates at all except for the way they all looked. The only one that seemed like he didn't belong on the deck of a pirate ship was Billy. He strolled across the deck as if he were in a different place all together. It was like he was on a walk through the country side, and had all the time in the world.

"Come with me," he said and led me into his cabin.

The cabin was quite large, but it was very organized, except for the table. It was covered in bottles, charts, books, and all manner of other things that I had no idea what they were. The rest of the cabin looked like a library with a hammock hung in the corner.

"Please sit." He pulled out a chair and motioned for me to sit down across from him.

I sat.

"I believe that you're smart enough to realize why you're here."

I nodded.

"I have two children that I know of," he said. "Only one of them had red eyes like me. I guess that would make you the son of Gabriella Penney."

"Yes," I nodded trying to keep my voice deep, but not knowing exactly how long I could hold out. "The governor's daughter."

"That's funny," he smiled. "I was told that she gave birth to a girl with scarlet eyes, not a boy."

"Maybe she did maybe she didn't," I shrugged. "You weren't around, how would you know?"

He laughed a little. "You're not a boy are you?"

"You're quicker at figuring things than all the men on that ship," I told him. I cleared my throat and allowed myself to talk normal. "What do you want?" I had talked with my normal voice every day, even if only for a few moments, since I had come aboard *the Victory*, but it was still odd to hear myself every time.

He thought for a moment as if he really wanted to ask the right question. "And is your name really Billy, or did you just make that up?"

"My name is Billy," I answered.

"That would be short for Sabil or Sabilla I'd imagine," he said.

That surprised me. I had not known that he knew my name. "Sabilla," I answered. "How would you know?"

"You remind me of your mother," he smiled, as if he were remembering. "You hardly look like her at all, but I can tell that she's your mother. She was the most beautiful woman that I had ever met. When we first met she looked so innocent and sweet, but as I soon found out, that was just a show she put on to keep her parents happy."

"What do you mean?" I asked.

"Well, you see," he sighed. "She would be all prim and proper by day, but she would sneak out at night and dance in the local bars. She loved to sing and dance. She had the voice of an angel. When I asked her why she did those kinds of things, she said that it was simply because she could. We met in a bar where I was spending the night, and one thing led to another and, then came you."

"Are you trying to say that my mother wasn't a good girl?" I asked.

"She seduced a pirate," he laughed. "What do you think?"

"Oh yes, I'm sure you had nothing to do with it."

"I didn't say that." He shook his head. "She came into my room after hours and...."

"Stop," I cut him off. "Please. All that matters is that I'm here now. I don't need any details. Good Lord, are all men like this?"

He just laughed. "So we have now established that you're not my son, but in fact, my daughter."

"Yes," I nodded. "Can I leave now?"

"If you left now where would you go?" He examined his fingernails. "Your friends are gone, we're very far from any land, and I'm the only family you have besides your mother. So therefore, you will stay with me. That is, if you don't have a husband somewhere, but something makes me doubt that."

"What makes you think that I'm not married?" I asked.

"Well, you are of age I guess." He looked at me sideways. "But what would a married woman be doing on a ship with a bunch of strange men, unless of course, you're married to one of them?"

"Maybe I am." I crossed my arms across my chest.

"Then it would be the lieutenant," he said. "Am I correct?"

"I'm not married," I laughed a little. "And if I was you think I would be married to Apollo?"

"Well," he shrugged. "He seemed to really care what happened to you. What's wrong? You don't like it when a man cares about you?"

"How would you know if he cared about me or not?" I huffed, feeling bombarded with more question than I really cared to answer. "You don't know me and you don't know him either and besides, when we were on the ship with them, you still thought I was a boy."

"True," he nodded. "So, who is he to you if not your love interest? He must know that you're a girl. There's no other explanation for why he would be so protective of you. I mean, I've been on navy ships before and men don't act like that about each other. Not real men anyway. But by the way you're acting, it seems more like you love him, but you're afraid to tell him that."

"Look damn it," I was getting upset. "Stop acting like you know everything about me. I'll bet this is the first time that you've ever seen me, and all you want to do is assume that you know every little detail of my life."

"You know," he said coolly. "Any one of my crewmen would get a couple of lashings if they spoke to me like that."

I just sat there with my arms crossed across my chest. I was so angry at that moment that I felt like my chest was going to burst. How dare he do this to me? He left me to be raised at an orphanage and had never once come to see me, but then when I did meet him he was going to treat me like he had known me all my life. I didn't think so.

He heaved a great sigh. "Even though you sort of remind me of your mother, the two of you are complete opposites. It's funny how two people could be exactly alike, yet completely different at the same time." With that, he stood up. "You're right Billy. I don't know you, but there is only one way for me to get to know you. So, when you are ready to talk, I am ready to listen," He walked out.

I sat there and looked around the room. I noticed that there was a mirror in the corner. It struck me as odd, because Billy didn't seem like the kind to look in the mirror very much. I went over and looked at my reflection. I was quite surprised at what I saw. I looked almost just like my father. A lot of the reason was that I was dressed like a boy, so I decided to change that. I let my hair down, tightened my belt a little, unbuttoned the bottom three buttons of my shirt, and tied up my shirt tail, then looked back in the mirror. I looked so different from what I had when I would look in the mirror every day. For the first time in a long time, I looked like a girl. I didn't think of myself as a boy, but the strange thing was, that I didn't really think of myself as a girl either.

I adjusted my sword strap and then I went up on deck.

I don't know what I was expecting when I came up on deck, but I wasn't expecting everyone to stop and stare at me. I scanned the crowd until I saw Billy. He was standing at the helm and he was staring at me as well. He was looking at me as if I were a memory of long ago.

"Everyone," Billy said. "This is my daughter Sabilla. If anyone messes with her they will be keel hauled, after thirty lashes. Understand?"

"Aye sir!" all the men yelled.

I was mildly horrified that he spoke such a threat in a tone that was more like he was discussing the weather, but at least I knew that he wasn't going to let anything happen to me.

As I walked up the steps someone let out a loud whistle a yelled, "Swing 'em honey!"

I didn't bother looking back. I just went on up the steps and stood next to Billy.

"So you want to get to know me?" I asked.

He nodded.

"I lived in an orphanage in the Barbados until I was fifteen. I had three friends there and one of them died five years ago, when the island was attacked by pirates. The other two were on the *H.M.S. Victory* with me. The three of us got onto the ship as ships boys. One of my friends was a girl, so the two of us had to dress up as boys. I was promoted to a midshipman after I was on the ship for a week and a half, because I saved the gun division that I was working for. I know it sounds ridiculous, but it happened and I had a lot of trouble at first, but

I did fine. Is there anything else you would like to know?"

"Which of your friends died?" The question surprised me.

"His name was Garth McHale," I answered.

He looked down at the deck and nodded. "I knew him. Despite your saying that I had never seen you before, I came to see you many times when you were a baby, and I was the one that took you to the orphanage. I knew that Garth would take care of you. As a matter of fact, the day that I took you to the orphanage was the same day that your friends Clara and Davy were taken there."

"I didn't tell you that my friends were named Clara and Davy."

"Never mind that," he shook his head. "I have some things to tend to," With that, he walked away leaving another man at the wheel.

I wondered for a moment why Billy had been so upset. I knew that it must have been a shock to find out that his friend had been killed, but I felt like there was something more to it. Otherwise, he would not have asked which of my friends had been killed, or Clara and Davy's names.

I walked down to the quarter deck, then decided that I would climb up to the foretop. It turns out that the men found it quite amusing to see a girl climb up the lines the way that I did.

"Maybe she should do it with a skirt on," one of the men yelled.

I sat down in the foretop and looked down at him. "And why is that?" I asked.

"Why shouldn't you?" he laughed.

"Well if it's a flash of pussy that you want, then all you have to do is look in the mirror," I hollered down to him.

His face turned red. He shook his head and got back to work, but all the other men started teasing him. I only felt bad for him for a minute or so. He disserved it. I mean, what could I say? I was a sailor.

I leaned back and breathed a deep breath of salt air.

"Oh, yer a sight fer sore eyes," came the voice of an Irishman from behind me.

I turned around to face him. He looked to be about twenty or so. He had curly, auburn, hair, dark green eyes, he was pretty well built (I could tell by how his shirt was tight across his chest), and he had a dimple in his chin. Needless to say, he was rather good looking.

"Excuse me?" I raised my eyebrows.

"Yer the most beautiful thing that I've ever laid my eyes on in all my life."

For a moment I wondered how many girls he had ever said that to.

"What's yer name, beautiful?" he asked.

"Billy Scarlet," I answered. "And yours?"

"Domonic," he said. "Domonic O'Rielly. I think I'll just call ya Scarlet if ya don't mind. Yer the captain's daughter I'd take it, the one that we'll get thirty lashes and a keel haulin', if we mess with ya."

I nodded.

He came over and sat down next to me. "Tell me Scarlet, ya gotta man on that pretty navy ship o' yer's?"

I laughed a little. Domonic was as cocky and flirty as he was muscled and red headed.

"What does it matter?" I asked.

"I'd take that as a no," he smiled. "Or it means that ya do, but ya really don't care. Either way I think I could win ya over."

I liked the compliment, but I figured that the main reason he was being that way was because he hadn't been ashore in a while. I knew men, and that's just how they were. I didn't understand it, but I had learned to live with it.

Just then the supper bell rang.

"Ladies first." Domonic nodded toward the line that was closest to us.

"Let's just see who gets down first," I said.

He smiled. "Very well." He got up and jumped to one of the lines that was farther away. It was a long jump and it kind of startled me, but he grabbed hold of it then winked at me. "See ya at the end o' the line." With that, he began sliding down.

I grabbed the line closest to me and slid down as fast as I could. When I got to the bottom he was standing there waiting for me.

"What took ya so long?" he asked.

"I let you win," I told him.

"An' why's that?" he smiled a smile that was so cocky that he was rivaling Apollo.

"Cause I felt like it," I answered.

"Billy," my father called. "You'll be dining with me in my cabin tonight. I don't want any of these men bothering you." He gave Domonic a warning look.

"See ya later, Scarlet," Domonic nodded, and followed the other men to the galley.

I went into Billy's cabin.

Me and him ate roasted fish with lemon.

"I try to make sure that the men get some kind of fresh fruit or vegetable at every meal," he said. "I don't want any of them getting scurvy. Lemons are especially good for preventing it. You know what scurvy is, don't you?" He winced at his own comment as if he suddenly realized what he had just said and how neither he nor I really would want to think about a horrible sickness while we were eating.

I just nodded.

I could tell that he was just trying to make conversation, but it wasn't really working. After that comment, he must have decided that the prevention of scurvy was not exactly a good meal time conversation, because he stopped talking altogether.

I tried to think of something, anything to say, but nothing came to mind, so I just sat there quietly, hoping that he would say something to break the awkward silence. It seemed that both me and Billy were alike in the way that it was hard for either of us to find something to talk about.

"Why are you so quiet?" he asked, finally.

"That's like asking someone why they're tall," I said.

"Really?" he smiled.

"Yes," I answered. "I don't know why I'm quiet. I just don't know what to say, most of the time, and when I do think of something to say, it all comes out sounding stupid, so most of the time I find it easier to not say anything." I paused for a moment.

"You can keep talking if you want," he said.

"Why?" I asked.

"I like the sound of your voice," he answered.

"What do you want to talk about?" I asked.

"What rank were you on that ship?"

"I was a midshipman, in charge of gun division three," I answered.

"Impressive," he nodded. "I was a midshipman once. Back when I sailed on the *H.M.S. Bounty.*"

"You were in the king's navy?" I asked.

"Yes, I was," he answered.

"How did you become a pirate?" I asked.

"I got involved with the wrong yet somehow, right people," he answered. "One thing led to another. I didn't like England's view on things. I truly believe that the English can be quite twisted, but so can other people, so I mustn't generalize. Anyway, I couldn't stand for some of the things that I saw happening, anymore so I abandoned ship."

"I don't understand a lot of England's reasoning either," I said.

"So," he sighed. "We agree on one thing so far."

He looked at me for a moment then said, "I never really have been a pirate, Billy. It's sad when days have come down to where a man cannot sail the seas under his own flag without being accused of such horrid and hellish crimes that are committed by men who engage in true piracy. I was accused of being a pirate because one day I sailed up on an American ship that was being attacked. It was a merchant vessel. The ship that was attacking it was flying no flag, so I sailed over and assisted the Americans in their fight. The other ship, as it turns out, was a French privateer. The Americans thanked me well, but in the eyes of the French, I was a pirate. I soon became so in the eyes of the people on many of the Caribbean islands. I don't know where I stand with the British, but with them I guess it would depend on who you ask as to where I stand."

I nodded.

"And what of you?"

I cast him an odd glance. "What of me?"

"This Apollo," he said. "He reminds me of someone. It matters not if you give two cents for him, that's not what I'm asking."

"Why do you say that?"

"I just don't want you getting all offended over that again," he laughed a little. "Anyway, who is he?"

"He reminds you of Garth McHale," I told him.

"Why?"

"Apollo is Mr. McHale's grandson."

He laughed. "I noticed that he had quite the swagger about him as Garth always did. I've missed old McHale over the years."

I nodded. "So have I."

The two of us stayed up most of the rest of the night talking about the past few years and about how we grew up. He told me about how he left his navy ship when he was eighteen, after the captain had him lashed for something that he didn't do. And I told him of all of my adventures at sea and how I had dressed up as a boy so that I could go sailing. By the time we got done talking it was well past midnight.

He showed me into a small room that seemed like it was his closet. It was through a sliding door in the back of his cabin.

"Do you have everything that you need?" he asked just as I was about to doze off.

"I'm fine," I told him.

"Let me know if you need anything," he said.

"I will," I answered and went on to sleep.

***

The next day I got to meet some of the other crewmen. I met the man that said that I needed to wear a skirt. His name was Jack Emmerson. He was a blond haired, blue eyed Englishman. He said that he wasn't mad at me for what I had said, but I could tell that I had hurt his pride a good bit and I didn't mind that one bit. He disserved every word of it, along with all the teasing that he got.

I also met a man named Art Smith and a Spanish man named Jase. Art was a middle aged, rugged man. He had mousey, brown hair, dark eyes, maybe three teeth and he looked (and smelled) like he had never bathed in all his life, but he seemed to be a nice guy.

I liked Jase. He was the first Spanish man that I had ever met.

"So you are the captain's daughter?" he asked. He said "captain" like "capyton".

"Yes," I answered.

"You look a lot like him," he told me.

There was something very familiar about him. It was almost as if I had met him before, but I knew that it was impossible. He wasn't as tall as all the other men. He was about the same height as Billy. He had long black hair, pretty big muscles, and eyes that were so dark brown that they almost looked black.

He looked at me the same way that Billy had. As if he was remembering something from long ago. I only wondered why for a little while, but I just figured that if there was a reason for it that I should know about, they would tell me, otherwise I should not worry about it.

Later that evening, when things had settled down from their usual hustle of the day, the men decided to have a drinking game and for some reason, that at the moment escaped my knowledge, but later came to light, much to the amusement of many, they wished for me to join them.

"I don't think so," I told them.

"Oh come on, Scarlet," Domonic urged. "Don't be a wuss."

"I'm not a wuss, I'm being a lady," I said. It was not a very convincing argument for someone who had pretended to be a man for the past five years, so I added; "For the first time in years."

"Come on, Billy," my father said. "You're a sailor. We all know that and there is nothing to be ashamed of there. I assure you, no one will think the less of you for joining in. In fact I'd be worried about the exact opposite if I were you," He cast Domonic a sideways glance. "I have no doubts that you could out drink all of them if you took a notion."

"Don't worry," Domonic told me. "I won't get upset if you beat me."

"Fine," I sat down at the small table, in between Art and Domonic. They were the only other ones that were in the game.

I started to say that I wasn't worried about upsetting anyone else, but instead was worried how I would react to such fast drinking. I didn't want to tell them that I couldn't hold hard drinks well. As a matter of fact, when I had become a midshipman and was allowed a full ration of rum, I had insisted that I'd still only get a half ration, if any at all because even a small amount gave me a headache.

I watched as Jack Emmerson poured the shots. I got a terrible tingle of anticipation at the back of my throat as the small glasses were placed before us on the table. Each of us were to get six shots and whoever drank them all fastest, would win. I had a strange feeling that Art was going to win, but I figured that I would try anyway.

"Ready," Jase said. "Go!"

The first shot went down easy, so I drank the other five faster. Me and Domonic finished at the same time, before Art.

I was surprised, with the drink as well as myself. The stuff wasn't near as harsh as rum. As a matter of fact it tasted kind of good. I had never expected that I would have been able to drink like that. Somewhere in the back of my, somewhat clouded mind, I had a feeling that, despite the good taste of this drink, it was stronger than any other I had taken before.

Me and Domonic slammed our last glasses down on the table, which was met with a loud cheer. I'm sure Art would have cheered as well had he not passed out five seconds before. If I had been in my right mind, I would have realized that it was terribly stupid to continue, but I was far too gone to even think of that.

"We have a tie!" Jack yelled. "Time for the tie breaker!" With that they refilled the glasses.

"Hold yer horses," Domonic rubbed his forehead as if he was already starting to get a head ache. "Can the lady handle it?" He looked at me, slack eyed.

It was almost as if I were in a dream and I was just watching wishing I could slap myself in the face. "Of course I can handle it. What do you take me for?"

"Billy, I think you need to slow down," My father told me.

I could tell that he was very concerned, but me being a natural show off, not to mention I was hopelessly drunk, I would not back down to such a challenge.

I shook my head. "I'm fine."

"Go," Jase said, in a tone that showed that he had his doubts about me holding the stuff very good. It was almost as if, both him and Billy knew that I wasn't a good drinker. They seemed to know a lot about me, even things that I wasn't sure of myself.

They sat the drinks in front of us and we were off again. I finished first, but I was beginning to feel odd indeed. I got this tingly feeling that was spreading throughout my body, and the world began to spin in ways that I had never seen before.

I looked over at Domonic, who for some reason seemed even better looking than I had first thought. I smiled and laughed so stupidly that what brain I did have left in my head wanted to beat me even more senseless than I already was.

"I let ya win," Domonic said.

"Oh really? You just don't wanna say that ya lost ta a girl," I found it harder and harder to speak with every word that I said.

He looked at me all slack eyed. "I let ya win 'cause I'm in love with ya."

"That's a load o' shit Dom," I huffed.

"I'll prove it." The next thing I knew Domonic's mouth was locked onto mine. That was the last thing that I could remember until I was in my bed in Billy's cabin with my head throbbing.

I moaned and looked over at Billy. He was sitting in a chair beside my bed. "What happened?"

"You got very drunk and went stark raving mad, if you must know," he said.

"I figured as much." I tried to sit up, but the world spun around and I had to lay back down. "What did I do? The last thing that I remember was getting kissed by Domonic."

"Oh my dear, kissing him was just the beginning," he laughed.

"Oh Lord," I whispered. "How many more guys did I kiss?"

"You didn't kiss anyone else," he laughed. "Would you like me to tell you what happened?"

"Not really, but I would rather hear it from you than from Domonic, after I get to feeling better, so have at it," I sighed. "Hopefully I'll be able to say that I've done worse."

"I'd like to think not."

And so he began:

After Domonic kissed, me I slapped the hell out of him.

"I'll say!" I scoffed. "I never thought that when I got kissed for the first time I would be drunker than a dumb ass in a brothel."

"A what?" Billy asked.

"What'd ya hit me for?" Domonic asked.

"Cause you're an idiot," I told him. "I can't believe that I let ya talk me inta doin' that. I've never been able ta hold strong drinks well, and though I find ya very easy ta look at, I can't believe that you gave me my first kiss."

"So, Scarlet," Domonic smirked. "I'm the first man that ever kissed ya? How'd ya like it?"

"I can't say," I answered. "I've nobody ta compare ya to and besides if you ask me I think that it felt like kissin' a wet mop."

"Billy," my father said. "You need to go lay down or something."

"Lay down?" I asked. "I don't need to lay down, I feel fine."

It was about that time that somebody began playing a song that I knew.

"I know this song!" I exclaimed. "Play it louder!" They of course listened to a horribly drunk moron, meaning myself of course, and played it louder, while I, said moron, jumped up on the table and sang along with it as loud as I possibly could.

About halfway through the last verse of the song, I started dancing and the small innocent table just couldn't take that. It fell over and I fell on top of Billy.

"Okay," he said. "You're coming back to my cabin."

After that I said a bunch of off the wall things and he wouldn't tell me what they were.

Once he was done telling me all the stupid things that I did I just moaned. "You at least have to tell me some of what I said."

"Well, there was something about a man you said you knew a long time ago. I don't know who he was or much of what you were talking about, but it sounded odd. You said that you saw him in a lot of your dreams, but you weren't sure what his name was, though did tell me what he looked like and that you thought that his name might be James. I might have an idea of...." He paused, cleared his throat and moved on. "Of course you chose the perfect moment to tell me about how you found out about what goes on in brothels. It was the moment that Domonic had come in to check on you so he got the full run down on it as well. Poor bastard, you wouldn't be satisfied until both of us had heard the whole story. You told me a good bit about Apollo and you tried to tell me something about Domonic, but you were much too far gone by that point for me to understand. That just some of the stuff. Do you care for me to continue? I could get into greater detail of some of the moments during your, how should I say, colorful story about brothels or perhaps when you decided to go tell Domonic off and I had to stop you. Would you like for me to?"

"No," I shook my head.

"Who told you that anyway?"

"Told me what?"

"About the brothels and all. It sounded like a story told by a drunk Irishman."

"It was my ship's dad, on board *the Victory*. He was Irish, so it seems you have your story tellers straight. Though by what you say, I probably embellished it a good bit, which, in fact, frightens me."

"Let's just hope that Domonic doesn't remember any of it."

I moaned once more, hoping beyond hope that Domonic had been too drunk to remember my rantings. "Yes, let's."

"Of all the dumb things that were done, I do believe that the dumbest of them all was when Domonic said that he let you win because he loved you. Dumb ass. I can't believe he would say something that stupid, even if he was drunk." He shook his head and looked into my eyes that were almost certainly bloodshot. "If you weren't a very good drinker, you could have just said so. You only told me that after you were in here babbling on."

"I thought you knew," I said without really realizing the words had come out of my mouth.

He gave me an odd stare. "And how would I know that?" he asked in a way that almost convinced me that he didn't know.

"I don't know. I just need some rest I guess. I feel like my skull is being crushed."

"That's what happens when you get that drunk," he laughed a little. "You just stay down here until you feel better. I'll see you in a little while."

***

I didn't feel better until that next morning, and after I that I didn't even want to smell rum, whiskey or anything like it, therefore I did not want to go into the galley or the hold. I either stayed on deck or in Billy's cabin.

That evening I was feeling mostly better so I decided to sit in the foretop. After a few minutes Domonic came up and sat down next to me. I was mildly terrified at the thought of him remembering anything that I had said while drunk, but I wasn't going to let on. I just sat there as awkward silence filled the air, hoping that he would be the first to speak. Finally he did.

"Feelin' better?" he asked.

"Jackass," I muttered.

He laughed. "That's hardly complimentary, but I'd take that as a yes."

"You let me win because you loved me?" I huffed. "What kind of stupid lie is that? I can't believe that even you would say something that pathetic."

He just laughed.

"You let me win because you wanted to see what I was like when I was drunk," I said. "You weren't very drunk at all were you?"

"Not as drunk as you. Not so drunk that I don't remember certain stories that you found it necessary to tell when I came to see you."

I could have beat myself senseless for that one. "I seem to have quite a way with words when I've had a little too much to drink."

"I'd say," he smiled and started to climb down. "Oh by the way, thanks for yer compliment."

"Oh dear God, which one?" I rolled my eyes.

"I'm glad that you think I'm very easy to look at." With that he slid down the rope.

I wanted to throw something after him, but I didn't have anything so I just sat there. I thought for a minute about tossing my boot after him, but decided against it because I probably wouldn't hit him anyway. Besides, I had embarrassed myself enough. There was no doubting the fact that I was bad at making good impressions.

Just then, someone yelled, "Ship off starboard stern!"

I slid down to the deck and joined Billy at the helm.

"It looks like your navy friends have come to collect you." He handed me his scope.

I looked through the scope and saw that it was in fact the *H.M.S. Victory* with captain Hector at the helm. I could tell that he was ready for a fight.

I took the scope away from my eye and when I did I noticed the letters *W.S.S.* on the side of it.

"What do those letters stand for?" I asked.

"My name," Billy answered. "William Sabill Scarlet."

"Sabill?" I asked.

He nodded.

I had truly been named after my father. I had thought that his name was

William and people called him Billy and it was just a coincidence that we were both called the same thing, but that wasn't right. I really was named after him.

"I have a plan," I said. "They're mostly here for me. I can get in a long boat and while they slow their speed to pick me up, you can get away."

"I won last time," he said simply. "Why should I not win this time?"

"Please," I begged. "They're more prepared this time. They know what to expect from you." 'And I don't want anybody on either of the ships to get hurt,' I added in my mind.

"Very well," He sighed. "I don't want to put you in any danger, but if this is what you want to do. Are you sure?"

No, I wasn't sure. I wasn't sure that captain Hector would not make chase after they got me on board, I wasn't sure that I wanted to leave my father's ship so soon, but I was sure that I wanted to protect the crews of both ships and I would do everything in my power to see to it that none of them got hurt. I didn't know if my plan would work or not, but I would do the best that I could.

I turned to him and nodded.

"Ready a lifeboat!" he called.

I went over and stepped into the boat that they had ready.

Billy came over to me. "I'm going to miss you, Sabilla. I hope to see you again very soon. You know, I always thought that you were going to turn out this way," The next thing that he did really surprised me. He kissed me on the forehead and whispered, "I love you."

"I love you too, father," I said.

When he smiled at me, I knew beyond a shadow of a doubt, that he did love me. He may have left me at an orphanage and he may have had many faults, but I knew, for the first time in my life, that my father really did love me.

I motioned to the men who were holding the lines and they began lowering me down into the water.

"Hey, Scarlet," Domonic called down to me. "Try not to miss me too much."

"I'll do my best not to," I rolled my eyes.

After that they let the life boat loose and I paddled as fast as I could toward the other ship. All of a sudden, the wind blew across my face causing my hair to blow into my eyes. I then, realized that I still looked like a girl.

'Oh well,' I thought. 'They were going to have to find out about it sooner or later. It's better they find out in this way than in some other. At least this way, Apollo will be accused of nothing. I would not have him demoted for this.'

Captain Hector called for the order for the for'ard sail to be lowered. Doing this slowed the ship down so that they could pick me up. They hauled the boat up and I climbed out. It felt good to be back on the *Victory*, but in a way it felt strange, to be there as a girl. Not only because I looked different because I knew that I was no longer going to be treated as an equal. I was going to be treated as if I was lower than the rest. As a girl, I was no longer an officer, I was no one. The five years I had spent on the ship, the respect and the position that I had earned no longer applied. I was a woman and there was no more hiding it.

I looked off into the distance and saw that Billy's ship was now a good ways off and definitely out of firing range that made me feel a good bit better about life in general, but it still didn't help the fact that I felt like I had just threw away all that I had worked for. However, I knew it was worth me being discovered to be a girl, to ensure the safety of all the people I cared about.

Davy came running over to me. "Billy, thank God you're all right." He hugged me.

"Where's Clark?" I asked once he was done hugging me, hoping they had not yet found out about Clara.

"I think you mean, Miss Clara Honeycut," Captain Hector said as he came across the deck toward me. From the expression on his face, I could tell that he was a little less than pleased.

"What?" I asked. "What's going on?"

"Everyone knows, Billy," Davy said.

"Where is Clara?" I almost yelled.

"She's in the brig," Apollo answered.

"Why? What happened?"

"After we found out that she was a girl, we figured that it would be the best thing to do for her safety," Captain Hector said. "And that's exactly where you're going."

"What?" By that point I was getting really mad.

"Billy, it's only until we get you to land," Apollo told me. "You and Clara will be paid for your time aboard the *Victory* and put ashore. We can't have women on the ship. You must understand."

"I'm not going to the brig," I huffed. "I have been a girl this whole time, and I haven't been in the brig. I can't believe this."

"Girls don't belong on ships," he said sounding very much like a strict officer.

"Well, I've been here for five years, so why didn't you put me off to begin with?"

He just shook his head and walked up the deck a ways.

I couldn't believe that Apollo was acting like he had never known about any of it, in the first place. I had not wanted him to get in trouble and I wasn't sure how I thought he would act, but this was certainly not it. I figured that he would at least stand up for me in some way.

"Look, I may be a girl, but I am an....."

Just then, I got splashed with some very cold water from behind cutting off my words. I turned around and saw Apollo holding a bucket of water.

"Cool off sugar puss," he said in his cocky voice. "Okay. Just give it a rest."

"With all due respect, lieutenant." I walked over and slapped him across the face as hard as I could, then went down to the brig of my own free will.

The brig was dark, wet, and dank. It smelled strongly of stagnant sea water and rats. The only light was coming from a single port hole. An eerie creaking came from a lamp that was swinging on a hook next to the entrance.

I did not want to go in, but I had resigned myself to the fact that no matter how much I fought, I was still going to be put down there, so there was no use making it any worse than it had to be.

They put me in the same cell as Clara. It was the least wet of them all. As a matter of fact, it seemed that they had made it quite comfortable.

"So, you're back," she smiled. "I've been locked in this damn, cell since the day after you left. They let Patrick Arthur take me for a walk around the deck every day at noon and every night at sun down, other than that I have not left this wretched slop pit. You know, I never thought that I'd get locked in prison for being a girl."

"Don't I know it?" I sat down next to her. "It's stupid."

She sighed. "Men will be men and us women have to deal with it. So, what all happened to you? Why are you wet?"

"It's something of a long story," I told her.

"Yes," she nodded. "And I'm bored."

So, I told her of my time on my father's ship. Including the part about me getting drunk and telling my father and Domonic about brothels, which caused us both to laugh furiously. I told her of how good a man my father really was and that me and him really did have the same name. I also told her of my, not so happy, return to the ship and how Apollo had splashed me with the bucket of water, but we mostly dwelled on the main event. My getting drunk of course.

"I can't believe you got that drunk," she laughed after I was done telling the story.

"I can't either. You should have seen me. I'm sure all of you would have gotten some good laughs out of it. And I will never be able to think of Domonic for the rest of my life, without being embarrassed."

The two of us sat up talking well into the night. Sometime after Clara had gone to sleep Davy came in.

"You all right?" he asked.

"Yea," I nodded and took his hand through the bars. I just held his hand like I did when I was little. It made me feel better. "How did they find out about me and Clara?" I asked.

"We had to tell them," he answered. "It was the only way to get the captain to go after you. I have to get back on watch. Apollo is covering for me right now. Goodnight, Billy."

"Goodnight," I whispered.

With that he walked out.

I sat down and heaved a great sigh. Though Clara was in the cell with me and there was a guard not too far away I still felt alone. I shivered, slightly with loneliness, and slightly with fear. Where would we go if we got put off the ship? As I had told Apollo, I had no other home. Me and Clara would have nothing and would have to start over from the bottom up if we were to be put off the ship.

I looked over at the guard. I recognized him. It was Patrick. I guessed that he must have been put in charge of watching after us girls because Clara had mentioned him being there before and then he was there guarding the cell that night as well.

"Hey, Patrick," I said.

"Hello, Billy," he smiled. "So, Billy Scarlet is a miss. It's not quite as much of a shock to me as it is to most. I always knew that you were too prissy to be a boy."

"Prissy or not, I saved your ass on more than one occasion," I laughed a little.

"That you did." He leaned against the bars. "I'll be sad to see the two of you go." He glanced through the bars at Clara, then whispered. "You've been very good sailors."

"I wish that everyone felt that way," I said. "Or at least some of them."

"The captain doesn't want you to go either," he told me. "He just doesn't want either of you to get hurt, is all. He has his reasons, I assure you."

I sighed. "I didn't mean the captain."

"I know," he nodded. "You meant Apollo. I don't know what goes on in that head of his. He's been like a brother to me ever since we were ship's boys, but that doesn't mean I ever have, or ever will understand him."

"It's going to be really strange for the two of us to live on land after all this time on a ship," I said. "I don't know what we're going to do."

"Just do me a favor," he told me.

"What's that?" I asked.

"Take good care of Clara for me."

Just then, Apollo walked in. He was in his uniform, but he wasn't wearing his hat and his hair was down. His shirt was not tucked in and unlaced at the top and I caught a glimpse of a crescent moon tattoo on his chest. He was his usual dashing self. Most girls would have simply, swooned at the sight of him when he walked through that door, but I was almost too angry to see how good he looked.

"Patrick," he said. "I would like to have a moment alone with Billy."

"Yes, sir," Patrick nodded and walked out.

"I'm sorry for the way that I acted on deck," he said.

"I'll bet you are," I huffed. "I am too. Where are we going to get put off?"

"Florida," he answered.

"Good," I nodded. "I hope it doesn't take too long."

"Billy," he sighed. "I said that I'm sorry. Look, you must understand the reasons for my actions."

I could tell by the tone of his voice that he really was sorry, but that didn't make me feel much better about what he had done.

"I understand that you were so scared that the captain would find out that you didn't tell him about me years ago, that you pretended that you have never known anything about any of it. You didn't stand up for me at all."

"That is not it, Billy," he huffed. "You don't know how bad things would look for your reputation if the captain found out that I had known all along. Rumors will seem to create themselves on a ship like this and I didn't want to put you through anything like that."

"You're saying that the men will start saying that the two of us have..."

He cut me off. "They will say that I was keeping you on board as my mistress."

"And how do you know that?"

"Because I've seen it happen to men on other ships before. The men came out of it clean, because people said that they were just being men and that's what men do, but the woman was disgraced many times over. I didn't want that to happen. And am I so wrong as to want to protect the job that I worked so hard to get to? I've worked my whole life to get to where I am."

"And it would be a shame for you to lose all of it just because of some girl."

"Billy," he sighed.

"No, I understand." I felt tears coming, but I would not dare let them fall. My next words came out as a mere whisper. "I didn't ask you to tell all of everything that had happened. I just wanted you to stand up for me out there."

"I tried, but you wouldn't give me the chance." He looked me straight in the eye, and for a moment I wanted to give in and say that I had already forgiven him, but my mind went back to him splashing me with water and saying what he had said, as if I had never been anything or anyone at all to him. I got mad all over again. I took a deep breath, trying to calm myself down before I spoke again, but it didn't work as well as I had hoped.

"I was happy to see you when I got back on this ship," I scoffed. "Are you just too busy trying to be more than you are to see how you treat people? I thought that you were my friend."

"Billy," he said. "I chose to put you off in Florida for a good reason."

"Why is that?" I asked. "So that you'll know where to find me?"

"No," he answered. "I see you haven't cooled off any."

I grabbed a cup of water that was on the floor beside me and splashed him in the face with it. "Cool off yourself," I huffed. "Sugar puss."

"Very well," he nodded and walked out.

A minute or so later Patrick came back in. By the look on his face, I could tell that Apollo must have been in something of a huff, when he left. "Didn't go so well, I'd take it."

"Not really," I answered.

"Just sleep it off," he said. "It'll all seem better in the morning."

***

I awoke the next morning to Patrick calling my name. I got up and walked over to the door of the cell. "What is it?"

"Apollo wants to see you," he answered.

"Okay," I yawned and followed him to Apollo's cabin.

"Good morning, Billy," Apollo said when he saw me.

Without a word, Patrick left the room.

"Have you calmed down any?" Apollo asked. "I had something that I wanted to give you last night, but you wouldn't let me."

"I'm fine," I told him.

"Good." He handed me a small piece of paper.

"What's this?" I asked.

"It tells where your mother lives," he answered. "I found out that she lives in Florida, so I told the captain to drop you off there."

"Thank you," I said.

"I know you don't believe me when I say that I'm sorry about what happened yesterday," He sighed. "But I really am. I was being an ass."

"That you were," I nodded.

"I have one more thing that I wanted to give you before you left."

"What...." I had no time to finish my question. He kissed me full on my still open mouth. When he stopped it took me a few seconds to get back steady on my feet.

"I'm gonna miss you, sugar puss," he whispered.

I put my arms around him and just leaned into him. I was going to miss him more than words could say. "I'll miss you too, but do me a favor."

"What's that?" he asked.

"Never call me that again."

He nodded. "No problem there."

I laughed a little, but it turned into a slight sob.

He stroked my back. "It's okay." he sighed.

"Do I have to go back to that cell?" I asked.

"No," he laughed a little. "We're only a few miles out of the harbor."

"I have to go get my stuff together," I said. "I'll see you in a few minutes," I went down to the midshipman's berth and got my sea bag. Clara and Davy were down there, waiting for me. It was then that something occurred to me. "Are you coming with us, Davy?"

"I can't, Billy," he told me.

"Why?" I asked.

"My life belongs to the navy for the next few years," he answered. "I have to stay with them until I get discharged."

I sighed. I wasn't surprised to hear that they were keeping Davy with them, but all the same I couldn't imagine life without him. I couldn't remember a time that me, Clara and Davy had not been together. I had always figured that we would possibly go our separate ways one day, but I had never wanted it to happen. Moving on in the world and having our own lives had always seemed like a far in the future kind of thing, but then there it was right in front of us. It was time to move on, just like we had when we left the orphanage. Things were changing and we had to learn to deal with it if we wanted to survive. I felt tears in my eyes, but I blinked them back. I could tell that Clara was doing the same.

"If either of you start crying I'm going to lose it," Davy laughed. "The two of you have never been the kind to just cry your eyes out about small stuff and if you start it now, I'm not going to be happy."

"Small stuff?" Clara asked. "You say that us getting separated for the first time in our lives, for God only knows how long, is small stuff?"

"I'm saying that it's not that bad. We're grown up now. Our lives have to be what we make them. You two are going to be just fine, and so am I. It's how Mr. McHale used to say."

"Just another step towards forever," we said at the same time.

It had been many years since I heard those words spoken and they gave me a new kind of confidence that I could not explain. "To hell with this," I huffed. "I'm not going to cry damn it. We're all okay. We're alive and well and we will see each other again. If not in this life, I know we'll see each other in the next one. I mean, we've been more of a family than most people that actually are related. No matter what happens no one can take that away from us, so come on you damn sea rats, let's get a move on. We have somewhere to be."

With that we headed up on deck. We were in a busy little Florida harbor. It looked like a pleasant town, but it didn't look like a place where I wanted to live. Buggies clattered up and down the cobblestone streets. Vender's wagons were set up at the far side of the docks and continued on into town. Each wagon contained different kinds of goods, from sweet cakes to silver ware, there was a little bit of everything and something for everyone. Not only that, it seemed as though everyone decided to come and see what all was going on. There was a sea of people wandering about and I wasn't at all eager to join them. It looked like an alright place, but it didn't look like my home and I didn't intend for it to be.

They docked the ship and set out a gang plank. Captain Hector gave each of us a bag of gold coins which was our share of pay for our time on the ship.

"You two have been good men," he told us. "Or well, sailors. I hate to see you go."

"We're going to miss sailing with you, sir," I saluted.

"Goodbye, midshipman Scarlet," he said. "And goodbye, midshipman Honeycut."

"Goodbye, sir," we both said and then headed down the gang plank.

Once we got onto the dock I looked back at the crewmen. Arnold was looking at me as if I were his own child. Danny and Simon saluted. Patrick looked like he wasn't sure what to do or say. He stared at Clara for a long moment then disappeared below decks. Apollo gave me his cocky smile and winked at me. Finally, I looked at Davy, my brother. He smiled and waved to us.

"Farewell, my beloved crew of the *H.M.S. Victory*," I called. "I will miss all of you and I wish you God speed."

With that the two of us walked up the dock.

Clara took my hand and squeezed it. "We make an oath here and now," She whispered. "It's only forward from here. We will never look back."

"Yes," I nodded. "Never."

So we walked down the dock and mixed into the sea of people. We tried to blend in, but no matter how hard we tried, it did not feel right. Land had not felt like home in years, but we had to try it. We seemed to melt into the crowd a head off in an unknown direction, a new direction, and no matter how much we wanted to, we never once looked back.

Part 2
A new life

Chapter

Six

Our first night away from the ship, me and Clara stayed at an inn that was on the top floor of a bar. It was a nice place, kind of quiet and cozy. It wasn't the kind of place that two women would stay by themselves, but we had found out that the reason for the town being so crowded earlier was because it was market day, and there were no other vacant rooms in town besides the rooms in the bar.

That night when we were eating we chose to sit at the table that was farthest from the door. I wasn't sure why I had chosen that place, but I felt safer there. Ever since we had come into the town I had felt like we were being watched. I didn't know who would be watching us or why, but I liked being able to see everything that was going on in the place.

I sat there drinking a cup of ale, and fiddling with my jade eye medallion. Suddenly, I felt so much like someone was watching me. A feeling came over me that I had not felt before. I could not explain it, it was a feeling that I had only felt in my dreams, the dreams that I would have about battles when I was younger. Someone was watching me; I could feel it in the depths of my soul. I looked around the room noticed a man standing next to the fire place. He was standing in the shadows so I couldn't see his face, but I could tell that he was staring straight at me. He turned, took a few steps and sat down at a small table that was next to the window. Smoke came out of the fire place and swirled around him as if it were trying to hide him. I flinched slightly under his gaze.

"What's wrong?" Clara asked.

"That man over by the fire place," I whispered while staring into my cup. "He's staring over at us."

"It's probably because we're two girls in men's clothes," she said. "Or it could be that we are in a place like this, alone. Don't worry about it, Billy."

I nodded and took the last sip of my ale then went up to the counter to get another. When I turned to go back to the table I almost jumped out of my skin. It was almost as if the man appeared out of thin air right next to me. I looked over at him and when I did, my heart skipped a beat. I wasn't sure that was a good, or bad thing, but I felt like I had seen him before. As a matter of fact, I knew I had seen him before. I wasn't sure where or how, but I knew that this had not been our first meeting. In the few seconds that he was standing there, I tried to think back to every man I had met in the time that I had been a sailor, but I knew, even without thinking too hard about it, I had met him before then, but when and where, I had no idea.

I glanced over at him casually. He had a sharp jaw and chin. He had a beard that looked like it had only been growing for a day or two. He had long wavy, brown hair, brown eyes, and a dimple in his chin. Needless to say, he was terribly handsome.

I opened my mouth to speak, but he spoke first.

"Be careful where you show off that jade eye, Miss Scarlet," he said, paid the bar tender and walked upstairs to a room.

I looked down at the counter and noticed that he had left a small piece of paper. I picked it up and looked at it. It was a small corner of, what I guessed, had been a large piece of parchment. I was stained and yellowing, and he had folded it over three times. I gently unfolded it so as not to rip it, for in seemed very fragile. Though there was not much at all written on it, what was written chilled me to my very core. I read it two or three times before I even believed what was written. It said:

Sabilla Scarlet #14

I went back to the table and sat down.

"What did he mean by that?" Clara scowled. She looked over at me. "Are you all right? You look like you've seen a ghost. What's wrong?"

"I'm not sure, but he left this on the counter." I showed her the note. "I think he wants me to go to his room or something."

"Something about this doesn't sound right." She looked over at the chair that he had been sitting in as if it could tell us who he was and what he wanted.

"You're damn right," I huffed. "Not very many people in this world know that my name is Sabilla. I've never met him before so how would he know? At least I don't think I've ever met him."

"What do you mean you don't think you've ever met him?"

"You didn't get an odd feeling when you looked at him? Like you've seen him before, but don't know when or where?"

She thought for a moment. "Now that you mention it, I do think I've seen him before."

I looked up at the room that he had walked into. This was more than I wished to handle on my first night away from *the Victory*, but I had to go into that room and speak to him, no matter what I thought would or would not happen when I got there.

"I don't think that you should go," she said as if she could read my mind. "He could be dangerous. I'd be careful about speaking to a strange man like him. I mean, he knows your name, there is something very frightening about that."

"That's the reason that I'm going," I told her. "I have to find out how he knows me. I've never been to this place before in my life, and I don't think that my reputation precedes me quite that well. If anyone in these parts knew me, they would know me as a man, a sailor named Billy Scarlet, unless news travels on the wind here."

"Do you want me to come with you?" she asked.

"If you want to," I answered.

When we got done eating we went to our room, put up our bags, then went down the hall to room number fourteen. I took a deep breath and knocked on the door.

"Come in," came the man's voice.

My hand shook as I reached out and turned the door knob. I pushed the door. It creaked open and the two of us went inside. The room was very dimly lit. The only light came from a small fire that burned in the fireplace. The man was sitting in a chair next to the window.

"How in the bloody hell did you know my name?" I asked. I knew it wasn't really the nicest way to greet a stranger, but he had not exactly been very nice with his greeting either, so I guess that made us even.

"Calm down, Miss Sabilla," he laughed slightly. "I'll explain that in good time." Despite the fact that he seemed very mysterious and slightly alarming, there was something warm and welcoming about him.

"What's so important about my jade eye medallion?" I calmed myself down a good bit. Something in the tone of his voice made me feel sort of at ease.

"I haven't yet introduced myself." He ignored my question. "People call me Shadowlark. About your medallion, it symbolizes something from another world."

"How do you know that?" I asked.

"Because." He lit a few candles that were on the mantle. The only thing that was strange about it was the fact that the fire to light the candles, seemed to come up out of the fireplace and onto his fingertips so that he could light the candle. "I have a brother named Nathaniel, but he's now called Grayheart and he's linked to that world. Very few people will recognize the jade eye, but the few that do you will not want to be around. As for how I know your name, I've known that for many years. You see there are a lot of things that I can't explain right now, but I will watch out for you. If someone ever says anything about the medallion be cautious of them. You have no knowledge of this, so be careful where you wear that thing."

I thought back to when I had first bought the medallion and the boy had told me that most sea faring men would shy away from it and how his father had told him not to sell it to anyone who didn't recognize such a trinket. The medallion itself was odd enough just to look at because I felt like I had seen it before, but then to meet a man that I got the same feeling about, only ten times stronger, I began to feel very odd about all of it indeed.

"What does any of this have to do with either of us?" Clara asked. "If your brother is part of this thing with the jade eye then why are you acting like it's a bad thing?"

"If you have even seen the jade eye then you're part of this," he answered. "And as for the other question, I don't approve of what my brother stands for. It may be a good thing that you wear the jade eye, or it may be a bad thing. It all depends on how brave you are."

"What do you mean?" I asked.

"If you are brave enough to face people like Grayheart and the Rossaletta, then by all means wear it. I just don't want you to get hurt." He propped on the window sill. "Rossaletta is heartless and cruel. The only thing that really bothers me is that she is very close to being able to come into this world."

"Who's Rossaletta?" I asked, but somehow I knew the answer before I had even asked.

"The *Dragon's Empress*," he answered. "Beware of her. She is very powerful. You will know if you see her, of that I am certain, but don't worry. I'll watch out for both of you."

"How are you going to do that?" Clara asked. "Are you going to come with us where ever we go?"

"I'll be with you for some of the time," he answered. "Just don't worry. I won't let anything happen to you."

"I still don't understand any of this, but I think I believe you," I said. "The only thing that I don't get is, how this could put either of us in any danger, and if it does, how much are we in?"

"I can't explain this right now, but be on your guard. Ill news was carried on the wind tonight. I hope it was not true. If it is true then that means he is coming and we must be extra careful not to let him find us, but I cannot say just yet if he is here," he said. "All the same, I'll stay with you. You may return to your room, now. The two of you need your rest."

After him saying that, we left. We went back to our room and got ready for bed. All the things that he had said confused me. Long after Clara had gone to sleep I was still awake thinking about all that had happened. What had he meant by ill news had been brought on the wind? What did any of it have to do with me or Clara, besides the fact that I had my jade eye medallion? Why did he not tell me how he knew my name? (And the biggest question on my mind.) Who exactly was this man called Shadowlark? As very odd as it seemed, his name sounded very familiar to me. Something kept telling me that he was the man from my dream, but I knew he could not be. The man in my dream was named James, or something similar. None of it made much sense to me, but I tried not to let it bother me.

No matter what I tried I could not sleep so I decided to read some out of Mr. McHale's book. It had been quite a while since I had looked at it. As a matter of fact I had not read any from the book since I had shown it to Apollo when I found out that Mr. McHale was his grandfather.

The first few pages were only a few sentences about how he had been very busy, but on the sixth page he wrote:

It is me of course. I am so
tired. I did not know that a
person could get this tired.
Anyway, something quite odd
happened today on my morning
watch. I spotted a ship not too
far away from us in the fog.
When I looked at it through my
scope I saw that it was hideous.
It had snakes for masts and the
bowhead looked like a dragon's
head. The name on the back of
the ship was, as I recall, *The
Dragon's Empress*. The "a" in
the word dragon was looked like
a red eye and it was made out
of what looked like it was made
out of jade. I called on the helmsman
to come and look and I was glad
that he came because not three seconds
after he saw it the ship vanished into
thin air. We were the only two that
saw it, which is strange because there
were a lot of men on deck at the time.
I must go now. I have to get some sleep.

I sat there feeling like my heart was about to beat out of my chest. *The Dragon's Empress* was what Shadowlark had called the Rossaletta woman and Mr. McHale had wrote that there was a red jade eye on the back of that accursed ship. I felt the medallion around my neck. At that moment I felt like taking it off and throwing it out my window, but instead I looked back at Mr. McHale's book.

I have found out a bit more about this *Dragon's Empress*. I'm told that it's a ghost ship that is captained by an immortal man named Nate Grayheart. That's about all that I've found out so far. Odd things have been happening lately. We have been caught in a fog all day long and yesterday we kept spotting rocks, but every time we got sort of close to them, they would disappear. I believe that all of this has something to do with that accursed ghost ship. We are lost. Our compass is broken so we cannot tell which way we are going and we haven't seen land in a very long time. To tell the truth, I want to go home, but how am I to do that when we don't even know what direction we're sailing in? I have a feeling that this is only the beginning of my worries. Someone is calling me on deck and by their tone I can tell the news will not be good.

I quickly flipped the page and read the next entry.

It is hard to believe all the things that have
happened in the last hour. When I was called
onto the deck I saw land. The lookout said that
it had appeared out of nowhere. The land was
odd looking. It was like a mountain sticking up
out of the ocean. At the top of it was some form
of structure that was unlike any other that I had
ever seen. It looked like a castle only a lot more
sinister than any I had seen. None of that was
as surprising as the roaring sound that came from
within the mountain. Suddenly the ground began
to shake and out of the side of the mountain flew
a dragon. It was like one that you would see in
stories only five times as terrible. Its scales were
red, blue and gray, his wings looked paper thin,
but they carried him like a bird. He had talons
like a hawk and his eyes shone like fire. Though
I was scared I did stare in awe at this beast.
Never in my life had I thought that I would ever
see something such as that. After sailing past the
mountain we came into such deep waters that they
looked black. I wondered for a moment if we were
in the black sea, but that was almost impossible
because we had been in the Atlantic and I had heard
of there being any dragons in that area. So I don't
know where we are. All I know is that we are in
very deep water. I must go now.

After that I put the book down. Was the place with dragon the same place that my medallion and Shadowlark had come from? I didn't know and the only way for me to find out about any of it was to ask this mysterious man that knew too much about me already. I wasn't sure if I trusted him or not. As a matter of fact I wasn't even sure why I wanted to trust him, but for some reason I did. It took a lot to gain my trust and very few people had my full trust at all.

It could not just be a coincidence that this man had told me of the same places that were in Mr. McHale's book. There had to be something more to it. There was some deeper, underlying meaning to all of it that I felt like I knew, but could not quite say.

As I lay there, I found myself drifting to the point where I was almost asleep, but not quite. I was in between awake and dreaming and somehow, I knew how all of it connected. I knew every detail of how I knew Shadowlark, or why my father looked at me like I was memory, but when I found myself all the way awake, I had once again forgotten everything that I had dreamed of and had no way to remember any of it.

   ***

That next morning me and Clara got ready to go. We weren't quite sure where we were going to go, but we did know that we weren't going to stay in one place for very long, at least not in this place for long that is. We weren't sure where, when, or if we were going to settle, but the one thing we knew for sure was that we were going to settle in the Florida harbor. It was nice, but to be honest, a place such as that was a little too tame for us. Somewhere deep inside, we still wanted adventure.

I got my sea bag and went outside in front of the inn to wait for Clara. I wasn't outside for very long when Shadowlark appeared seemingly out of thin air beside me. He seemed to have an odd habit of doing this, but for some reason his appearing out of nowhere didn't bother me near as much as I would have thought.

"I see that you are brave enough to wear your medallion," he said.

I had not thought about since I had gotten up and for some reason I felt like taking it off then and there, but I didn't. "Yes. I've worn it every day now for the last five years. Nothing has bothered me about it before and if it does now then I'll deal with it."

"I'm glad to see it. I hoped that you would be," he nodded with a blank expression on his face, so I could not interpret what he meant by saying this, but I could tell that he was not being sarcastic. "So, where are you going?"

"I'm not sure yet," I answered. "Why?"

"If you insist on wearing such a trinket then you may be in more danger than ever before," he told me. "The news that came on the wind last night is in fact true and that makes it even more dangerous to wear anything baring the symbol of the jade eye."

"And what did the wind tell you?" I asked, not half believing him.

He smiled for the first time as if he knew my thoughts. His smile caused my heart to beat strangely, and I smiled back at him.

His smile slowly faded and was replaced by a look of concern. "It told me that the *Dragon's Empress* is sailing these waters. This is the first time in twenty years that my brother has dared to enter this world which could only mean one thing." He paused and rubbed his chin. "He's looking for someone," He cast me an odd glance and for the first time, I could read his expression.

"You're suggesting that he's looking for me?" I asked.

He just nodded slightly.

"Why would he want me?"

"What is the color of the jade eye that you wear, Miss Sabilla Scarlet?"

"Red of course." Just as the words came out of my mouth I began to understand. "The same as mine."

"And are you aware that there is no red jade in this world. Not scarlet red, anyway," He let that sink in for a moment then he went on. "There once were people in my world that had that same eye color."

"What do you mean by once were?" I asked.

"It was a certain race," he answered. "They weren't like mortal men, but they weren't immortals either. Every one of them had red eyes. Some say they were the descendants of angels others say they were the descendants of devils, but no one knows for sure. One day the wicked men of the eastern mountains began killing them. They were good fighters, but they were no match for the army that was sent on them and half of the people turned on their own and joined the wicked men. Very few of my people survived and the ones who did came to this world. After that they pushed aside all of their powers because they figured that they would be found too easily if they were to use them. All of them decided to forget who they once were and become part of this world."

"What kind of powers did they have?" I asked slowly becoming mesmerized by the story, but most of all, by the way he spoke when he was telling it.

"They could speak to wind, water, and fire," he answered. "They could tame the dragons of the Defentar Mountains and islands and their power to speak to wind and water allowed them to be able bring air into the water so that they could swim into the deepest parts of the bottomless ocean."

Just then Clara came out of the inn.

"I'm ready," she said, only briefly glancing at Shadowlark.

"So the jade eye stands for that race?" I asked.

"Yes," he answered. "They found the red jade when mining years ago and they carved pieces of it into the shapes of eyes, so that our people would have their own symbol."

"So what does it have to do with your brother?" I asked.

"Me, him and the woman Rossaletta are descendants of that race," he answered. "As are you, Miss Sabilla."

"So why would he want to hurt me?" I asked. "If I am part of this race, would he not want to have me on his side?"

"No, he hates his own people," he answered. "They would not allow him to rule after he joined the wicked men. He hates the ones that stayed in our world, but he really hates the ones that came here."

Clara looked at the two of us with a confused expression. "So from what I've taken from this is that your brother wants to kill Billy because she is the descendent of someone that he doesn't like?"

"Yes," he answered. "That's about it."

"And why are we worried about this?" she asked. "I thought that you said your brother was in a different world."

"Well, he's come back to this world," he told her. "This the first time he's been in this world in twenty years and he is definitely looking for someone."

"I know where we're going," I pulled the note that Apollo gave me, out of my pocket.

"What's that?" Clara asked.

"It tells how to get to my mother's house," I told her. "Apollo gave it to me yesterday when we left the ship. Do you think we could go there?"

"We don't have anywhere else to go," she shrugged. "We may as well."

"I have some horses," Shadowlark said. "Three of them. They're not much bigger than pack mules, but they're good riders even if you've never ridden a horse before."

"He's coming?" Clara asked me in a tone that said she did not trust him in the slightest way. I could not blame her for being so skeptical about him. She did not know what I did. She did not know that Mr. McHale had been in the world that this man said he was from.

"Yes," I nodded and cast a glance in Shadowlark's direction. He smiled once again, and I knew that I was doing the right thing by having him come with us.

I knew that it was odd for me to just let him come when we didn't even know him, but for some reason I felt safe around him and it made me feel better to know that he would be with us.

After Shadowlark brought his horses we headed off. It didn't take too long for me and Clara to get the hang of riding, but it still felt quite awkward to me. I wasn't sure if I liked all the bouncing, but I figured that I would get used to it.

***

As it turned out, my mother's house was only two towns away from where we started and the man we asked for directions said that we should be there before night fall. We traveled on the smaller roads that didn't lead through the middle of the towns Shadowlark seemed uncomfortable with the idea of going through the towns when his brother might be in any one of them searching for any of us. It, to me, seemed an odd notion that anyone should be looking for us, but I didn't push for him to tell me more of his brother, nor did I mind travelling through the less populated areas. In fact, I enjoyed the solitude.

"So," Clara said breaking the long held silence. "Shadowlark. Is that your real name or is it only a nick name?"

"It's not the name that I was given by my parents," he answered. "But it's what I've been called for many years. I am known by many other names, but that is what I'm most widely known as."

"So, why do they call you Shadowlark?" I asked.

"There is a kind of bird in my world that is much like a lark from this world only he is transparent. He looks like nothing but a mere shadow. The fact that they can hardly be seen makes them do things that most birds wouldn't. They are brave, reckless and at times, quite foolish. I have often heard them called arrogant and very sure of their own ability, but one cannot judge the character of such a bird unless they have observed it for themselves. From my observation of the bird, it merely seems fearless, neither arrogant nor foolish, but all the same reckless. It is odd for me to describe it in such a way seeing as that it's what I'm named for, though I'm not sure that it's very befitting."

"Why do you say that?" I asked.

He smiled as if slightly embarrassed. "Because I cannot be the judge of my own character and I have never been told if the name is truly fitting, but simply that I have been given the name. To be completely fearless is a gift that I have only known of one man possessing. Do not think I boast upon myself by telling you this, for I have borne the name for years and always figured it was mine because I have the ability of keeping myself from being seem from time to time. I do not feel that I hold any of the real characteristics of such a creature."

We rode in silence for another minute or two. I just sat there trying to sort out all that he meant, but my mind soon drifted to other subjects that seemed to press harder on my mind.

"I wonder if my mother will even know who I am," I sighed.

"Of course she will." Clara gave me a teasing smile. "How could she forget her little red eyed bastard?"

I laughed a little. Most people would have taken that as an insult, but I didn't because it was the truth. I was a red eyed bastard so to speak. Not to say that I liked the title my point was that there was nothing I could do about it.

I just sat on my horse worrying. What if my mother did want to see me? What if she said that she didn't want me then so she didn't want me now? (Or even worse) What if she knew who I was, but she pretended not to because she didn't want me hurting her reputation any more than I already had? The latter seemed to be the most likely of all of the questions.

I tried to push all those thoughts out of my mind, but it was harder than I thought it would be. All my life I had wondered what it would be like to see my mother. Not that I really cared to do so in particular, but I had wondered about. I don't know any child that would not, under the circumstances. Now that the time had come for me to meet her, I was terrified.

It was around five o'clock in the afternoon when we got to her house. The house was rather large and for the most part was white. It had three stories and the porch was made out of red bricks. Out behind the house was a large red barn and a field that with about twenty horses running around in it.

All of it seemed to loom above us, hoping to scare us away. Such a place was all too fancy and up-town looking for my taste. Not to say that I didn't like nice things, but this place was not the kind of house that seemed all too welcoming, but I would not allow myself to be intimidated.

A young boy was running around in the front yard playing with a big, shaggy, black dog. His blond curls were wet with sweat and sticking to his face and his clothes, which looked as if they had been very fine and clean only a few hours earlier were grubby and stained. When he looked up and saw us he stopped.

"Can I help you?" he asked. He didn't have an accent like mine, Clara's and Shadowlark's. He had an American accent.

"Yes, I think you can," I nodded. "We're looking for a woman named Gabriella Penney. We were told that she lives here."

"Well." He scratched his forehead. "Mama's name is Gabriella Meyers. I think that her last name might have been Penney before she got married to daddy."

"Is she here?" I felt my heart beating faster.

"Yes ma'am," the little boy nodded.

The three of us dismounted.

"Can we see her?" I asked.

Just then a girl dressed in what looked like a maid's dress, came out the front door. "Henry Harold Meyers the third get back in this house right this minute." She was about to say something else when she looked up and saw us. "Oh." She seemed very surprised at the sight of us. "Can I help you, miss?"

"Yes," I nodded. "Could you tell Mrs. Meyers that miss Billy Scarlet is here to see her?"

The girl looked at me doubtfully, but she nodded. "Right away, miss." She headed back into the house with Henry in tow.

Not two minutes later a woman came out onto the porch. She had smooth pale skin, long flowing blond hair, big blue eyes and she was wearing a dark purple dress. She looked like she was in her middle to late thirties which would have put her at about anywhere from fifteen to seventeen when she had me. A radiant smile spread across her face. I could see why Billy had thought that she was beautiful.

She came down the steps and walked over to us. Her big blue eyes studied my face.

"Oh Sabilla, is that really you?" she asked.

"Billy," I said. "And yes, it's me."

She threw her arms around me and held me for a minute. I tried to hug her back, but I wasn't sure what I should do. The embrace was more than awkward and for some reason, I felt like she was putting little, if any feeling at all, into it. When she stopped hugging me she looked over at the others.

"This is Shadowlark and Clara," I told her.

"David!" she yelled so loud that I jumped. A man in his mid-twenties came out of the barn.

"Yes ma'am," he said.

"Take their horses to the barn," she told him.

He nodded and did as she said. I was wishing he had not taken the horses away because it made me feel like my only way of escape was being cut off. It made me feel bad, but for more than one reason, I was already wanting to leave, but I decided to relax and go with it.

"Heavens above," She looked at us as she led us to the house. "Why are you girls dressed the way that you are? You look like you came out of the back allies somewhere."

For a moment I felt like calling David back, getting on my horse and leaving, but once again I convinced myself to calm down and at least give it a chance. I figured that we could at least give it one night.

"We just like dressing this way," I told her as we climbed the steps. "It's the way that we've dressed for the past few years."

"I'll get each of you girls a good dress." She opened the door and led us inside. "Harold!" She called once we were inside, using a tone so loud that it made me want to cover my ears.

A very preppy man came out of one of the rooms. He was tall and lanky with straight brown hair and sleepy looking brown eyes. He was wearing dress clothes that made him look like he belonged on some sort of court.

"Yes darling?" The way he talked made him sound as if he were extremely bored.

'She left Billy for this guy?' I thought. 'She must have married for money.'

"Do you remember me telling you about my daughter, Sabilla?" she asked.

'Okay, this is the most odd family I have ever met," I thought. 'She's married to this man and has had children with him, but she speaks so nonchalantly of the child that she had out of wedlock with a pirate and gave to an orphanage. Very odd indeed.'

Henry nodded. "I do believe so, yes."

"You can call me Billy," I told her, but she seemed to ignore me.

"This is her," she told him. "And these are her friends Clara and...." She looked blankly at Shadowlark. "I'm sorry I can't remember what your name is."

"Shadowlark," he answered.

"Ah yes," she nodded. "Shadowlark."

Harold gave us a very bored smile and walked away.

"Now." Gabriella clapped her hands together. "I want you to meet your twin sister."

"What?" I asked, more taken aback than I had ever been in my entire life. "I have....." The words did not want to come out. Every fiber of my being fought the thought that was now trying to cripple me. "I have a twin sister?"

"Emmaline!" Gabriella called up the stairs.

"I'm coming," came a very sweet, almost angelic, voice.

A few minutes later a girl came down the stairs. She walked with the countenance of an empress. She looked just like Gabriella only she was wearing a pink dress. She was my complete opposite. She was everything that anyone would use to describe perfection in a woman. Everything about her was seemingly flawless, from her dress and the way she walked, to her complexion and her crystal blue eyes. It was more than I could believe to think that she was my twin. She sort of wrinkled her nose at the three of us or maybe just me.

"Emmaline do you remember me telling you about your twin sister?"

"Yes." She cast a hopeful glance in Clara's direction, then gave me an odd look as if she knew what Gabriella was going to say next.

"This is her," Gabriella said. "Emmaline, this is Sabilla, Sabilla this is Emmaline."

"You can just call me Billy," I said. "Good to meet you."

She smiled and looked away as if I had spoken to her by mistake. I could tell that she was thinking the same thing that I was, only for different reasons. How could the two of us been born of the same parents?

She looked behind me at Clara and Shadowlark as if hoping to find out something about them that would counter her feelings about finding out who I was.

"Oh yes," Gabriella said. "These are Sabilla's friends, Clara and Shadowlark."

She took no notice of Clara, but her gaze lingered on Shadowlark. As a matter of fact I really didn't like the way that she was looking at him. "Mother," She finally said. "I must get back to my room. I was fixing to bathe."

"Oh no, dear," Gabriella laughed a little. "We're fixing to eat dinner. It will be done in a few minutes."

"All right," Emmaline huffed and walked back up the stairs.

"Well we really have to get going," I said. "We were just passing through and I figured that we would come see you, but you can get to your dinner and we'll see you later."

"But you must at least stay the night," Gabriella said cheerily. "Please, Sabilla. It's the least that I could do."

After seeing my twin sister I was really not wanting to even stay the night or even another second, but I figured that we could at least get a good meal out of it all.

"We'll stay the night I guess," I told her. "And I would like for you to call me Billy if you don't mind."

"Very good," Gabriella smiled. "I'll show you to the guest rooms then you can come to dinner." She seemed to leap up the stairs.

She showed me and Clara to one room and Shadowlark to another that was right down the hall from us. Both of the rooms were on the top floor. We washed up a little and went down stairs to the dining hall.

It was a large room that was well lit with candles and the now dim light that came in through the windows. There was a long table with six chairs on either side of it and a chair at each end.

I sat right across from Emmaline. Clara sat next to me and across from Henry and Shadowlark sat in between Henry and a little girl that I had not yet met. She had dark hair, fair skin, big blue eyes and looked to be about seven.

After Harold said the blessing Gabriella told Henry and the little girl, whose name was Sarah, who I was. Emmaline just sat quietly eating her food and doing her best not to look at me.

"So," Gabriella said. "What do the three of you do?"

"Me and Clara are sailors." I answered and I could tell that Emmaline,

Harold and Gabriella were about to choke, but I got nothing but satisfaction from that.

"And you?" she looked at Shadowlark.

I looked at him blankly. I had not bothered to ask what he did.

"Well ma'am," he said. "I'm a man of many trades I suppose you'd say."

Gabriella just smiled and nodded.

"What about you Emmaline?" I asked, hoping that I could make some kind of conversation with my newly found sister. I wanted to get to know her and hoped that we would get along, better than it seemed like when we first met earlier in the day. "What do you do?"

Emmaline started to speak, but Gabriella interrupted.

"Dear child," Gabriella laughed. "You cannot expect Emmaline to be as rough and tumble as you and your friends. She is a high society woman. She is consumed by her study. She can sing, dance, speak French and Latin, she can play the piano and the cello, she has riding lessons every day, and has an extensive knowledge of how to be the lady of a large household. All we have to do now is find her a good husband so she can put all of that knowledge to good use. I mean she's twenty years old, she needs to do something with her life before she becomes an old maid."

It annoyed me greatly to hear Gabriella speak of Emmaline as if she was not even in the room and I could tell that Emmaline did not like it either, but she was not about to say anything about it.

"So, Sabilla," Gabriella continued. "Are you married?" She smiled in Shadowlark's direction.

This seemed to amuse Shadowlark, while it embarrassed me greatly. "No, ma'am. I am not."

"Well, we're going to find a husband for Emmaline soon; perhaps we can do the same for you."

At this Clara snickered loudly, but pretended to cough, so that no one would notice. It took some effort for me not to laugh and I could tell that Shadowlark was facing the same issue.

"No thank you," I smiled as sweetly as I could manage. "I thank you for your concern and willingness to help me in such a way, but I fear that it is not necessary."

"Very well," she shrugged and continued to dominate the conversation for the rest of the meal.

After I got done eating I looked over and noticed that Shadowlark was staring intently at one of the candles. I looked at the flame and it was dancing in an odd way. It moved around in ways that I had never seen before and deep in the middle of it I began to see pictures. I saw small dancers, birds, lions, snakes and all manner of other things that seemed to be enchanted by words that could only be felt, not spoken. It was as if I was watching another world unfold before my eyes. I could almost hear music playing softly. I could see the ocean and I could hear it, the sounds of the waves crashing against the shore. It was mesmerizing. It sucked me in and I felt as if I was being pulled into a dream.

When he noticed that I was looking at the flame he looked away and as quickly as it had started all of it was over and I was back in the real world. I just sighed. There were so many mysteries about this man. More than I could even count.

Chapter

Seven

That night I couldn't sleep. The place was too unfamiliar to me. It was warm, dry and comfortable, but it was unfamiliar all the same. For some reason, I felt like I was trapped. I had no idea how a place that was comfortable and home like, could feel so much like a prison.

I got up out of bed and went down the hall and out onto the balcony. I liked it better in the open air. Even when the entire world seemed unfamiliar the night was the one thing that was always the same. I took a deep breath and, for a moment, tried to imagine the feeling of the deck swaying beneath my feet. It worked for a moment. I could feel the deck, see the stars reflecting off the water, and smell the salt air, but all too soon, it faded away and I was back on the balcony.

I took a deep breath of the cool night air and noticed that Shadowlark was on the other side of the balcony. He seemed to be imagining that he was in another place and time as well. He took a deep breath and let it out very slowly. I wasn't sure if he was aware of my presence, so I walked over to him.

"Are you okay?" I asked.

He looked over at me as if he had thought I had been out there with him, but was not quite sure. "Yes," he nodded.

"You said that your people could speak to fire," I said. "Is that what you were doing with the candle at the table tonight?"

"Yes," he answered. "I was taught to speak to fire many years ago."

"What is the easiest to speak to?" I asked. "Wind, fire, or water?"

"Of the three wind is the easiest." he answered. "And water would about have to be the hardest."

"Why is water the hardest?"

"Because there are so many different forms of it. There are ponds, lakes, rivers, oceans and even the rain. Each of them has a different voice."

"Can you teach me to speak to the wind?" I asked.

He blushed a little.

"What?" I asked.

"The more exposed to the wind you are the easier it is to speak to it," he answered. "That's why I sometimes take off my shirt when I speak to it."

At that, I could feel myself blushing.

"It's okay," he smiled. "It's not hard to do if you try. Just listen to it." He came up behind me and rubbed my shoulders. "Feel the wind on your face," he whispered in my ear.

I closed my eyes and listened. I could hear the same tune that I had heard when he had made the flame dance. The tune was wild yet calming, and seemed to be a living thing instead of just a sound or and feeling. I took a deep breath and it as if I were breathing in the music itself. The air and the music mixed together and swirled all around me. It was as if I was in a completely different world for split second. I felt like I had gone into a trance of some kind. It enveloped me and made me relax completely.

"Do you hear it?" he whispered softly. I could feel his warm breath on my cheek and it warmed the chill that had come in the night air. I leaned against him and the warmth of his body sunk deep into my skin and coursed through my entire body.

"Yes," I sighed. The song slowly died away and I looked at Shadowlark who was, at that point, standing behind me.

"That music was beautiful," I said. "But I don't understand anything that just happened."

He smiled. "In time you will."

I wasn't sure why, but for some reason I felt like he was looking deep into my soul and I felt my guard go up. I quickly stepped away from him, feeling as if I had just exposed my soul to him. "I have to get to bed. I have a feeling that Gabriella will want me to do some stuff with her in the morning even if I don't want to so, I need to get some sleep." I started back inside. When I got to the door I turned back around. He had his back turned to me.

I walked back over to him and gently touched his shoulder. "Thank you for showing me that," I said.

I wasn't sure if I had felt it right or not, but he seemed to shiver slightly when I touched him. "You're very welcome, Miss Sabilla," he said without turning around.

"Goodnight, Shadowlark," I whispered and walked back to my room to get back to bed. I felt so strange. It was almost as if I was falling in love with him, but I kept telling myself not to. I wasn't the kind of girl that got all strange about a man, but I could hardly help it. There was something deeper in my feelings for Shadowlark than I had felt with any other man that I had ever met, but that only made me more cautious.

***

The next morning I awoke to the sound of Gabriella beating on our door and calling to us. "Sabilla, Clara! Good morning! The two of you need to get up and bathe!"

I moaned. I was used to getting up early, but there was something in the tone of her voice that just annoyed me and made me sure that I was fixing to be put through intense torture.

We got up and followed her to a room that she called the wash room. There were two large brass tubs that were full of steaming water. Even with how much I wanted to leave I couldn't help but feel a bit of excitement at the thought of getting a real tub bath. I had not bathed in a tub since I was at the orphanage. We both bathed and I must say that I enjoyed it very much and I didn't want to get out.

"So," Clara said as we dried off. "This is how rich people live? I could get used to this."

We put on robes that Gabriella had given to us and then headed back to our room. When we got there we saw that two maids and Gabriella were waiting for us. They had each of us a dress. Clara's was pale blue with light pink trimming. Mine was cream colored with light yellow lace around the neck.

I was more ready to leave than I ever had been. I did not want to wear that dress at all and I could tell that Gabriella knew that, but she didn't care.

"I'm not wearing that," I said.

"Oh, it won't be that bad."

With that they began dressing us. The dresses themselves weren't the worst part. The worst part was when they began smashing us into corsets. That was the underlying tone of torture that I knew I had heard in her voice when she had woke us up. They tied them as tight as they would go and not only did it feel like it was crushing my ribs, it also made it where I could hardly breathe and it nearly made my breasts come out of my dress. I had worn the top half of a corset to hide the fact that I was a girl, back when I was sailing on *the Victory*, but with the way that those women fixed that corset, there was no way that anyone would mistake me or Clara for boys.

After they got us dressed they fixed our hair. They did the same thing with both of us. They pulled our hair up in buns on top of our heads and left a few strands hanging down. They used a hot iron that was shaped like a stick to curl those few strands and that gave me illusion that they were trying to cook the side of my head. Once they were done with that they were done with that they dabbed rose water on us.

Gabriella then informed us that we would be going to town with her and Emmaline.

Before I left my room I put on my medallion. Clara cast me a sort of worried glance, but I just shook my head. I knew that I would be okay.

We went down stairs, ate a small breakfast of toast, jam and tea which left me feeling a slight bit hungry because I was used to a bit larger meal for breakfast, then we went outside. There was a carriage waiting for us.

When I looked across the yard I saw Shadowlark with Henry. He wasn't wearing the same clothes that he had the day before. Instead, he was wearing black pants and a white button up shirt. When he saw me and Clara he just stopped and stared.

"What is it?" I heard Henry asked with a curious expression.

"Nothing," Shadowlark answered. "I just never figured those two to be the kind to wear dresses."

"They didn't seem to be the type that would wear something like that," Henry laughed a little. "And personally I liked the way they looked before. They look too much like noble women now. They looked much sweeter before."

Suddenly, Shadowlark looked like he was fixing to start laughing. I also noticed that Gabriella was staring intently at my left arm. That was when it hit me. Our dresses had short sleeves.

"Is that a naked mermaid?" Emmaline asked in a disgusted tone.

"Yes," I smiled. "As a matter of fact it is. Why? Do you like it? I got it in Puerto Rico when I was fifteen. It's not something that you're used to, I'm sure, but it's quite common among sailors."

"Well, I must say that it does compliment your earring," she huffed and got into the carriage.

"I know," I laughed as though she had meant it as a compliment, but to myself I thought, 'Damn it, I thought I had taken that thing out.' Instead of saying this out loud I just smiled. "I got them both on the same day. Maybe someday me and you can go there together and get matching tattoos. You don't seem to be the type to get anything as hard core as a naked mermaid, but we could get something more sweet, that will fit into your nature. You know like a rose or something. It'll be like a sisterhood bond thing."

She just scoffed and shook her head.

Just then, Shadowlark came over and helped me into the carriage.

"Are you coming to town with us?" I asked him.

"No," he shook his head. "I promised to show Henry a few sword tricks."

"Okay," I said.

He kissed me on the hand and walked back over to Henry.

It wasn't long after that that we got going.

"So," Gabriella smiled. "What's the story with you and this Shadowman?"

"Shadowlark," I corrected her. "It's hard to explain."

"If you ask me a decent man like him doesn't belong with two rough sailor girls like you." Emmaline said.

"Then where does he belong?" I asked. "In the arms of a rich fancy woman who will take him for granted and cheat on him at every chance that she gets? A confided life that will keep him in one place for the rest of his life, stuck performing duties that are placed before him by a board of advisors? I hate to disappoint you, but I don't think that a life such as that would please him very well. And besides, I don't recall anyone asking you about any of it in the first place."

She stuck out her jaw and crossed her arms across her chest. "So he belongs with two pirate women that get tattooed and pierced and wear pants instead of dresses?"

"Emmaline, that's enough," Gabriella snapped.

"We're not pirates," I told her. "We're midshipmen on the *H.M.S Victory*, under the command of Captain James Bernard Hector. If you don't believe me I could show you some of the things that I have in my sea bag at the house."

"That would be delightful," Gabriella said. "We would love for you to show us some of your navy things. I have always had a fascination with the sea."

"So," I could tell that Clara was trying to change the subject. "Why are we coming to town anyway?"

"We have to make sure that everything is in order for the ball tomorrow night," Gabriella answered. "We're just getting a few things like perfume and jewelry and anything else that we happen to fancy."

"Maybe while we're in town we can get those matching tattoos that you were talking about," Emmaline said mockingly.

"I knew that she would come around," I laughed. "I suppose we'll get them here since we really don't have the time to go to Puerto Rico. We need to get them now so we can show them off at the ball."

"You are impossible," Emmaline huffed. "Why can't you just keep your little mouth......"

"How can you tell me to keep my mouth shut when you were the one who was making a jibe at me? Were you expecting me to just sit back and take your insults? I'm not sure of the type of people you are used to dealing with, but I can assure you that I am not as dim witted as they are."

"It seems that you might be," Emmaline scoffed. "You are just more upfront and literal about it, but so much is to be expected from a woman who has spent her life as if she were a man. One such as you could not be expected to have very good manners. I suppose that we will all have to deal with your barbaric ways."

"Emmaline enough!" Gabriella almost yelled. "Good grief. Sabilla why do you have to act so much like your fa...." she stopped. "Just stop it okay."

It took every bit of self-control that I had in me not to reach across and slap the daylights of Emmaline. I just clenched my jaw and fought every urge to jump out the wagon.

We rode in silence until we got to town.

The first place that we went to was a dress shop. Inside there were a bunch of racks of cloth of all different colors. There were ladies sewing fabric faster than my eyes could keep up with. I had learned a bit of sewing when I was younger, but I had never been near that fast with it.

A tall slender lady came out of the back room and walked over to us. "Good afternoon Mrs. Meyers. I have your gowns ready and I must say they are very beautiful."

"Thank you, Mary," Gabriella smiled. "I was wondering if you could get two ball gowns ready for tomorrow night. Sabilla and Clara each need a good gown."

It was making me mad that she would call me Billy and every time I told her to she would ignore me.

"I'm sure we can," Mary answered. "We have two or three dresses that would be fit, that we have already started work on, but just need to be sized and have some trim added."

"Very good," Gabriella nodded then turned to me and Clara. "Go let them take your measurements and pick out some cloth and trimmings. Emmaline and I will be across the street buying jewelry."

The ladies took us into the back room and stripped us into our underwear, measured our waists, arms, chests, shoulders and hips, then sent us to pick out styles.

Clara decided to get a low cut rosy pink and yellow dress that had a fluffy skirt and sleeves that came down to her wrists. Mary said that it would be perfect for dancing.

I picked out a dress that was not quite as low cut. Its sleeves came to the elbow and then sort of billowed out. It had a nice full skirt that would frill out while dancing. The colors of mine were crimson, navy blue and white. I knew that red wasn't exactly a proper color, but I didn't really care. I just liked the color.

"Okay," Mary said as we headed out of the store. "You two are perfect for these dresses. We will not even have to do much sizing. All we have to do is put on the last few touches, like the colors that you want and the lace. We will deliver them this time tomorrow maybe a little later."

"Thank you," I told her.

The ladies had already started working on them. It made me feel sort of bad to know that they were going to be working that hard for me, but I figured that they were going to get well paid for it and they did not have too much work to do since they already had them mostly done.

We found Gabriella and Emmaline in the store that they told us they would be in. They weren't only looking at jewelry, but they were also looking at perfumes. I recognized the smell of them as of the kinds that we had found on smugglers ships.

"All done I see." Gabriella came over to us. "Try to find a perfume that smells the way that your dress looks. At a ball such as this, all things must match."

That confused me, but I figured that I would try my best. I just figured that it must be some strange woman thing that I had never been told of. Mistress Lora had never told me, and all my other teachers had been men. I would not have expected Mr. McHale, Apollo, or Arnold to have known anything about perfumes. I just figured that it would be fun to try and see if I could find one that would fit such a description, so we went and started smelling perfumes.

"So we have our dresses and now we have to find a perfume to match?" Clara laughed. "Good Lord, this corset is killing me."

"Mine too," I huffed. "I wonder what idiot came up with such a torture device."

"I'll bet it was a man," Clara smelled a perfume, made a bad face and sat it back down. "A man that wanted his woman to look perfect even if it meant her collapsing because she couldn't breathe."

"And what if it was a woman?" I asked.

"Then she was very vane," She answered. "She wanted to look perfect no matter how much damage she caused herself and then there were a bunch of women that were impressed by her stupidity that they wanted to do the same thing."

I picked up a perfume and smelled it and right away I knew that was the one that I wanted. It was something from Asia and it smelled beautiful. It was a little expensive, but I had enough money so I decided to buy it. Clara bought a different one, but it smelled just as beautiful. Emmaline seemed to get mad at the idea that we could afford something like that because she bought something that was twice as expensive.

Next we picked out jewelry. Gabriella insisted on buying our jewelry. I got a golden hair comb with diamonds and pearls and Clara got a pearl necklace.

While I was walking around the store waiting for Gabriella to get done shopping, an old lady got really close to me and I could tell that she was looking at my tattoo. Her blatant staring didn't bother me at first, but then she put on her glasses and got really close up to me.

"Yes, it's a naked mermaid," I told her.

When I spoke the lady jumped and pulled her glasses off and looked away as if she was very interested in the flowers that were sitting on the counter. I couldn't believe that she did not expect me to notice her staring at me the way that she been.

"I got it while I was on liberty in Puerto Rico. I got my earring in the same day. Do you like it?" I made myself a promise that the first chance I got, I would pierce my other ear so that I wouldn't look like such a sap, with just one.

The lady blushed and walked away shaking her head.

Not long after that we headed back to the house and I was very glad because I was tired of women looking at me all strange because of my tattoo. The way that I figured it was if they were embarrassed by a naked woman then they should have been boys. I mean, what did they think they were, under their clothes? Heck, I had seen boys that were less embarrassed by a naked woman than some of those women were.

***

By the time we got back to the house the sun was going down and there was an odd orange glow coming from the back yard.

"What's that back there?" Emmaline asked.

"It almost looks as if something's on fire," Gabriella remarked. "Quick, Martin," She called to the driver. "Pull around back there and see what's going on."

When the carriage stopped we went around behind the house and saw Shadowlark juggling. He was tossing sword in one hand and a torch in the other. Henry and Sarah sat in the grass watching them with their eyes wide.

I climbed out of the carriage as quickly as I could. I wanted to watch him. I knew that he must be speaking to the fire to keep it under such control. Clara got out behind me, followed by Gabriella and Emmaline.

I stood there, as captivated by the spectacle as the young children were. Sweat dripped down his bare upper body, causing his skin to glow in the torch light. He was completely relaxed. The fire would flare up really big, or the sword would almost graze him, but he would not flinch away from it. Each move seemed so fluid, and if any one of them was mistaken, it could be fatal, but he made no wrong moves. He tossed each item and caught it again, as if it was the easiest thing in the world to do.

After catching the torch three times, he threw the sword high and let it fall and stick into the ground, then he blew on the torch and it exploded into a large fire ball that hung in the air.

The exploding sound caused Emmaline to scream that made Shadowlark stop and look over at us. I was glad that he had not been juggling anything anymore. Her screaming could have caused him to hurt himself.

'Thanks Emmaline,' I thought. 'Now he's going to stop.'

He put the torch out, pulled his shirt on, and came over to us. "Have a good time?" he asked. He had not bothered to button his shirt back up, and needless to say, it was somewhat distracting.

"Yes we did," Gabriella nodded. "That was amazing, what you were doing with those things. Where did you learn that?"

"I was taught by a friend, many years ago," he answered. "But I mostly just taught myself. I'm sorry if I scared anyone."

"I'm fine," Emmaline blushed. "It just startled me is all."

He just nodded and went back over to Henry and Sarah. "Okay," he told them. "Time to get inside and get ready for dinner."

"Thanks, Emmaline," Henry huffed. "Now the show's over." He took Sarah's hand and they went inside.

When we got inside we went straight to the dining hall. We all sat in the same places that we had the night before.

After saying the blessing Harold looked over at Shadowlark. "I was watching you outside putting on a show for Henry and Sarah this evening," he said in his usual bored tone. "I thought it was quite amazing. Where did you learn that?"

"I learned from an old friend," Shadowlark answered, casting a glance in my direction. "Many years ago."

Harold nodded. "I've seen people in shows do that kind of thing. I've always enjoyed watching people play with fire."

"I don't only use fire," Shadowlark told him. "I also juggle swords and throw daggers. I can do lots of things like that."

"Yes, I saw you tossing the sword as well," Henry nodded. "That bit seemed rather alarming to me I must say."

"It's not as dangerous as the fire," Shadowlark said. "It takes a while to learn to do it without hurting yourself, but after you learn, it comes as a second nature."

"My parents would die if I ever did anything like that," Henry said. "Or they would kill me, one of the two."

"I would have a fit if I saw any of my children juggling swords," Gabriella said. "I'll bet that your mother didn't like it at all."

It made me feel odd to hear her say that she would worry anything about her children, when she had not even bothered to raise me at all. I could have been kidnapped by gypsies and made to do all kind of dangerous stunts and she would have neither known nor cared.

"My parents thought that I had gone quite mad," he laughed a little. "When I started doing shows for a living my father didn't like it very much. He said that it was odd that I would receive compensation for my lunacy. He thought I was rather odd at first."

"I don't think that kind of thing is odd at all," Emmaline said. "As a matter of fact, I think that it's amazing and very brave to do something of the like."

"Yea right," Henry huffed. "That's why you squealed like a frightened rabbit when he blew a big fire ball. I'd love to see you at one of the big shows where a lot of people are doing that at the same time."

Me, Clara, and Shadowlark snickered a little bit and that made her really mad.

Everything was quiet for a few minutes then Emmaline said, "So Shadowlark, are you coming to the ball tomorrow night?"

"I'm not sure," he shrugged.

"Please come," Sarah begged. "You have to come. It'll be the first time that I get to go to a ball and I really want you to be there."

He glanced over at Gabriella. "I'm not sure that I have been invited to come."

"I guess it would be fine," she said. "As long as you have something nice to wear."

"If you don't have anything I'm sure I have something that you can use," Harold told him.

"Thank you, sir," Shadowlark nodded.

After supper me and Clara bathed and went to bed. A few hours later I woke up very thirsty so I went down stairs to the kitchen to get a glass of water. There was the same creepy feeling to walk around in the house in the dark as I it had been when we used to walk around in the church at night. I tried to get there and back as fast as possible, but I kept running into chairs, or getting lost in places that I had not yet seen in the house before.

Finally I found my way to the kitchen. As I headed back to my room I walked past a room that the door was open and there was a slight glow coming from inside.

"Who's out there?" came Harold's voice.

For a minute I wanted to run back to my room and pretend that I had not even got out of bed, but instead I went into the room. "It's just me," I said.

"Oh, hello Sabilla," he smiled.

"Please," I sighed. "Call me Billy."

"Okay," he nodded. "Well Billy, I've been wanting to talk to you, but I haven't gotten the chance."

"What is it?" I asked.

"It's about Gabriella," he answered. "By now you have probably seen how very impulsive she is."

I nodded.

142

He continued. "I love her very much, but in some ways she is much like a child. She wants what she wants until she gets it, then she grows increasingly bored with it. I don't want you to take this the wrong way because I like you and your two friends, but you must be very careful when it comes to Gabriella. You see everyone thought that she would never get married because they thought that she would get too easily bored if she was to stay with one man for too long. She'll take up things like horseback riding or sewing, she spends lots of money on it then she'll quit after a few days. My point is that right now she is very excited at the thought of you, but tomorrow she may not care if you're here or not."

I nodded. "The same way that she was with me when I was a baby and how she was with my father."

"Exactly," he nodded. "So be kind of careful. I don't want you to get hurt."

"I understand," 'But it's too late for that,' I added in my mind. I had known it all along, but to hear him say it made me feel like I had had the wind knocked out of me. I just stood there for a moment wishing that I had never come.

"Are you alright?" he asked. "Shall I call the nurse maid? You don't look well."

"No," I shook my head. "I'm fine. I'm just tired is all."

"Goodnight, Billy."

"Goodnight," the word came out as a mere whisper.

I went back upstairs, crawled in my bed and pulled the covers up to my chin. I had never felt so unwanted in all my life, even when I had first heard the story of my mother leaving me to be raised by strangers. Just to be under the same roof as her and to know that she still did not really care to have me around and at any moment might just tell me to go away, made me feel like a street urchin who was just living off of someone else's charity.

Clara propped herself up on her elbows. "Are you all right?"

"Yea," I answered. "I just don't want to stay here for much longer."

"It'll be okay." She lay back down and rolled over to where she was not facing me.

I sat there for a very long time thinking about a lot of things. I wished that I could believe that things would be okay, but something kept me from doing so. Harold had not told me what he had because it might happen. He told me all of it because he knew that it was going to happen, it was only a question of when, and how bad it would hurt when it did.

I wanted to leave; I wanted that more than anything. The only thing that made me think that I should stay and go to the ball that the women at the dress shop had to work so hard on my dress and I didn't want their efforts to be wasted. I also continued to wonder about all of the things that Harold had talked about. How long would it take for my mother to get bored with me for the second time? Why exactly had she given me to Mistress Lora? I knew the answer to that, it was because I had red eyes, I just didn't want to hear her say it. Why had she kept Emmaline while she gave me up? I knew the answer to that question too, but all the same, I did not want to hear it spoken aloud. That would hurt even worse than just knowing. My thoughts were then brought to the question of why she wouldn't call me Billy. When we were in the carriage, she had almost told me that I was acting like my father, but did not say it completely. She must not have wanted to think of Billy, therefore would not say his name even if he was referring to me when doing so.

I decided to push all the thoughts out of my mind and go to sleep. Once I was asleep my mind was plagued with nightmares. Every dream that I had was about the *Dragon's Empress* or the dragon coming out of the side of the mountain. If I wasn't seeing that I was seeing my friends on the *Victory* getting hurt or even killed in battles. Needless to say, I was glad when the sun came up.

***

With the sun came more preparations for the ball. It was going to take place in the huge ballroom that was on the bottom floor of the house.

A little after noon our dresses were delivered to the house and so we began getting dressed for the ball hours before it was supposed to take place. It truly got on my nerves to think that any event could be thought of as so important that it would take hours to get ready for. That is unless it was a battle and I was hoping that there wasn't going to be any of that going on. It was supposed to be an enjoyable affair.

The first preparation that we went through was the whole kill-them-with-the-corset routine then we started getting our dresses on. It was a lot more complicated to get the ball gown on than it was to get the dress on that I had worn the day before. They were made up of at least three pieces, not including the petticoats, or the corsets.

Gabriella gave us both a pair of shoes. "These should suit you well. I didn't think to get the two of you some shoes while we were in town."

"It's okay." I pulled the shoes on. My feet felt so cramped that I just felt like it would be better to kick off the shoes and go barefoot. "Oh my goodness, these things are so tight."

Gabriella laughed. "We pay a high price to be beautiful sometimes. They will do you just fine. You'll get used to them."

"I don't think that I will," Clara told her. Her feet were bigger than mine so we would have to get her a different pair.

"Here you go." Gabriella handed her another pair that was a good bit bigger. "These are some of Emmaline's. Her feet are about the same size as yours, they should do for you."

"Thank you," Clara smiled and put the shoes on.

Next we got to work on our hair. We both wore our hair down and a maid named Lucy helped us get it curled.

"Are you coming to the ball?" I asked her.

"No," she answered. "It's not my place."

"Would you like to come?" I asked.

"If I could," she nodded. "But I don't think that would be possible ma'am. I'm a maid here. It would not be proper for me to go if I'm not invited."

"Wait right here," I went down the hall to Gabriella's room.

She was standing in front of her mirror dabbing on perfume when I came in.

"Can I help you?" she asked, only looking at me out of the corner of her eye.

"Yes," I nodded. "Would it be all right if I brought the maid Lucy with me to the ball as my guest?"

"That's fine," she nodded. "Look in the closet in your room. I think there's a gown in there that she can wear."

"Okay," I nodded and went back to the room.

"Where did you go?" Clara asked.

"Lucy." I went over to the closet and got out the dress that Gabriella told me about. It was a beautiful light green gown. It was the color of the bottom of a new leaf.

"What?" She looked at the dress, then at me.

"You're coming with us," I told her. "You have been invited to come as my guest. It's all settled and there's use arguing with me. Now come over here and get this dress on. It'll go great with your red hair and green eyes."

"What?" She was aghast. "How?"

"Don't ask questions just come on."

We helped her get ready. I let her use my perfume and since I was wearing my hair down I let her use my hair comb.

"Oh, but I couldn't," she said when I offered it to her.

"Yes you can," I told her. "It's mine to give or lend if I wish and I'm not going to be wearing it, so you can."

We finished getting ready and headed to the ballroom. I made sure to wear my jade eye. It went well with the red on my dress.

Gabriella and Harold stood at the door greeting the guests as they came in. He looked thoroughly bored and she looked completely thrilled. Her perfectly happy smile faded away when she saw the red on my dress. She just took a deep breath as if trying to regain composure and she plastered her constant smile back on her face. "Good evening, dears. Your friend Shadow-whatever is here already and if you wish to join Emmaline she's over there on there on the far side of the room."

"Thank you," I nodded and we walked on. As I walked I thought about the color on my dress. I had not come to offend my mother or make her uncomfortable in any way, but after her and Emmaline had treated me with such contempt, I felt it necessary to fight back in whatever way I could. Besides, the red in my dress went with the color of my eyes, unlike most other things that I would wear and Gabriella had said that at an event such as this one, all things should match.

The place was very crowded and I had never seen so many dressed up people in one place at one time. I also noticed that there were a bunch of men that had come there alone.

"Suitors," Lucy said when she saw me looking at them. "They're here to court Emmaline and all the other young girls that are here tonight. Gabriella is dead set on getting Emmaline married off in the next few months. Emmaline doesn't really seem all too eager to get married just yet though, but her mother won't have it. She tells Emmaline that she is far too beautiful to sit around and let herself become an old maid. She has invited every single, rich, and eligible man from here to southern Georgia. The two of you will probably get a dance from some of them tonight."

"As will you," Clara said. "No one here can tell the difference between you and a princess."

Lucy just smiled. "It's hard for me to believe that I'm here as a guest and not a worker. I have never had it this way before."

"Who knows," Clara said. "You might meet the man that will be your husband here tonight."

Lucy blushed then looked over toward the suitors. "Maybe I will."

Just then a man came over to us. He was a little taller than Clara (her being the tallest of the three of us). He had dark brown hair, big blue eyes and looked to be in his middle twenties.

"I don't believe that I've met you ladies," he said. "My name is Will Jarvis. What are yours?"

"My name is Billy Scarlet," I told him. "This is Clara Honeycut and Lucy O'Connor."

A smile spread across his face. "Well, Miss O'Connor, may I have the honor of this dance?"

"Yes, you may," she nodded and let him lead her out onto the dance floor.

A few minutes later a man named Theodore Reynolds came over and asked Clara to dance and I was left on my own to watch all the other couples.

Shadowlark came over to me. He was wearing a fancy black suit and boots. Little Sarah was clinging to him for dear life, but when she saw Henry, she jumped down and ran to him.

Shadowlark smiled and just as he was about to open his mouth to say something another man came over and stepped in between us. He was a little taller than Shadowlark. He had dark, greasy looking hair, a goatee and he was rather round.

"Hello, beautiful," he said in an oily voice. "I have singled you out of all the ladies in this room. I've been watching you since you walked in the door tonight."

The notion creeped me out a good bit.

He continued. "Never in my life have I seen something as beautiful and elegant as you. My name is Vernon Mitchell. What is your name my, sweet?"

"My name is Billy Scarlet," I answered. 'And I'm not your sweet,' I added in my mind.

"Just like the pirate with scarlet eyes," he mused. "And I see that your eyes are that same color as his. Though red eyes are rare I find that yours are very beautiful."

It was then that one song ended and another one began. It had a faster beat than the one before it.

"Billy," Shadowlark stepped in between Vernon and myself. "Would you like to dance?"

I nodded and he led me out onto the floor. That really seemed to make Vernon mad. He seemed to be a very rich man who was not used to being rejected by anyone.

"Thank you for saving me from having to dance with that guy," I told him.

"You are very welcome," he smiled. "Now let's see if we can really piss him off."

"What do you mean?" I asked. I blushed slightly at his language, but I was not sure why. I had spent the last five years on a ship full of sailors and had heard much worse things said. I supposed that hearing him say something like that made it different.

"Just follow my lead," he answered and we started to dance.

It was a fast paced song and it took a lot for me to keep up. I had never danced like that before, but it was quite apparent that Shadowlark had. It was easy to figure out what he was going to do next. He would spin me around and we sort of flew across the floor as if we were the only ones that were dancing. Soon we had cleared the dance floor and everyone just stood back and watched us.

Every now and then I would notice him looking over my shoulder and smiling. I figured that it was because he was trying to make Vernon mad and I could tell that it was working. Vernon was standing on the side lines with his face all red.

Somewhere in the midst of all the faces I saw Emmaline who stood there with her eyes wide and her mouth hanging open in the most unflattering and unlady-like manner. I didn't really care though. I was having fun.

As the dance progressed I felt like the two of us had become one. We were definitely moving as such. He would spin and twirl me, but I would never be out of his reach for long. At one point, he caught me in his strong embrace and pulled me so close to him that it made me tingle from my head to my toes. He leaned his forehead against mine and closed his eyes for a brief moment, breathing a gentle sigh, then he swept me around once more. He finished off the dance by doing a deep dip.

"How did you learn to dance like that?" I asked as we walked off the floor.

He leaned a little closer to me and sort half whispered, "As I said before, I'm a man of many trades."

Suddenly there was a loud crash in the corner that was closest to the door, followed by a loud scream. I looked over to see if I could tell what it was when suddenly a chimp came running out of the corner followed by a young man who looked to be about in his middle to late teens.

The monkey ran over to me and grabbed onto the skirt of my dress. The young man came over and tried to get the monkey to let go, but he wouldn't.

"Come on, Monkey," he urged. "I'm so sorry about this."

"It's okay," I told him.

The boy was dressed up, but he didn't seem to like it very much. He had reddish blond hair, bluish green eyes and fair, slightly freckled skin. His monkey of course, looked like a monkey, only he was wearing clothes.

Just then, he was joined by a girl who seemed to be about the same age as he was. She was elegantly dressed, in a light blue gown, but there was something about her that was distinctly pirate-ish.

"What's wrong?" she asked.

"It's this stupid monkey again," he emphasized on the word stupid, causing the monkey to snarl a bit. "He's acting like he's gone completely mad."

"Monkey," the girl urged. "Let go of her skirt or you are going to be in big trouble."

The monkey shook his head.

"Monkey," he threatened. "I will drag you out of here and toss you off the end of the nearest dock."

At that comment the monkey to let go.

"My name's Jonny, by the way," he said. "Jonny Ford, and this is my friend Claire Evans."

"I'm Billy Scarlet."

Jonny nodded. "I saw you with Shadowlark. He's a good guy unlike his brother Nate, who has suddenly decided to give me trouble." His eyes strayed to my medallion. "Nice medallion. The only place that I ever saw a symbol like that was in the death rocks."

It made me nervous to hear someone talking about my medallion because Shadowlark told me that I should be cautious of anyone that recognized it.

"You must be from his world or something," Claire said.

"I've been told that." I involuntarily shifted my weight from one foot to the other. "Your monkey is cute," I told them, trying to change the subject. "What's his name?"

"Well," Jonny said. "I've only ever called him Monkey."

Claire, then began looking around as if she had lost something. "Where is that blasted monkey, now?"

Not two seconds after he said that, someone let out a loud scream.

"Found him." Jonny looked up. "And not in a very good place either."

My eyes followed his all the way up to the chandelier.

"Oh dear, God," Claire exclaimed.

"Oh no," Jonny huffed as the monkey began blowing out the lamps. He ran to where he was right under the monkey. "Stop it Monkey!" he yelled. "Get down here now!"

The monkey shook his head and blew out another lamp.

"Monkey," Jonny sounded threatening. "Don't make me get my rock salt gun."

The monkey stuck his tongue out at him, made a laughing noise and blew out another lamp.

Jonny pulled out a small gun and the monkey screamed.

"If you don't get down from there by the time I count to five," Jonny threatened. "I'll put a piece of rock salt in your butt cheek and you won't be able to sit down for a week. One..."

The monkey didn't wait for him to count any more. Instead he took a flying leap, landed on top of Jonny, then went and grabbed onto Emmaline's dress. She screamed like a crazed lunatic.

"Get that thing away from me!" she yelled, all the while, trying to climb up on the man that was standing next to her.

Claire helped Jonny to his feet.

"I'm very sorry." The two of them went over got the monkey away from her. "It won't happen again." They came back over to me.

"We have to go before this crazy monkey goes and does something that'll get us thrown in jail or shot," Claire laughed. "We're going to be in town for the next little while. Maybe we'll see you again sometime." With that, the two of them left.

Just then the man, or well male, man was not quite the word to describe him; that was standing next to Emmaline came over to me. He had blond hair, green eyes and a very sharp nose and chin. He had thin lips and a sort of pale, pasty complexion. The way he was smiling made me want to run away.

"You are beautiful." The sound of his voice made me want to wrinkle my nose. "Dance with me." He held out his hand.

"No thank you." I started to walk away, but he put his arm out to bar my way.

"If you could clear the dance floor with that other man imagine what you could do with a younger and much more handsome man like me."

'You obviously don't own a mirror.' I so badly wanted to say. 'And you certainly must not know that I know a lot of ways to hurt people really bad.'

"I don't want to have to ask again," he gave me a creepy smile.

"And I don't want to answer again. It gets tiring after the first two times," I told him.

"Then save the energy of rejecting me and dance with me. I know that you want to. I can see it in your eyes. Besides, I am just going to ask you again if you don't dance with me now."

"Fine," I huffed and grabbed his arm and pulled him out onto the dance floor almost causing him to fall over. I took on a very stiff frame and was very jerky with my movements.

"So what is it that you do, miss?" he asked, trying to move a little more fluidly, but I wouldn't let him.

"Billy Scarlet," I answered. "And I'm a sailor."

"Oh," he laughed a little. "How appropriate, Billy Scarlet is a sailor. I thought that women weren't allowed on ships."

"I have my ways of doing things." I so badly wanted to get away from him.

"I'll bet you do." He started to rub my back, but I just squeezed his hand really hard until he stopped. "You're hurting my hand," he whined a little, but I ignored him.

When I stopped squeezing his hand he started back rubbing my back. "And what are some of your ways of doing things? I certainly would like to find out about that. It sounds too interesting to pass up."

I pushed him away from me. "Look, I didn't want to dance with you in the first place and if you keep this up I'm going to embarrass you more than I already have."

"Very well." He held out his hand for me to keep dancing.

"No thank you." I walked off, but before I could get off the dance floor Vernon caught me and swept me all the way back to the middle of the dance floor.

'Oh dear God, what did I do to deserve this?' I thought. 'I should have known that I was right in thinking that I was preparing enough for this to be a battle.'

"May I ask how old you are?" he asked.

"I'm twenty," I answered. "And you?"

"I'm forty-two," he said.

'Oh Lord,' I thought. 'This man is more than double my age and he thinks that he's in love with me.'

"I know you are a bit young for a man of my age, but I have needed to take a wife for some time and I think that you would make a good one."

"Enough!" I pushed him away from me. "You don't even know me and I don't know you well enough to even want to dance with you. I hate to disappoint you, but I'm not ready to get married to anyone much less you. Get away from me," I knew I was causing a scene, but I was tired of these men acting the way that they were.

Just then, Shadowlark walked up to me. "Hello Billy. Is this man bothering you?"

"Yes, he is," I nodded.

Shadowlark glared at Vernon. "Leave her alone. I'm only going to say it nicely once."

Vernon seemed to growl. "What's it to you?"

"None of your damn business," Shadowlark answered in a very calm tone. "But I suggest, in the interest of your health, that you leave her alone when she tells you to. If you touch her again I promise that you will regret it with all of your being. Do I make myself clear?"

Vernon nodded, with a look of panic on his face.

"Good," Shadowlark smiled. "I'm glad to know that we can communicate effectively." He took me by the arm and led me off the floor.

"Thank you for doing that," I told him.

"That's what I'm here for," he smiled.

Just then I saw a woman that I recognized. It was Mistress Lora.

"Excuse me for a minute," I said to Shadowlark and walked over to her. "Hello, Mistress Lora," I said.

She turned to me. She had hardly changed at all. She looked me over then put her hand on her chest. "Sabilla Scarlet," she smiled. "Heavens child, is that you?"

"Yes, ma'am," I nodded.

"I have not seen you in what seems like a life age. You disappeared after the pirate attack that night. I thought you had been taken away," she said. "You and two other children. Davy and Clara. Are they here?"

"Clara is here," I told her. "But Davy isn't. He's a midshipman on the *H.M.S. Victory.*"

"Where's Clara?" she asked.

I looked around the dance floor and spotted her, then pointed her out to Mistress Lora.

"The two of you have grown so much." There was no mistaking the admiration in her voice. "And look at how beautiful the two of you have gotten. You certainly look like accomplished young ladies. I wish I could see Davy again too. He was such a sweet boy. I remember the three of you getting in such trouble. Oh I miss those days."

"Do you still have an orphanage?" I asked.

"Yes," she answered. "It's here in Florida. The old church crumbled and all the blocks were hauled away. I don't know if anyone else built anything there.

After the church was gone it was like life started over. It's almost as if those times were in another life."

"I know what you mean," I nodded. "When they were moving the old blocks away they didn't mess with Mr. McHale's grave did they?"

"No," she answered. "I made sure of that."

It was strange to talk to Mistress Lora after all those years. It had only been five years, but as she had said, it felt like another life and even though it hadn't even been a week since I got off of the *Victory* it felt like I had been away from them for years.

"Are you okay?" she asked.

I nodded. "It's just that things have changed so much. I miss those days as well. You don't know how many times I have wished on stars or prayed that I would wake up back at the church, all of this having been a dream, but things do get better."

"Yes they do," she patted me on the arm.

"I just feel like I'm back where I started every time I think of the night that the town was attacked. Of all the things that have happened in the past five years that is the main thing that I think I could have lived without."

"I know what you mean, but look at you now. You seem to have a nice life, and the man that you were dancing with." She nudged me, jokingly. "I have never seen two dance partners who were so passionate in all my years of going to these balls."

I laughed. "And to think that I had never even danced with him before," I half whispered so that no one else would know.

She smiled. "By the look of you two, it will not be the last. It's been good to see you. I do, so much wish that I could stay longer, but I have to go. I have to get back the orphanage before vespers."

"Okay," I smiled. "I'll see you later," And once again she was out of my life.

Just then Clara walked over to me. "So miss-clear-the-dance-floor," she laughed. "You have made all the other girls out here, wildly envious. I could practically feel the heat coming off the two of you while you were dancing."

"Don't be ridiculous," I scoffed. "We were only dancing and....."

She gave me a silencing look and I could feel my face turning red.

"Was it that obvious?" I was beginning to get somewhat embarrassed. If Clara and Mistress Lora had noticed all these things about me and Shadowlark while we were dancing, everyone else must have.

"I don't think that it's even rational to ask if you are having fun," She smirked. "Have you met anyone interesting?"

"Besides the fact that there have been creeps messing with me and watching me since I walked through the door," I answered. "I just saw Mistress Lora."

"Really?" she asked. "Where is she?" Her tone made her sound kind of distant.

"She just left," I answered. "She's doing good. She has a new orphanage now. It's here in Florida. She said that the old one is gone now, but she's doing good."

"That's good," she said in a mesmerized voice.

"What is with you?" I asked. "You seem all..... I don't know... girly."

"I don't know what you're talking about." She bit her lip.

"Yes you do. Who are you looking at anyway?" I said when I noticed that she was looking at someone across the room. I looked closer and saw that she was looking at a young man that looked to be about twenty. He had blond hair, blue eyes and he was staring right back at Clara.

"Is Miss Honeycut smitten?" I teased.

"Stop it." She blushed.

"What's his name?" I asked.

"David Hunt," she answered.

Suddenly I got this strange feeling. This man would be the man that she would marry. It made me feel happy, but it also made me sad because if she got married then she would want to settle down and I wasn't ready to do that, but it would be strange to go on by myself. I don't know how I figured that he would be her husband, but the second I saw him I just knew. I always knew right away when someone would be really important in our lives and I got that feeling a lot when I looked at him. The only thing about it was that most of the time it was a good feeling, but with this man I got a very strange feeling and to tell the truth I didn't like it. There was something dangerous and alarming about this man. I did not point this out though. I just hoped that Clara would see it for herself.

Just then, he came over to us.

"Hello," he said in a preppy sounding voice. "My name is David Hunt. You must be Billy. Clara has told me about you. It's good to meet you." It was almost as if he was reading every word that he said and from the start I had no idea what Clara saw in him. "Clara would you like to dance again? I hope I'm not tiring you out, but I can't stand to be away from you for a moment."

"I would love to dance," she smiled. "And you aren't tiring me out. I love dancing with you."

With that he whisked her away leaving me standing there.

Gabriella then came over to me. "Do you know who the man was that you left on the dance floor?"

"Which one?" I asked. "The older or the newer?"

She did not seem to find my joke amusing. "The younger man."

"He's a creep as far as I know," I huffed.

She shook her head. "His name is Mavis Tucker. He's the governor's son. He is very rich and he has a lot of influence around here. You are of the right age to get married and he would be a very good prospect. Imagine the life you could have if you married him."

"What about Emmaline?" I asked. "Have you found a husband for her yet?"

"No, but we'll find her one tonight," she answered. "But I think that Mavis likes you."

"Oh yes," I huffed. "If that were to happen then it would be the exact opposite of you and Billy. A governor's son and a sailor girl. It doesn't sound like a good match to me."

"Don't you say his name here," she said.

"Whose?" I asked. "Billy's?"

"I said don't say his name!" she began to raise her voice. "And stop making such a spectacle of yourself!"

"Why can't I say his name?" I asked keeping my voice down, hoping she would follow suit. "He's my father and he's Emmaline's as well, so why can't I mention him?"

"Because I said so!" she yelled. By that point everyone was staring at us. "I don't want to hear that name! He is my past and I don't like it! I don't want to hear it! Your name is Sabilla, not Billy! Your father will never be a part of my life again so just stop it!" Her eyes were starting to glaze over with tears, but she blinked them back. When she said this, I heard and saw that she regretted all of this, but somehow she couldn't give it up.

"What is this all about?" I asked. 'It's happening,' I thought. 'This is it. This is where it all comes out and she tells me the truth of it all.'

"It's about my life!" she huffed. "The life that I have now! I don't want you to ruin the life that I have now! You almost ruined it once why do you have to come in here and act like you want to bring that part of my life back?!"

It was then that Emmaline joined in. "Can't you see that you don't belong here?!"

"Look damn it!" I huffed. "I didn't come here to ruin your lives. I just wanted to see what it was like to have a family. Gabriella, you think that *I* ruined *your* life? Think of what you did to mine. I was put in an orphanage for the first fifteen years of my life. I never knew what it was like to have a real mother or father. I did have a man that was like my father, but he died in my arms five years ago; and Emmaline you will always have one thing over me. Our mother chose you over me. She gave me away because I showed her past that she didn't like, but with you she could at least hide the truth. If you have a problem with me, then get over it, but don't worry because I won't be here much longer." With that I left. I ran outside, sat on the steps and cried. I hadn't cried that much since Mr. McHale had died. I knew it had been coming. Why could I not have just left before it was all out in the open like that?

Suddenly, I felt a hand on my shoulder. I looked up and saw Shadowlark. He sat down next to me. I leaned up against him and he just held me while I cried.

"Shhhh," he whispered. "It's okay."

"Thank you, Shadowlark," I said. "But it's not okay."

"Maybe not now, but it will be someday," he told me. "Life goes on and God has his way of fixing things and He will mend your broken heart. I know you came here to feel wanted and loved and got the opposite, but think of your whole life. You've had love all of your life without the help of your mother or sister." He stood up in front of me and looked at the house. "You don't need all of this to be loved. You don't need a life of money or of fancy dresses and everything that most people would want." He knelt down in front of me and looked me in the eye. "It's what's in your heart that counts. It doesn't matter what they say. They don't control your life. They never have and they never will. They gave up that right years ago. So what if your mother didn't want you. It's her loss. You don't have to let them tell you what you're worth." He gently wiped the tears from my eyes. "Don't let her rule your life. You're much stronger than that."

"Thank you." I stood up. "There's something I have to do. Will you come with me?"

He took my hand and nodded.

The two of us walked back into the ballroom. When we came through the door everyone turned and looked at us.

Clara came over to me. "Are you all right?" She could obviously see that I had been crying.

I nodded then turned to the rest of the people. "I just wanted Gabriella to know that the worst part of her past will be leaving soon." I walked over to her. "You can have your life. You can have this dress. You can have all the riches in the world, but you can't have me. I'm done trying to get all of this right and to tell the God's honest truth I don't give a flying damn and a half what you think of me. You don't control my life. You gave up that right a long time ago. I'm done. I tried, but you didn't want me years ago so why should you care now. Keep this life that you have chosen for yourself. The fake, sad, pathetic, loveless, life that you have now. I'm not sorry that I came; it just let me know what you really are.

"I am Billy Scarlet. One of the two that you left in your past twenty years ago. You may be able to hide me from the world, but you will never be able to hide it from yourself. You may be able to hide the past with Emmaline, but no matter how much you try to hide it she will always be half Billy Scarlet. Running from your past will only make it catch up with you quicker. You're not free here, you're trapped and you know it, but what I say doesn't matter. Nothing about me ever mattered anyway, did it?"

Gabriella looked away from me.

The only thing that kept me strong was Shadowlark taking my hand and Clara standing next to me.

"I'm going to bed now, but this night will most likely be the last one that I spend here. You don't have to worry about me anymore. I won't be coming back," I said and walked out followed by Clara and Shadowlark.

That night I lay in bed trying to sleep, but sleep would not come no matter how hard I tried. I just laid there wishing that I was anywhere other than Gabriella's house.

"So what do you think about David?" Clara asked.

"He seems like an all right guy, I suppose," I answered. "Did he kiss you?"

"No," she laughed a little.

"But you wanted him to," I said.

She threw her pillow at me.

"Clara," I said after a minute. "Do you ever with that we could go back to how things used to be?"

"Yes," she sighed. "Sometimes I just want to be back at the orphanage getting trouble with you and Davy. In the past few days I have taken to wishing I was back on *the Victory*, but we have to be careful about those kinds of wishes."

"What do you mean?"

"You don't want to get caught up in the past, Billy," she said. "There comes a time to move on. Remember, we made an oath when we left the orphanage that we would never look back, and when we left the ship. If we spend too much time wanting what was taken from us and wanting to live in the past, we will never be able to live in the present, much less the future. Stop looking back. It's torture. Don't do that to yourself."

"I've never really thought of it that way," I sighed. "I need to live the way that Mr. McHale would have wanted me to. He would not have wanted me to look back."

"Yes," she nodded.

We talked for little while longer, mostly about David, but then after a while she finally went to sleep. I laid there listening to the rhythmic sound of her breathing. She was right. It was time for me to stop wishing for the past, but instead looking to the future.

It wasn't long after she went to sleep that I heard someone go out the back door of the house. I got up and went see who it was. I made my way down the stairs. The ball was over and everyone was asleep except for a few servants who were cleaning up. I did not want to talk to anyone, instead I walked straight to the back door and I went outside.

When I got into the yard I saw Shadowlark standing near the edge of the porch. He stood there for a minute then headed to the barn. I followed him.

"Where are you going?" I asked.

He looked up briefly. "I have to leave." He led his horse out into the yard. "I know that it's kind of, out of the blue for me to leave like this, but bad news came on the wind tonight and I must find out if it's true or not. I pray to God that it's not."

"What news?"

"I dare not say it aloud for they may hear me and I don't want danger to be brought upon you and the others in this house."

"They?" I asked, confused.

"The Linthrids," he answered, but I still had no idea what he was talking about. "They are here and they must not hear the news. It is too dangerous for their kind to know this." He cast a glance toward the path that led to the barn, as if whatever he was speaking of was over there watching us.

For a moment I thought that I saw a shadow pass across the path and I was sure that I heard an odd fizzy clicking noise. It sent chills from the top of my head to my toes. "What are they?"

He did not bother answering and in a way I was glad, for I was not sure I wanted to know. "Don't look at them," he said. "I don't want them coming over here."

"I don't see anything," I told him.

"Good." He tightened the horses' saddle. "They are not anything that you will want to see, especially not just before you go to bed. I'm sure that there will come a point when you will be able to see them, but that does not need to be tonight. They will return to our world with more information than they need to already, but it's best if they do not try to talk to either of us. You need to get back inside. They should be gone after I leave."

"Can I please come with you?" I asked. "I can be ready in a few minutes."

I could tell that he was going to say no just by the look on his face. "You need to stay here, but if I'm not back by sun down in three days you must leave."

"Why?" I asked. "What's going on?"

Once again, he ignored my questions. "I will find you no matter where you go."

"So you're going to leave me too?" I could feel the tears coming back. "You were even going to leave without saying goodbye."

He stopped what he was doing and faced me. "I called you out here. You may not have heard my voice, but it was because I called you that you woke up and came out here." He reached up and took the horses reins.

"Shadowlark." I grabbed his hand. "Please don't leave me here alone," I had never felt more pleading in all my life. "Clara is probably going to get married to that man and no one else here really cares about me. I'm begging you, don't leave me here alone."

He sighed and looked at me. "Billy, I have to go and you must listen to me. I can't take you along and I know you don't understand right now, but you will. Don't make me answer any questions here. It is not safe, not while they are listening. There are so many things that I wish I could tell you, but those things will show themselves soon enough." He reached out and stroked my cheek gently.

I nodded and took his hand in mine. He squeezed my hand, then softly kissed my knuckles.

"If you do have to leave I will find you." He let go of my hand and mounted the horse. "I promise." He kicked the horse and disappeared into the night.

I hadn't felt so alone in all my life. I felt tears in my eyes. I just stood there staring into the darkness, but it was no use because he was gone.

Chapter

Eight

The next few days went by in a very slow and boring fashion. I slept in the barn loft with the servants, because I flat out refused to stay in the same house as Gabriella and Emmaline. Call me prideful or whatever you wish, but I could not speak to either of them anymore. I could not wait for the third day to come, so that either Shadowlark would return and we would leave together, or I could leave on my own. Either way, I wanted to leave as soon as I possibly could.

Clara got worse and worse when it came to David. I could hardly talk to her anymore. It was as if this man had completely taken over her mind, and not in a good way. I did not like him one bit. He had turned Clara into something that she had never been before. He had turned her all girly and up town. She had even started to act like she was better than others, which was something that she had never done before.

On the morning of the third day Clara announced that her and David were going to get married. The news broke my heart because I most likely wasn't going to get to see the wedding and I felt like she was basically leaving me to fend for myself in the world.

"Where did Shadowlark go?" she asked me in between girly fits. "I have not seen him in a few days. Is everything okay?"

"He just had to leave," I answered. "He left the night of the ball."

"Why?" she asked.

Personally, I didn't want to talk about it to anyone, much less someone who was having such delusions as she was. I mean, don't get me wrong, I wanted her to be happy and I hoped that someday she would find the right man that would make her so, but I could tell that she wasn't really happy with this guy. She was deceiving herself. She wanted this man to make her happy, but he wasn't so she was telling herself that he was and doing everything she could to make herself believe that it was true. Such deception was something I never thought her capable of doing, and I didn't know that she would.

"Well?" She had grown slightly impatient with my delay.

I didn't want to say anything, but I told her anyway. "He heard bad news on the wind and he had to go see if it was true. It kind of makes you wonder if the wind would lie or something." The words didn't sound true when I said them. They just sounded sort of flat and hollow.

She nodded and went back to being all girly.

"I'm not sure what color I should wear for the wedding," she sighed. "I mean, white of course, but I don't know if I should add in some pink or yellow, or perhaps a little of both; and my hair. Oh, heaven only knows what I'm going to do with my hair."

I could not believe what I was hearing. This was not the Clara that I knew. She had completely changed and not for the better, in my opinion.

"I've noticed that you only wear long sleeves when you're around him," I said. "Does he know about your tattoo?"

"No, of course not. I'll cover it with make-up to make for certain that he never sees it. Heaven knows what a fright and shock it would give him if he saw that his future bride had a naked mermaid tattooed on her arm."

I wanted to scream. What had happened to the Clara that didn't care a lick about what other people thought? What had prompted this sudden change of character? Only a few days ago, she would not even cast this David Hunt a second look, much less agreed to marry him after such a short time.

"Clara," I said. "Are you sure that marrying David is the right thing to do? You've only known him for three days. I mean, do you want a life like this? You've seen what it can do to people."

"Well," she sighed. "He's a really good guy. He's funny, he's nice, and he's great with children. We want the same things. I think that we fit well together."

"What do you mean, you want the same things?"

"We both want a family and a nice home, and he wants a farm too."

"Clara, everyone wants family and a nice home. Hell, I would like that someday too, but I'm not going to go off and marry the first man who comes along, saying that he wants the same thing."

She scoffed. "You just don't understand, Billy."

"You're damn right, I don't understand, so please help me with that. I don't know all of the details of what has gone on with the two of you, but I want you to answer one question for me. Do you love him?"

"Oh my goodness," she laughed. "I have never met a guy like him before. He said that I'm the best thing that ever happened to him and he would never let me go."

"Do you love him?" I asked again.

"Of course," she shrugged.

"That's not the answer that I wanted," I told her. "You know, when we left the ship Patrick told me something. He told me to watch out for you."

She looked at me in an odd way. "It may not be the answer that you wanted, but it is the answer you are going to get."

"I don't think Patrick would have said that about a boy."

Her face turned red and she looked down.

"Don't push me away, Clara. I need you. I need you now more than ever. I have no idea what has been going on and to tell the truth, I'm scared. I know that leaving the ship was hard, but just because we had to go, doesn't mean you have to forget everyone that was on board. Neither I, nor Patrick meant for any of that to happen, so please don't blame us for it."

She walked over to the door. "I have things to do. I'll see you in a little while." And so, she left me standing there alone.

"Never let you go huh?" I asked into the silence. "Do you think that's what Patrick did?"

***

Later that day I sat in the kitchen with Lucy. I was writing goodbye letters to Clara and Gabriella. Lucy was the only one that I had told that I was leaving. She had been very good to me in the days after the ball and I hated to leave her, but I knew that I had to. Somehow, she seemed to understand Shadowlark's warning. She listened without question and promised that if someone that she, or Clara did not know, came asking about me, she would tell them that I had not been there.

"I'm going to miss you, Billy," she said. "You've been a really good friend to me. I'm really sorry about the way things turned out when you came here."

"You have no need to apologize. You have been nothing but kind to me since I came here," I smiled. "You didn't cause Gabriella to snap and basically tell me that she didn't love me. You have been a great friend to me and I wish there was a way that I could repay you for helping me like this."

"The best way to repay me is to come back here and see me again after all of this blows over."

"If it ever does," I huffed.

"You just wait. In a week or two your mother will have forgotten that any of this happened. At least she will pretend that she has forgotten it. I do wish that there was something that I could do to make Gabriella change her mind about you. I would give anything to keep you around for a while longer. Things will get dull here without you and your friends."

"There is only one more thing that I need you to do," I told her. "If they ask you where I've gone don't tell them anything. Tell them that you haven't seen me since breakfast. I don't want you getting in trouble over any of it though I doubt that they'll care. The only one you can tell is Clara, but make her promise that she won't tell."

"Okay, if that's what you wish. Though, as you said, I don't think anyone will bother with asking about you besides Clara," she nodded. "Well." She stood. "I have to go refill these water jugs. I'll be right back." She walked out of the room.

I was going to miss her. I was going to Miss Clara as well, but there was nothing I could do about it. I had to leave and there was no way around it. As I sat there alone I read over my two letters making sure that I had gotten them how I wanted them.

Dear Gabriella,

I'm sorry for how things turned out.
I never meant to bring your past back to
hurt you. All that I wanted to do was
meet you. I want you to know that I
do forgive you and I will always love you
because you are my mother. Tell Emmaline
that I was very glad to meet my twin sister
even though it was very awkward. Well it
seems there is nothing more to say. Goodbye.
Billy Scarlet

Dear Clara,

I'm really going to miss you. I do
wish you all of the luck in the world with
your life, but I think you know why I
can't be part of it. You know that I love you
and that even though I now know that
I have a real sister you will always be the
only true sister that I have. I have to
leave now. It's best that I don't write
down the reason, but if you ask Lucy she
will tell you. Well, I guess that it's time for
a goodbye that I never hoped would take
place. I suppose that it's me against the
world now, but don't worry for me. We
both knew that it would come to this someday
and I want you to be happy. Live your life,
Clara and don't ever look back. I hope to see
you again someday. It's just another step towards
forever.
Love,
Billy Scarlet

I folded both of the letters. I put one in Harold's office and the other on

Clara's bed. After doing that I packed my sea bag and got dressed and ready for a long ride. I ate supper Lucy in her quarters that night. She had warmed some salted pork and cooked some bread for the both of us.

"So, where will you go?" she asked.

"I'm not sure. My plan is to find a boat and get on it. I don't really care where it's going. I wish you or Clara would come with me."

"I would love to come. I have always wanted to see the world, but my family is here, and I would not dare leave. Not now anyway."

I took a sip of water. "I understand. I ....." I felt myself start to choke up. I wasn't about to cry, it had just come to the point where words did not want to come anymore. I saw sympathy in her eyes and that made me feel worse than anything yet. I did not want anyone feeling sorry for me. I cleared my throat and took another bite of bread.

"Are you okay?"

I nodded. To tell the truth, I was scared to be alone. I had never been alone in all my life. The thought of facing the world on my own made me feel terribly small. "It's just going to be odd to be on my own is all, but don't worry. I can take care of myself."

We finished supper and for the rest of the evening I wandered around waiting and hoping beyond hope that Shadowlark would get there before sun down. I stood in the yard watching sun fade away over the trees, hoping that just maybe, I would catch a glimpse of him riding up, in the distance. The last bit of light faded away and there was no sign of him.

I had hoped so badly that he would return and I would not have to strike out on my own, but he didn't so I got my sea bag, and headed out to the barn.

My horse whinnied loudly when I came through the barn door. I went over and soothed herby stroking her soft mane, praying that she had not woken anyone up. She seemed more than ready to come out of her stall, but she waited very patiently for me to get her saddle on.

"I'm as ready to go as you are," I whispered to her.

I walked her, quietly out of the barn and into the fresh air, to get her bridle on. When I got outside, I felt a chill run through my body. Something was watching me. The popping and fizzy noise that I had heard the night that Shadowlark left was now coming from the corner of the barn and seemed to be getting closer to me. I turned my back on it and started walking the horse around the front of the house.

"Dear God, don't let them follow me," I prayed.

I saw a shadow move across the edge of the house. Whatever the creatures were, they did not want me to leave without me telling them something. I felt them come closer. I looked directly at the place where the noise was coming from. I felt as if I could see them, but somehow I still could not. I felt something reach out to me. The air close to me grew very cold. I shiver ran through my body. Whatever this was, I did not want it touching me. I felt something brush my cheek, it did not feel like much more than a spider web but it was cold and shocking.

I pulled away and quickly mounted my horse. I got settled in the saddle and was just about to kick her into a trot when I heard someone come out onto the front porch.

I quickly turned around, hoping that it was not one of the strange creatures trying to get into the house. It was only Emmaline.

"Where do you think you're going?"

I turned to face her. "What the hell do you care? I don't belong here. You had no trouble letting me know that, so I'm leaving."

"Wait," she said.

"What?" I asked. "I'm leaving. You don't have to worry about me ruining yours or Gabriella's lives anymore. You don't ever have to see me again. All you have to do is forget that I even exist. I'm sure that won't be too hard for you. You can get back to your normal life a pretend that my coming here was only a bad dream. I'll never be anything to either of you, so just let that be how life is from now on. You may have known that I existed, your whole life, but I'm sure that just seemed like some sort of distant fairy tale that was mentioned in passing, so let be that now and forever."

"I came out here to apologize," she said. "I know that you're going to leave and I don't blame you. When you first came here I thought mother was just forgetting me and tending to you because she suddenly loved you more than me, but the truth is she was trying to change you. All these years she has regretted what she did, by giving you up, so she tried to make it up in the wrong ways. She wanted you to be like everything else in this perfect little world that she has created for herself and when you weren't exactly how she wanted you to be she got mad," She sighed. "I'm sorry for the way I treated you. I had no right to be that way. You were right. I have had a family all my life while you have had nothing, but it seems that you are far happier than I have ever been. To tell the truth I wish that I were more like you. I wish that I could just leave and not worry about coming back to all of this."

"Well." I bit my lip and sighed. I had not been expecting any of this. "You are lucky that you have a mother and father who love you."

"I just wish that I could get away from this marriage that mother has set up for me," She told me.

"Who are you getting married to? I asked.

"Mavis Tucker," she said the name as if she was forcing herself not to gag.

"Well, you said that you wanted to be more like me," I smiled. "What do you think I would do in that situation?"

"Oh no," she shook her head. "I would never be brave enough to leave."

"Okay," I dismounted. I casted a glance in the direction of the creatures that had decided to take up their time by watching me, but they had fallen silent. "There comes a time in your life when you have to do what you have to do to survive. You don't have to be like me to be strong. You are the daughter of

William Sabill Scarlet. You have to have a little bit of pirate in you somewhere. You just have to ask yourself a question. Do you want to marry Mavis and look back twenty years from now, wishing you had done things different? I think you are strong enough to do whatever you put your mind to."

She smiled and reached into her pocket. She pulled out a small angel that was made out of pure gold. "I want you to have this. I don't want you to think that I'm bad or anything, but it's for if you get in a pinch and need some money. It's not much, but it's the least that I can do," she sighed. "Or you could just keep it so that you won't forget me."

"I could never forget you." I put the angel in my pocket. "You're my sister," I hugged her. "I wish you luck with whatever path you choose to take," I mounted my horse and took the reins. "But don't spend your life wishing you had taken another road." With that, I waved goodbye and rode off into the darkness alone, as if I knew where I was going, but the truth was that I had never felt so lost in all my life. "Once again," I whispered. "I take a vow that I will never look back." And for the first time, I really meant it.

***

I rode until sun up and by then I was in a small harbor town. I paid for passage on the first passenger ship that I found. It was headed to Western Sahara in Morocco. It took up most of the money that I had left, but it was a way of getting out of that place. The voyage would take from three to five months depending on the weather. I knew that it was a long way away, but I had to leave. I loved Clara, but I wouldn't be able to live the life that she would soon lead.

When I had asked what it was like in Morocco people told me that there were deserts there. I found out that deserts were like oceans of sand that shifted with the wind. Hearing of it only made me want to go there even more. I only prayed that Shadowlark would be able to find me there.

I was able to take my horse on the ship with me even though they told me that a good bit of the time horses didn't do very well on ships. She was a small, red horse with a white stripe on her nose. I didn't know if she'd had a name before so I decided to call her Elizabeth.

As we cast off I stood there and watched all the people on the docks wave goodbye to their loved ones. I felt a pang of loneliness in my heart knowing that not one of those people were waving goodbye to me. As a matter of fact none of them probably even cared that I was there.

I went below deck to look at my room. It was small. It had a dresser with two drawers, a bathing basin, a mirror, a bed and enough floor space for me to put my sea bag down and be able to get dressed without bumping into anything. I liked the room very much. It reminded me of the midshipman's berth on the *Victory*.

I spent most of my time on deck. After sailing for about four days I met a woman named Winifred West. She looked to be in her early thirties. She had long, reddish blond hair, brown eyes, a slender face and a very pleasant smile. She was married to a former aristocrat named Edward. The two of them were now on their way to start a mission. They were hoping to start a church in Morocco. They had two children, a boy named Mark and a girl named August, and one baby on the way.

Mark was about four years old. He had dark hair, big brown eyes and rosy little cheeks. August was a year and a half. She had curly red hair and big blue eyes.

I really liked being with them. I would watch the children on deck while Winifred would take naps and I could talk to her about anything.

"Do you have a man out there somewhere Billy?" she asked one day while we were on deck. "You do a good job of hiding what you do, but something tells me that there is a man out there that you love, or at the very least, one who loves you."

"Well," I sighed. "I love three men, but I love one of them more than the other two."

"Well," she smiled. "Go on. Tell me about them. I love a good romance story."

"Okay," I nodded. "But I fear you will not get the romantic side from me. I've never been good at telling anything really sappy, and to tell the truth, I don't really think there is much romance in it." My mind strayed to the night that Shadowlark had taught me to speak to the wind, and I felt myself blushing, something fierce.

"Oh, really?" she smirked, and I knew that she had read my feelings.

I cleared my throat and laughed a little. "Anyway, I grew up with one of them. His name is Davy Mitchems. He was with me while I was on the *Victory*. He's like a brother to me. I miss him so much and I can't wait until we see each other again. I have so much to tell him. The second one was also with me on that ship. His name is Apollo McHale and the third one's name is Shadowlark."

She nodded. "Tell me about this Shadowlark. You blushed more when you said his name."

"What can I say about him?" I looked down, trying to hide my mixed feelings for the man. "He's the reason I'm here. I suppose that you can say that he's a man of many talents. He didn't even have to say that for me to see that it was true. He also juggles swords and torches, and throws daggers. He seems so fearless and there's just something about him that's strange yet so familiar."

"He sounds interesting," she nodded. "Tell me about the other one. Apollo."

"Well," I laughed a little. "That man is almost senseless. He helped me out a lot when I was on the *Victory*. He's well on his way to being a captain of his own ship now. I hardly know what to think of him at all, but the only real problem is that I can't stop thinking about him."

"And Davy?" she asked.

"Like I said," I told her. "I grew up with him. He was one of the two kids that left the orphanage with me. He's a midshipman now. I don't know what I would've done if I had not had him and Clara with me."

"So which one do you love the most?" she asked. "You speak of each of them as if you were in a faraway place, so I can't tell just by hearing you talk about them."

"Not telling," I shook my head.

"Oh come on." She nudged my arm. "If you don't tell me I'll start guessing. There are only three of them and you said that Davy is like your brother, so that means there's only two. I'm bound to get one of them right."

"Not telling. Not never," I told her. "It doesn't really matter anyway." I sighed and looked away from her, hoping that she would not see how I felt.

I felt her hand on my shoulder. "I think it does matter."

"I just don't really want to talk about it right now."

"Okay," she laughed a little. "Well, I have to go put Mark and August down for a nap."

"Okay," I nodded. "I'll see you in a little while."

After she had gone I noticed a young man standing by the rail. I didn't think nothing of it until he said, "Hello, Miss Billy Scarlet."

I recognized the voice from the night of the ball. It was Jonny.

"Hey." I went over to him. "How are you doing?"

"I'm fine. And you?" He was staring intently through his scope at something. "It's been a while."

"It's only been a week and a half since I saw you but, I'm doing good," I answered. "At least as good as to be expected when I'm heading off into the wild blue yonder," The whole time I was speaking to him he did not look at me and it started to get on my nerves. "What are you looking at?"

He took the scope away from his eye. "I've found you so we're getting out of here."

"What are you talking about?" I asked.

He pointed out to sea.

I looked and saw a pirate ship not too far away from us. "I have to go tell the captain," I started to run off, but he caught my arm.

"No," he whispered. "No one needs to tell anyone."

"How can you say that? I've been in pirate attacks before. I've been a sailor for years, I know what could happen. I'm not as ignorant of pirates as other girls that you may know. They'll attack us and most of the people will be killed."

"No one's going to get hurt or killed as long as you just follow along," he said.

"Follow along with what?"

"The other ship will be over here in a second and you'll see."

"We have to warn the people." I started off toward the cabin, but once again he grabbed my arm and stopped me.

"I'm not ignorant either, Billy. If you tell anyone about that ship then both of us are going to regret it for a very long time. Just trust me."

"Fine," I scoffed and pulled me arm away from him. "Why?"

"I can't tell you right now, but you'll see in a minute and about telling anyone about it, they're bound to see it sometime and if they don't they're stupid. I mean after all we are on a ship in the middle of the ocean and there is only one other ship in sight."

I just shook my head.

The closer the ship got the more the people panicked. The ship was in attack position. It had all guns showing and was moving into position to broadside. Our ship had a few guns, but not near enough to be a threat to the pirates.

The crew ran around the deck readying what guns we did have, but I knew that it wasn't much use. In my experience with fighting at sea, I knew there wasn't much chance for a ship full of people when they had these little guns.

"This isn't what I thought they would do," Jonny grimaced.

"What did you expect them to do?" I asked. "Say 'Oh look a pirate ship. That's pretty. Let's go have a civilized conversation with them.'?"

"I'm not talking about the people on this ship," he said. "I meant the ones on the other ship. Anyway, you need to go get your things."

"What? Why?"

"You really have a problem with trusting people don't you?"

"Yes, I guess I do."

"Just go get your things and stop arguing with me before somebody gets hurt because you're taking too long."

"What about my horse?" I asked. "I'm not leaving without her."

"How the hell are you going to get a horse across to that ship? We don't have time for this."

"I'm not leaving without out her," I crossed my arms across my chest.

"Fine," he huffed. "We'll set the gang plank across. Will you just get your things and get ready to go. Dang, you are so stubborn."

So, I went below deck, got my sea bag, then went to the hold and got Elizabeth. She had doing very well at sea, but as I walked her across the deck, she stumbled and hesitated slightly with the sway of the ship. At one point she stopped completely.

"Come on girl." I rubbed her neck and clicked my tongue. "We have to hurry."

She seemed to understand, because she started walking again.

By the time I got back on deck the two ships were right side by side with a gang plank across. Jonny was trying to get the captain of the passenger ship to believe that no one was going to get hurt.

"We're only taking one of your passengers and we're not even going to hurt her," Jonny told him. "We only need you to stay right here while we get her and her horse onto our ship."

"I will not help you. These ships are coming apart the second I get my hands on that wheel," the captain insisted.

"Don't think that I'll tell anyone if you help me. As you can imagine, I'm not very popular to most men in the king's navy."

"I'm a man of honor, sir," the captain huffed. "I will not help anyone of your type."

"I'm a man of honor too, captain. I promise I will not hurt any man, woman, or child aboard this ship, nor will I take any of your cargo. All I ask in return is that you return the favor and not hurt any of us as we pass across the gangplank."

"No man of honor would do things like you do. I don't strike bargains with pirates, nor am I permitted to suffer them."

"Fine," Jonny huffed. "Troy!" he called to the other ship. "Come help me out for a minute."

Just then a big built man came across from the other ship. He was very tall with long dark hair, tan skin and dark eyes. He was wearing a shirt without sleeves, showing that he had a tattoo of a jolly roger on his left arm.

"What is it?" he asked in an accent that I could not quite place.

"Help me out here," Jonny said. "We have to get them to stay here while we go across the gang plank. Also try to make him understand that we're not going to hurt anyone."

"We're not going to help any of you!" the captain yelled.

"Don't make us do this forcefully," Troy sounded annoyed at the idea.

"That's the only way anything is going to get done," Jonny told him, also sounding very annoyed at the thought of it. "They're not going to aid pirates of their own free will."

"Is that right?" Troy asked.

The captain nodded.

I looked over to the rail of Jonny's ship and saw Claire Evans. She seemed quite amused with the situation. More so than I would be, were I in her position.

"Fine," Troy said, while I was looking away and put the barrel of his rifle under my chin. "We take her or....I don't know.....we'll kill her?" The last bit almost sounded like a question.

"What?" The captain looked horrified.

"You heard me," Troy nodded. "And after her....." He paused, shrugged and looked at Jonny as if he were trying to come up with something else to say. Jonny gave no reply so he added what he seemed to figure any other pirate would say. "Well... you're next."

It then occurred to me that these men were not like any other pirates. They didn't seem very good at giving threats. As a matter of fact, it didn't seem like they were good at being pirates in the slightest way, but somehow it was scaring the captain and crew.

"I'd take it that all pirates are alike when it comes to taking one person off of a ship. It's all this if-we-can't-have-them-no-one-can business."

They all ignored what I was saying.

"If they don't have a captain they'll get lost and die," Troy said in a threatening voice. "Do you want that to happen to them?"

"Very well," the captain nodded.

"Okay," Jonny nodded. "Let's go."

We started across the gang plank. First we got Elizabeth across, then me, Troy and Jonny started across. When we were half way across the gang plank the captain of the passenger ship yelled an inaudible order to his crew, and they seemed to understand it perfectly. They set full sails, cut the roes that secured the gangplank, and turned the ship as hard away from us as possible. Troy pushed Jonny onto the other ship then jumped on himself. I threw my sea bag onto the ship, but I wasn't as fortunate as the others. I tumbled off the plank and into the water.

Once I hit the water I just kept going down farther and farther. I knew that there would be no bottom for a very long time. I pushed up with my legs. My lungs ached and felt like they were going to explode. I had not been able to take a very deep breath before I went in and it was very hard to keep going, but I wouldn't give up. I could see the surface, but the harder I worked at getting there the farther away it seemed.

'God help me,' I thought. 'Please,' It was then that I saw a rope in the water. I grabbed hold of it and it pulled me to the surface. I came up right beside the ship. I climbed up the ladder on the side of the ship. When I got on deck Jonny and Claire ran over to me.

"Are you okay?" he asked.

"I'm just fine," I huffed. "I would be much better if I hadn't just sunk almost to the bottom of the Atlantic Ocean. You know, I'm so sick of being kidnapped by pirates. None of you are good at giving threats by the way."

Claire just smiled as if she had known I was going to be in such a mood after all that had just happened.

"Will you just calm down," Troy said.

"Don't you tell me to calm down you giant son-of-a-bitch," I told him. "You let me go falling into the ocean and you held a rifle under my chin so you have no right to tell me to calm down, but I do thank whoever it was that threw me a line."

"What do you mean?" Jonny asked.

"Someone threw me a line," I said.

"We didn't throw you a line," Claire told me. "Jonny was just fixing to dive in after you, but you came up."

"Thank you God," I whispered.

"We were never going to kill you, or anyone else," Troy huffed. "We only did that so that those people would help us."

"Well in case you didn't notice none of your persuasion worked," I told him. "And I don't give a shit why you did any of it. The point is that you threatened to kill me and I don't take to kindly to people that do that," When I got mad about something I had tendency to go back to talking like a sailor.

"What do you think captain?" Troy asked. "Should I gag her, put her in irons and put her in the brig?"

"No," Jonny answered. "I'm thinking about doing that to both of you."

"Wait," I raised my eyebrows. "Aren't you a little young to be a captain?"

"Thank you," Jonny crossed his arms across his chest. "I bet you couldn't guess how old I am anyway, and now if you're done insulting my age then I'll explain to you what's going on."

"Sorry." He made me feel like a scolded child. "What's going on?"

Elizabeth whinnied and nudged me on the back. I rubbed her nose to calm her down

"We are under direct orders from Shadowlark," Jonny answered. "We were told to find you and take you to Puerto Rico."

"How can I trust you?" I asked. "I was told that I shouldn't trust anyone who recognized the jade eye."

"No, you weren't," Jonny shook his head. "You were told to be cautious of anyone who recognized it; and it's your choice to trust me or not. After all that you've been through, I can understand why you are very cautious about trusting people. Either way I'm taking you to Puerto Rico whether you like it or not."

"And what's in Puerto Rico?" I asked.

"A lot of things," he answered. "You'll see when you get there."

"How long will it take to get there?" I cast an icy glance in Troy's direction.

"It'll probably take about a week," Jonny answered. "And I expect everyone to behave."

"Where do I put Elizabeth?" I asked.

"Who's Elizabeth?" Jonny wrinkled his brow in confusion.

"My horse," I laughed a little. "Where am I supposed to put her? I doubt you'll want her on deck the whole time."

"You can put her in the hold," Jonny answered. "Troy will help you get her down there. There are a few other horses down there so she should have company."

"What about me?" I picked up my sea bag. "Where am I supposed to stay?"

"There's a bed down in the hold," Jonny answered. "You can stay down there. Unless of course, you want to stay with the men."

Troy shook his head with a look of panic on his face.

"Troy I'm joking," Jonny laughed. "Lord knows, if I were to let the two of you stay in the same room you would kill each other."

Without a word, Troy showed me to the hold, helped me get Elizabeth in her stall, then he left. There were a few bundles of hay in the far left corner, so I got some and put it in the stall with her. She quickly began munching away at it, as if she had not eaten in weeks.

I used a small lamp that was hanging by the stall to look around the room. The bed that Jonny had told me about was in the corner farthest from the horse stalls. It smelled pretty bad down there, but it was that or stay in the same room as all the men, so it really wasn't a hard choice. I had spent many a night in sleeping quarters with a bunch of men, but they had not known that I was a girl, and I wasn't about to take any chances. Jonny was a good captain, it seemed, but even the best of captain's could have a bad man among their crew, so I figured it best to stay where Jonny told me to. I sat my bag on the bed and headed back up on deck.

The first thing that I noticed when I got on deck was that the ship was swaying and that Jonny was yelling all manner of crazy things.

I looked over toward the helm and saw that the monkey had hold of the wheel and Jonny was trying his best to pry him off. I wasn't the only one that was watching this spectacle. As a matter of fact, the entire crew had stopped and they were watching as well.

"Get off the wheel you idiotic monkey!" Jonny yelled. "I'm the captain here! Let go you crazy thing!"

The monkey made a bunch of scary noises as if he were talking back to Jonny.

"Stop, you lunatic," Jonny growled. "If you don't let go I'll make you let go and when I do, you're going swimming."

It was then that I noticed a little blond haired girl sitting next to Troy. The two of them were talking about something, but between the facts that they were talking quietly and Jonny was yelling, I could not hear what they were saying. The little girl was really cute. I could not guess her age, but she did not look very old at all. Ten at the absolute, most.

"Monkey!" Jonny yelled. "If you don't stop, I'm gonna go back to Tortuga and I'm gone leave you there!"

'Oh wonderful,' I thought. 'He's threatening the monkey with what he's going to do to me, only he's leaving me on Puerto Rico.'

The monkey snarled at Jonny and made an odd squeaking noise.

"Monkey," Jonny threatened. "Let go of the wheel. Now."

"No," Was the noise that the monkey made, as if he could speak.

"Get me my gun," Jonny stuck out his jaw.

The monkey screamed, ran and hid behind Troy.

He just laughed and picked the monkey up. "Calm down, Monkey."

"What's that thing's name?" the little girl asked.

"I don't know," Troy shrugged. "Just Monkey I guess."

"Let's try this again," Jonny huffed and took the wheel.

I walked over and stood next to Jonny.

"So I'm supposed to meet Shadowlark in Puerto Rico?" I asked.

"I don't know," Jonny shrugged. "All I know is that he wants me to take you there."

"So if he's not there, then what am I supposed to do?" I asked.

"I told you," Jonny said. "I don't know."

"It's okay," I told him. "I'm mostly asking myself. I'm just hoping this isn't some sort of trap. By the way that Shadowlark was talking, it could possibly be something of the sort."

"It isn't," Jonny assured me. "I would only take orders such as these if I heard the from Shadowlark himself. Just like yourself, I trust very few people, especially in this situation."

"And what exactly is this situation?"

"It could be one of many things or it could be nothing, but either way it all points to Grayheart and Rossaletta. When they are in the mix, you can find very few people who can be trusted. Shadowlark is a good man, but he's running out of allies in this war."

The word "war" seemed so strong. To think that a small three letter word meant so much in so many ways. "No one said anything about a war."

"So small a word and so easy to say," he sighed. "Whether it has been said aloud to you or not it's what is before us. Two worlds are at war, but someone else will have to explain that to you, it is not for me to say."

I walked to the quarter deck and propped on the rail.

"Not what you're used to, I'd take it," Claire walked over to me. "You're a navy girl by the look of it."

"My father's a pirate, but I sailed on a navy ship for the past five years. How could you tell? Am I that obvious?"

"Well, I'm sort the opposite of you," she laughed. "My father is a captain in the American navy, but I have been sailing with Jonny for the past year or so. I suppose that after a while it's easy to tell who's pirate and who's navy. I don't think it's hard to tell that Jonny and his crew are not exactly your average pirates."

"They don't really seem to be."

"Jonny sails to keep from getting caught up in a war that he feels he doesn't belong in. Everyone wants him on their side. He is for the Americans and he helps them out when they need him, but most of the time, he has other stuff to deal with."

"Like what?"

"Usually, just regular pirates, but now it seems that you are not the only one that Nate Grayheart and others of the like are after."

***

Later on that day I got to meet the little blond haired girl. I was sitting at the rail and she just came over to me.

"Hey," she smiled. "Who are you?"

"My name's Billy Scarlet," I told her. "What's yours?"

"My name's Layla Morgan," she answered.

"So, what's a girl as young as you doing on a pirate ship?"

"Well," she sighed. "I'm looking for my brother Tylar. He's on another pirate ship and Jonny's gone take me to him. You see, me and Tylar are grandchildren of Henry Morgan and a lot of people wanna kill us and three months ago Tylar sailed away on a pirate ship with Tarus Addison and I miss him so I'm going to find him."

"How old is your brother?" I asked.

"He'd be twenty now," she sighed. "He wasn't home for his birthday. I really missed him then. Mother anf Fatherdecided to have another baby and then Fathersaid that Tylar wasn't his son anymore and he sent an American sailor after him to kill him."

"That's bad," I said.

She nodded then looked at my medallion. "I've got something sort of like that. I used it as a marker behind a rock in the wall of the tailor's shop at home so I wouldn't get lost in the alley ways."

"Where did you get it?"

"I found it in the marsh next to our house. It washed in on the full moon tides about a year or so ago."

I nodded wondering how something of the sort could have gone unnoticed by her brother or Jonny if they knew so much about the situation with the Jade eye. "So how do you know Jonny?"

"Me and Tylar met him when we got kidnapped by Mac Spade and taken to Nautilus island," she said as if it was the most normal thing in the world to get kidnapped.

She went on about it for a while. Her story was quite interesting. She told me about fighting monsters and pirates. She told me of Nautilus island. A magical island that held creatures that I could never have imagined. Creatures like the Golden Secrets, which contained magical powers that no one could fathom. It seemed like a place that would only come out of some kind of dream. She told me about how her brother fell in love with a girl that lived on the island, but she got mad at him when he told her that he was going to sail with the man named Tarus. She told me all the way up to how she got on Jonny's ship. A couple of times when she was talking about Tylar she had to wipe tears from her eyes. After hearing her story I wanted to meet the people that she was tell me about. Toby and Austin the Scotch Irish pirates that joined them, Natilie and Natalia Taylor, the twin island princesses, Ace the lone pirate that saved their lives, Pirate the macaw that thought he was human, the man that fought Mac Spade in the darkness, but most of all I wanted to meet Tylar the farm boy turned pirate who sailed all over the Caribbean to save Nautilus island. He sounded very fascinating.

I had never heard a girl that was Layla's age, tell a story in such detail and she told it with such enthusiasm.

When she was done she just sighed a stared out to sea. She truly was different from any other person that I had ever met in my life. I felt that she was going to grow up to be an amazing woman.

***

For the next few days I just wandered around the ship thinking about Layla's story. I also kept my distance from Troy because I didn't want to fight with him. It wasn't like we were really enemies or anything, but we had a passion for annoying the living daylights out of each other so I figured it would be best if we kept our distance from each other. Jonny seemed to have enough on his late without the two of us getting on each other's nerves and driving everyone else over the edge.

All in all, I liked being on Jonny's ship. I had fun talking to Claire and I enjoyed the time at sea, but for some reason I felt lost. I kept on wondering why Jonny didn't know what I was supposed to do when I got to Puerto Rico. Something didn't feel right about all of it. There was a warning deep in my heart, telling me that something was terribly wrong.

A few nights after I got on the ship I was sitting in the crow's nest trying to listen to the wind. I wanted to speak to it and see if it would tell me anything about what awaited me in Puerto Rico. I closed my eyes and focused hard on the sounds of the wind like I had done the night when Shadowlark had started to teach me. I wished that he was there with me, because hearing the words was easier when he was there to help me out. There, by myself, I could hear nothing. I strained my ears and tried with all my might to hear something, anything, but still no words came. Suddenly I heard something. I wasn't sure if I had imagined it or it had really happened. A voice softly said, "Don't try so hard. Let it flow."

I took a deep breath and closed my eyes. The wind blew across my face and ruffled my hair. It caressed my skin like a silk sheet gently fluttering from the sky. I began to hear something that sounded like a low whisper. It was speaking very clearly. I could tell each word apart and hear each bit being carefully pronounced with great articulation, but it was a language that wasn't familiar to me. I could feel the words rather than hear them, and it seemed as if the way to understand their meaning was lingering somewhere at the back of my mind. I just had to reach back far enough to find it.

"I don't understand," I whispered.

The whispering came again, but I could only understand one word, "*Empress*."

"*The Dragon's Empress*?" I asked.

It tried to answer and that time I understood a few more words of what it was saying. "*Empress*........... Grayheart.............. Shadowlark........................ Jameson."

"Jameson?" that was the only part that confused me.

"Grayman............. Grayheart.......... cautious.............. *Empress*........ waters........... Puerto Rico."

"What do you mean?" I asked, but it seemed that it was done speaking to me. The wind had gone completely silent.

I sighed. None of what it had said made much sense to me. I understood a bit of it, but I could not be sure. I wasn't what to believe or what not to believe when it came to hearing things on the wind, especially after Shadowlark made it sound as if the wind might not always tell the truth. I wasn't rightfully certain of what to think about any of it, but I had a feeling that I would have to be really careful in Puerto Rico.

That next morning we came into port. I got my things together and me and Elizabeth were set off the ship.

"Farewell!" Jonny called to me. "May you be successful in your quest, whatever it may be and where ever it may lead you."

"Good luck!" Claire called.

"The same to you," I called back. With that, me and Elizabeth headed down the dock.

I walked into town and stopped next to a building. The town looked as though it had just been attacked by pirates. It reminded me of the town that the orphanage had been in, the morning after the attack. Despite the mess the town was buzzing with life. Men, women and children of all ages were wandering the streets, but unlike me, all of them seemed to know where they were going. They were roaming around among tents that seemed to have been set up in a hurry. There was music playing somewhere, but I could not spot the person who was playing it though.

I walked on down the street listening to the seemingly endless chatter of the crowd. My eyes scanned the tents. Three ship's boys passed in front of me. They were going on about what seemed like a bet that they had made.

"If you don't do it, you don't get the money," the oldest looking one said.

"Fine, fine," the smallest of the three relented. "Is it going to hurt?"

"Like hell," the oldest one laughed, pulling up his sleeve, revealing an anchor tattoo on his forearm.

The tree of them walked on and I could not help but laugh out loud. They reminded me so much of my friends back on *the Victory*. I was surprised by the fact that the memory didn't bring even the slightest bit of sorrow. It only brought me happiness to think of my old ship mates. I still missed them, but it was not near as bad as it had been to start with.

I walked further down the road. It was still strange for me to be alone and even though I did not like it very much, I was starting to get used to it.

I came to a fairly busy street. It was so crowded that I had to stop and wait, so I turned down an alley way and came to a less populated part of the town. It was where all the taverns and inns were. It was odd that there were very few people in that area, but they all seemed more enthralled with the goings on, on the other side of town.

I stopped for a moment to figure out where I was going to go.

"Where in the bloody hell did you go?" a voice came from behind me.

I turned around and saw Clara propped up against the side of the building.

Her hair was cut short and she was dressed as a man. She looked at me with a sort of blank expression, all the while puffing on a thin cigar.

"Clara," I was very surprised. "I thought that you were going to get married."

She took a long draw on the cigar, blew smoke then said, "David Hunt is, was, and always will be an asshole. He has two mistresses and the only reason he wanted to marry me was because he thought that I was related to your mother." She puffed the cigar again. "You were right about all of it and I was stupid."

"No, Clara. You're not stupid."

"You've always seen the best in both me and Davy, but there is no need for it here and now. I know what happened and why. What I did was terribly foolish and I wish I could undo it, but I cannot. No one has any grounds to defend my actions, Billy not even you, or me. The whole thing is over and done. It doesn't matter anymore."

"Are you okay?"

She nodded. "I'm just glad that I got out of there when I did."

"I should've stayed with you," I said.

"No," she shook her head. "You were right to leave. Lucy told me everything. It's odd enough, but I think that her and Emmaline were planning to make a break for it," She took another draw of her cigar. I had seen her smoke before, but it seemed that, at this point she was doing it with a vengeance. "Anyway, the day after you left, a man came around asking about you. He said that he was Shadowlark's brother. I didn't speak to him. I didn't even see him, but I did hear Harold talking to him."

"He's looking for me," I said, mostly to myself. "We have to find Shadowlark. I was told that he was here somewhere."

"Okay." She put the cigar out on the wall. "How are we going to find him?"

"I'm not sure," I answered. "We'll look around at some of the inns."

The two of us went to a small inn. I tied Elizabeth out front and we went inside. It was also a tavern. There was a young girl behind the counter. She had long dark hair and looked to be about the same age as me and Clara.

She looked at me for a moment, then asked in a quiet voice, "Is your name Billy Scarlet?"

"Yes," I nodded. "Why?"

Without a word she handed me a small piece of paper and walked away.

I unfolded it and recognized the hand writing right off. It was the same hand writing as the note that I got in the bar in Florida.

Sabilla Scarlet La Rosa Rhojo #3

I read it to Clara.

"It could be a trap," she said. "But I think that we should at least look and see what's going on."

I was very glad to have Clara back with me. I was sad that she had gotten her heart broke, but I was glad that she was with me again because I was lost when I was alone.

"It's worth a try," I nodded. "Is this the place?"

"I'm not sure," she answered. "I didn't look at the sign."

We went and looked at the sign and sure enough it was the right place. We went back inside and headed up to the top floor where the rooms were. The third door to the left was room number three. I went over and knocked on it.

"Who's there?" A voice came from behind the door. I could not tell whose voice it was because it was hardly more than a whisper.

"Billy Scarlet."

Before I could even think the door flew open, me and Clara were pulled inside and the door was shut behind us. By the time the door had shut I had pulled my sword and held it at the ready because I had not even seen the face of the person that had pulled us in, nor was I sure that it was only one person.

"Put that thing away." It was, in fact, Shadowlark. "You pulled that thing so quick I was afraid you were going to run me through before you even saw who I was."

"Sorry." I put my sword back in its sheath. "Are you all right?" He was wearing a sword at his side, two pistols on his chest, and he seemed very on edge.

"When I told you to leave I didn't mean for you to go all the way across an entire ocean, but that doesn't matter now," he said. "The only thing that matters right now is the fact that we can't stay here. Grayheart has been on my trail ever since I left your mother's house. On top of that Arkola Terrell is here or at least she was and she knows that I'm here which is never a good thing."

"Who's Arkola Terrell?" Clara asked.

"Never mind that now," he told her. "Right now we just have to get out of here."

"So, what's wrong exactly?" I asked. "Why didn't you come back?"

"Because if I had've come back then Grayheart would have killed us all," he answered. "He knows we're here. It's only a matter of time before he finds us. We have to get a move on, and fast."

"So, If we can't stay here, then where are we going to go?" Clara asked.

He cast her a curious glance. "I thought you were supposed to be married," he shook his head as if he had remembered wrong. "Never mind that. Getting out of here will be the hard part."

"Why?" I asked. "What's wrong?"

"Not only does Grayheart know that we are here, he's here as well. His ship is anchored in the harbor," he told us. "We need to keep low on our way out and hope that he does not see us. I don't know whether they will recognize you or not, they will recognize me."

"I thought that the *Dragon's Empress* was supposed to be horrible looking," I said. "I was in the harbor a little while ago and I didn't see it."

"That part of it can only be seen in our world," he answered. "Here, you would not be able to tell it apart from your everyday average ship."

"How are we going to get out of here?" Clara asked.

"If we can get past Grayheart we'll try to find passage on a ship somewhere," Hhe said. "It won't be in this harbor, but I'm sure there will be another, a few miles from here."

"I have to get my horse," I told him. "She's out front. She was carrying mine and Clara's stuff."

"Okay," He nodded. "Let's go."

We went out front, got Elizabeth and headed toward the docks.

"Which ship is the *Empress*?" I asked as we got closer to the docks.

"The one at the very end." Shadowlark nodded toward the end of the dock.

I looked over at the ship. Like he had said, it looked like any other ship, but somehow slightly different. It was as if I was looking at the ship, but I wasn't looking at it. The sails were a bluish color that seemed to fade in and out, and I got a very strange feeling when I looked at them.

Shadowlark looked around as if he could feel someone watching us. The docks weren't very crowded and that made me very nervous. Then again, I would have been even more nervous had they been swarmed with people.

Suddenly I noticed a man standing not too far away from us. He was watching us. He had shoulder length, curly, dark blond hair, his eyes were the same dark blue as the ocean at night and he had sun tanned skin. He smiled a pleasant smile when our eyes met, but there arose an odd fear in my heart. I knew this man. I had seen him somewhere before, but I could not quite place where or when that had been. He seemed casual enough, but there was something about him that made me shiver.

When Shadowlark saw him he stopped. He walked over to us. His countenance was filled with grace and charm, yet there was something about him that made me feel like the air had become water and I was fixing to drown.

"There's nowhere else for you to go," the man said in a menacingly charming voice and oddly enough this man reminded me of Shadowlark. "Come with me and there will be no dispute. Try to escape and there will be bloodshed."

"You haven't said whose blood will be spilt," Shadowlark smiled.

"Don't try your childish antics on me brother," the man huffed. "They won't work and you know it, but you also know me and you know what I'm capable of doing to you should you choose not to come with me."

"I know that there was a time when the only men that you thought of hurting were the ones who would attack our people," Shadowlark said. "But then again, that was before your heart became like a burnt cinder, Grayheart."

I had realized who the man was before Shadowlark even said anything, but to hear his name spoken aloud and to see his face at the same time made my heart beat very fast. Up to that point, Grayheart had just been a shadow in my mind. A feeling that was more forbidding than anything else, but suddenly, right before my eyes, that shadow of a feeling had become flesh. He was there, standing before me.

Grayheart just smiled. "You can't say that I'm the only one with a change of name these days."

"The name has nothing to do with it," Shadowlark huffed. "What do you want with us?"

"Why would I want my little brother? Why would I want the ruler of our people?" Grayheart's voice was very mocking.

I realized that Grayheart had not been saying it because he meant it, he was saying that because Shadowlark was the younger brother, but he still got to rule.

Shadowlark just stood there expressionless.

"You will someday realize that our race is lost," Grayheart smiled. "The only ones that are left are of broken blood lines." He glanced at me.

"Then what do you care if the rest of them live?" Shadowlark asked.

"The rest of them," he mused to himself, then looked back at Shadowlark. "A race that each was born with a special talent." He stepped very close to Shadowlark. "Every child, born with a talent."

I could see a slight bit of anger in Shadowlark's eyes at the comment, while I could see amusement and triumph in Grayheart's expression. Somehow he had hit Shadowlark where it hurt.

"Come with me. You will be the guest of honor on board *the Empress*," Grayheart said. "I want to show you how far our world has come."

"And which route do you plan to take?" Shadowlark asked.

"Your favorite one," Grayheart laughed. "Through the death rocks."

"And if I refuse?" Shadowlark asked.

Grayheart nodded to someone behind us and before any of us could even blink, someone held a silver blade at Shadowlark's throat.

That made my heart beat even faster, but there was nothing I could do. I knew if I made a move to help Shadowlark, Grayheart would kill us. I felt that if my heart beat sped up anymore, that it would just fly right out of my chest.

Shadowlark laughed a little and said, "Hello Newheart."

"I don't think I have to explain." Grayheart looked me and Clara over. "I see you've brought friends. I know this one, of course," he nodded toward me. "But who's the boy?"

"That shows about how smart you are," Clara huffed. "I'm a girl, you witless bastard."

"Oh I see," Grayheart smiled. "Now I know who you are. Heaven forbid I forget your existence." He turned back to me. "So what of you?"

"What of me?" I asked. "If you mean that you are wondering what I think of you, then I'm sorry, I don't think you'll like that very much."

I saw Shadowlark suppress a smile.

"I'm losing patients here," Grayheart scoffed. "The three of you will come with me now or I will kill you."

"I don't think so," Shadowlark elbowed Newheart in the ribs, threw him over his shoulder, causing him to land on Grayheart, then yelled, "Run!"

Elizabeth bucked really hard and took off running. I couldn't keep up with her so I just let go of her reins.

We dodged our way through crowds of people all the way into town. I looked back and saw some of Grayheart's men coming after us.

"Quick, in here." Shadowlark pulled me into a barn.

After we got into the barn Elizabeth came in there after us. She was all in an uproar. I tried to get her to calm down, but she wouldn't.

"She's going to give us away," Shadowlark said. He went over to one of the stalls and got out two of their horses.

"You're stealing someone's horses?" Clara asked.

"Fine." Shadowlark set two gold pieces on the gate. "A piece of gold for each horse. Feel better?"

She just laughed and shook her head.

"We have to leave now," he told us. "Right now there is a rather large crowd of people outside. If we just fall in with them we may be able to sneak out of town unnoticed, unless of course they saw us come in here." He looked out of the barn. "Ready," he said. "Now."

We walked out of the barn and did our best to blend into the crowd. I tried not to look around very much, but that was hard. My eyes darted back and forth. I felt as if at any moment one of Grayheart's men would come out of the crowd and kill us. All the faces around us seemed to blend together and I could see any one of them being Grayheart's spy, hoping to catch us off guard.

We kept going until we were safely out of town. After we got into the outskirts of town, we left the crowd of people that we had fallen in with. We took a road that didn't seem well travelled. It seemed travelled enough that it would not arouse suspicion for us to go down it, but the road was sparsely travelled enough that there did not seem to be a threat of us encountering any unwanted company. There were no there any travelers, so it seemed safe enough. The road went through woods that were cleared well enough that we would be able to see if anyone was coming. We mounted our horses and began to trot slowly down the path.

I suddenly got this odd feeling inside of me that said something wasn't right. I got an odd tingling in my scalp. I looked behind us and saw a large man, all dressed in black, riding a horse that was the silvery color of moon light on water. The horse whinnied and huffed. Though this creature was quite majestic, something about the beast made it seem as though it were there by some doing that I could not explain. As if the being itself was pure enchantment.

"What's wrong?" Shadowlark noticed that I was staring at something. He looked back and saw the man. He breathed a deep sigh and gritted his teeth.

"What is?" I asked. "What's wrong?"

"That is a being that I believe was forged in the fires of hell," he answered. "There are few ways to kill him, but I may be able to stall him well enough."

"What are we supposed to do?" Clara asked.

"This is something you can't deal with. I'll fight him," he told us. "Now go, go!"

We kicked our horses and rode as fast as we could. Shadowlark rode with us for minute then he turned his horse around and stopped. I looked back and watched as the man came closer to Shadowlark. The enchanted horse pounded toward him with grace that I had never seen in any creature before. Where others would have tripped, the horse pranced lightly. Just as the man got right beside him Shadowlark jumped through the air and kicked him off of his horse. The man leapt to his feet as though he had not been hurt at all.

"Your lack of fear will be your undoing," the man hissed. "You call it bravery, I call it foolishness."

Shadowlark just smiled and kicked the man in the side of the face.

The man did not fall, or even seem hurt for that matter. With great speed and agility, he leapt through the air and caught Shadowlark from behind. The large man wrapped his bulky arm around Shadowlark's neck. He elbowed his attacker in the stomach and threw him over his shoulder the same way he had with Newheart. While he was on the ground, the man tripped Shadowlark, then got up and tried to step on his throat, but Shadowlark grabbed his foot and twisted it around, then got back to his feet.

"You might as well give up now," the man said. "It would be a lot less painful."

Shadowlark then began speaking a different language. I couldn't understand what he was saying, but obviously the other man could because he began to look very nervous.

The wind began to pick up.

"Stop that!" the man yelled.

"Stop what?" Shadowlark laughed.

"You know what I mean," the man huffed.

"What's the matter? Do you fear the words of your people?"

"Those words are not of anyone connected to me. They are words of cowards and peasants."

"Very well. How will you feel if I add something in it that might be familiar to you?" Shadowlark nodded then he began speaking a language that sounded completely different. A wall of water rose up out of the ground and joined the wind. Shadowlark began to back away, but he kept on talking. The water flew through the air and swirled around the man. It tangled around him and continued to grow larger and stronger, as if it were some sort of vine. It first wrapped around his wrists, then all the way up his arms and down his legs. It moved along his body until it had completely entrapped the man. It had him tight and it would not let him go.

Shadowlark quickly leapt onto his horse and caught up with us. We rode through the woods at a rather fast pace for a while. We only stopped when we came to a clearing in the woods.

"We can make camp here for the night," Shadowlark dismounted. "I don't like the idea of staying here any longer than we have to, but we should be safe here."

I dismounted and looked around. We were well hidden in the trees and underbrush. It seemed safe enough, but I was still sort of worried about that rider catching u with us again. I listened to the sounds in the woods for a second and I heard water flowing.

"I think there's a river over here," I told them. "I'm going to go get some water. I'll be back in a few minutes."

I walked through the woods a little ways and came to a river with water fall. The water looked so inviting that I could not resist. I walked over to the art that was still, for the most part, unstrapped my sword, took off my shoes, and waded in. The water felt so good. It was really hot outside and I had sunburn, so the water felt really good. I sat down on a rock that was on the bottom. Sitting down made the water come up to my shoulders. I looked down in the water at my toes. They looked cold and pale, but it felt really good to get cooled off. I closed my eyes and leaned back on the bank. Feeling the water in my skin made me relax and I was starting to doze off when I heard something on the bank. I looked up and saw Shadowlark standing there unbuttoning his shirt.

"Do you mind if I join you?" he asked.

"Not at all," I sat up.

He pulled his shirt off and got in. I noticed that he had a tattoo of a crossed sword and torch on his left shoulder. It also wasn't hard to notice how nicely built he was. I felt my cheeks burning with embarrassment when he noticed me checking out his bare chest and stomach, but I had to admit that he was quite a fine sight with his shirt off and his wet curls sticking to his face. He sat not too far away from me. When our eyes met he smiled slightly.

"What did that rider want?" I asked trying to make things a bit more casual.

He simply said, "To kill us." He took a deep breath and started treading water on his back. "Thank you for staying close by back there. Our race is stronger together than when they're apart."

"You're welcome," I said in a sort of stiff sounding voice.

He swam over and sat back where he had been sitting, and looked at me with a sort of half smile.

"What?" I asked.

"Tell me something." He propped against the bank. "Am I making you uneasy?"

"Why do you ask?" I shrugged.

"Well," he said. "For one thing, you haven't moved since I got in." He started treading water again. "You know, Miss Sabilla, I find that you are very quiet with most people, but you talk to me. Why is that?"

"I don't know," I said, blushing to no end.

"If you want me to go, I will. I did not mean to intrude on your quiet time," he said. "I don't want to make you uncomfortable."

"No, you don't have to go," I told him. "You're... I mean, I'm fine. In fact I enjoy the company. I've been alone far too much in the past few days." My mind was so jumbled that I could hardly think clearly. It was the strangest feeling.

He swam over and sat down next to me on the rock. "I do apologize about that. I didn't want to go alone and Heaven knows, I did not want to leave you." he sighed and looked me in the eye.

"Then why did you?" I tried to make the question sound light, but I could tell that it hit him like a load of bricks.

"I could not take you where I was going. I will someday, but it was not the right time. You saw how Grayheart acts about us and our people. If...." his voice trailed off. "The reason I did not come back was..."

"No," I shook my head. "You don't have to explain. You had your reasons and I'm not going to question that. I trust you."

He smiled and nodded. I could tell that he knew what a big deal it was for me to say something like that.

An awkward silence hung in the air for a moment. Finally, I decided to speak.

"How is it that you talk to water?" I asked.

"The first thing that you need to do is kiss the bottom of a pool just below a waterfall," he answered.

"Isn't that usually the deepest and most dangerous part of the pool?" I asked.

"Yes," he nodded. "It is quite difficult and if you're not careful the pressure of the fall can trap you at the bottom, but there is an easier way. I'll help you." With that he took a deep breath a dove under the water. He stayed down for about a minute and I was worried that he was having trouble, but soon I could see him coming back to the top. When he came back up, he swam over to me.

"Come here," he said, breathing slightly heavy.

I went over to him.

He put my arms over his bare shoulders. He then gave me a long full, open mouth kiss. The kiss gave me a strange tingling feeling from the top of my head down to my toes. He wrapped his arms firmly around me. It was unlike anything I had ever felt in my life. I leaned into him wishing the moment could last forever, but it was over as quickly as it had begun.

"There," he whispered. "The language of water is on your tongue. Speak to it."

I thought for a moment then, in a language that I could hardly understand, told the water to make a small whirlpool. It obeyed. It was as if I had spoken to it, yet all the same I had not said a word. I looked over at Shadowlark in amazement.

He smiled. "See. You can do it."

"What did you do?" I asked.

"I kissed the bottom of the pool then I kissed you," he answered. "Since I already knew the language, all I had to was pass it on to you."

"Thank you," I said.

He stroked my cheek softly. "You're very welcome, Miss Sabilla," With that, he got out of the water and put his shirt back on. He winked at me and walked back to the camp.

My heart fluttered around in my chest as if it were a butterfly. There was something about this man that just sent my mind reeling. I climbed out of the river, put my boots on and went back to the camp.

When I got back to the camp site, Shadowlark and Clara had already gotten a fire going and they were working on setting out some blankets. I walked over to help them. I was still very wet, therefore feeling quite water logged, but I managed to get a couple of the blankets set out without getting them too wet.

"We have to leave this island," Shadowlark said. "It makes me uneasy to think of staying here for the night, but I don't know what else we could do. It would be too risky to go into a town to stay the night so I guess this is as good a place as any."

***

Darkness slowly fell. We built the fire up good enough that no animals would come close, but we made sure that it was not big enough that anyone could see it from a distance. After we got done eating our small supper, Shadowlark stood up.

"Where are you going?" I asked.

"I'll stand watch." He dusted off his pants legs.

"Alone?"

"You two need rest. I'll be fine."

"I'll take over watch in a few hours. You'll have to wake me up though," I laid down and pulled my blanket over me. "I'm used to standing watch on a ship."

He smiled. "Okay. Goodnight."

"Goodnight," me and Clara said at the same time.

I laid there staring up at the sky for a few minutes. The stars shone so bright that it was almost as if I were staring into a dream. I looked over and noticed that Clara was still sitting up. She looked over at me as if she had something she wanted to say, but wasn't sure if she should or not.

"Is everything alright?"

She sort of half nodded, but I could tell that she wanted to say something.

"What is it?" I asked.

"Well," she sighed. "When you said the thing that you did about Patrick Arthur, you sort of brought me back to real life."

"What do you mean?" I asked.

"Patrick knew about me being a girl," she answered. "He guessed, I didn't have to tell him," She sighed and looked away. She laughed a little, but it almost sounded like she was being sarcastic about something. When she looked back at me she was fighting back small tears that were threatening to come. "We loved each other, Billy. It tore me apart when we left the ship. I didn't know what to do with myself. The only reason that I acted the way that I did about David was because I wanted to feel loved. For a while it was like I was blaming Patrick for what had happened. I thought that if I found another man, then that would make me feel better, but it didn't."

"I'm so sorry. I didn't know."

"It's not your fault."

"Why didn't you tell me about this before?"

She sighed and pushed back another sob. "What would it have mattered? What does any of it matter? No man in this world cares about me. I will end my life alone, as God intended."

"Don't say that, Clara. It does matter. You have as much of a chance of finding love as anyone."

"No, Billy, I think that there's a reason for me being alone and I just as well accept it. There's no use in fighting against life. I........ I will be just fine."

"Why didn't you tell me about you and Patrick?"

"It would have made no difference then, just as it makes none now."

"If you don't care and it makes no difference, why did you bother telling me at all?"

She lay down and pulled her covers up to her chin. "I just wanted you to know."

"Goodnight," I whispered and lay down as well. I wished with all my heart that she had told me sooner. I don't know what good it would have done, but it would have at least helped me to understand a bit more. I felt so bad for being so short and annoyed with her about David. I had not known all that she was going through, but I could not say much. I had not told her how I felt about the situation with my mother, nor had I asked her what was wrong or why she was acting the way she had been. Her breaking her heart was just as much my fault as it was anyone's. I had been so caught up in how bad my mother was treating me that I did not even take the time to help Clara when she had needed me the most. I would make it up to her somehow.

After a few hours, I got up and went over to Shadowlark.

He looked over at me. I could tell that he was beyond tired, but he would have stood watch the rest of the night if he had too. "Have you had any sleep?"

"More than you," I told him. "Go on and get to bed."

"Will you be alright?"

I laughed a little. "I can take care of it, Shadowlark. Just get some sleep."

"Keep a close eye out," he told me and went to lie down beside the fire.

I breathed in the cool night air and leaned my shoulder against a tree. The rhythmic noises of the night were beginning to lull me to sleep. I closed my eyes only briefly, then shook myself and walked a little ways from the tree, so that I would not lean on it anymore. It seemed that, as long as I was standing up straight, I was fine. I had not been away from the tree for five minutes when I felt a cold blade on my throat. I tried to pull away, but I felt an arm snake around my waist and arms. They held me so tight that I could not move my upper body.

"Call him," a man's voice whispered in my ear. It wasn't Grayheart or the rider that we had met earlier. The sound of his voice sent a chill through my whole body.

"Why?" I asked, hoping in vain that my voice would not shake when I spoke.

"Call him," he repeated. "Don't make me get forceful."

"This is already a bit more forceful than I would like." I wriggled around, trying to free myself, but his grip only tightened. "Why should I call him?"

"Because I said so." He pressed the blade down harder making it so I could scarcely breathe without it cutting me. "You know that he'll hear you."

"It would seem that Grayheart wants us alive, there would be no other way for us to see whatever it is that he wants us to see in that world of yours."

He laughed. "You still have the same way of reasoning."

'Still?' His saying that startled me worse than his knife at my throat. I tried not to let him see that he had rattled me with his words.

"What will it profit you to kill me?"

"It would profit me a lot. You have no idea." He breathed on the back of my neck. "But then again, I could take you with me. I'm sure that you would enjoy yourself on the *Empress*."

"Newheart," Shadowlark's voice rang through the woods and it was hard to tell which direction it was coming from.

I looked over toward the fire and Shadowlark was gone.

"Newheart." That time his voice was no more than a whisper.

Newheart's grip on me loosened. He took the knife away from my throat and stepped away from me as if touching me had burned him, all the while looking around nervously.

"Are you frightened, Newheart? Are you afraid because you cannot see me? Or is it that you are afraid that I'm going to do to you what you would do to me?"

"Show your face you gutless bastard," Newheart scoffed.

Shadowlark laughed. "You dare call me gutless while you are the one that stands there quaking in your boots. You've always been a coward, but you pretend to be more than you really are."

"Your name really fits you," Newheart huffed. "You hide like this and think that no one can find you, but in fact you're very foolish. I don't fear you. Now, show yourself!"

"Gladly," Shadowlark said. A blade then appeared at Newheart's throat as if it had seeped out of the night wind. "So Grayheart is still using you for his dirty work? Is it that he no longer has the stomach for it or was he just scared to come get me himself?"

"He's not scared of you," Newheart laughed. "Why would you think that? He's chasing you and all you do is run. So who is more of a coward, the chaser or the chased?"

"What's going on?" Clara came over to us.

"Stay back," I told her, stepping back a good ways, myself. The air around the two men felt as if it had turned to fire. I felt as if the air itself might explode at any given moment.

"He says that I rule nothing," Shadowlark tightened his grip. "If that is true then why is he worried? We aren't in his world, I don't pose a threat to him, he can do whatever he wants, what the hell does he want me for?" Normally Shadowlark was very composed, but he was getting more and more angry by the second. The more his anger grew the hotter the air around him got. His composure was held, seemingly, by a mere thread. I knew that if Newheart did not give him a good answer soon, Shadowlark was going to kill him. That much was very clear.

"If you're that curious, then you need to come with me," Newheart said.

Shadowlark pressed down on the blade so hard that a small stream of blood showed up on Newheart's throat. Newheart, gasped and winced, trying to pull away from Shadowlark, but even though he beat out Shadowlark with the size and muscle, Newheart was obviously no match for the other man's strength. I was almost frightened at the thought. Newheart had been strong enough to hold me so that I could not move, but he could not pull away from Shadowlark's grip.

"I know your style, Newheart. I haven't trusted you since I first saw you with Rossaletta. I'm not as ignorant as the men that you're used to dealing with. You tell Grayheart that if he wants me then he'll have to come get me himself."

"Are you suggesting that I go back to Grayheart without you?" Newheart asked.

Shadowlark nodded. "Yes Newheart, or I'll take this knife and pierce your *new heart* with it and you won't return to him at all."

"The captain may not like that," Newheart laughed a little. "I don't think your message will go over very well."

It was then that we heard a pistol cock. "It won't." Grayheart stood behind Shadowlark with a pistol held to his head.

Shadowlark released Newheart and dropped his knife.

"You've put on quite a show here tonight little brother," Grayheart scoffed. "Then again you were always good at that. It would disgust me to see the way that people loved the tricks you did with water, fire and all of your circus style antics. They loved you. I would say that they hated me, but they didn't know that I existed. No one knew me when I was Nathaniel Grayman."

"You were their king," Shadowlark huffed. "The greatest king our people had ever had. They loved and trusted you. They trusted you with their lives. Those people would have followed you to the end of the earth and beyond, and you threw all of that away and for what? Immortality that means nothing."

"Do not mock me brother," Grayheart hissed.

"It seems you can no longer tell praise from mockery," Shadowlark said. "I praised you for being a good king and scolded you for destroying our people with your own lust for power. You have lost all your former wisdom, brother and all I can do is pity you for it."

"I have gained more wisdom through my immortality than any of you could ever dream of having."

"Wisdom, brother, or ignorance?"

Grayheart thrust his pistol in Shadowlark's face. "I see life more clearly than you could ever dream of. It is you who is ignorant, but it is by your choosing."

"You have chosen to live blinded to everything but the will of the Dragon's Empress."

"My life is what I have made it. No one controls me.

"Is that what Rossaletta told you?"

Grayheart laughed. "Everyone knows who Nate Grayheart is. They all know and fear me. I rule our world now, just as I always should have."

"You always ruled our people," Shadowlark huffed. "Who put it in your mind that you never ruled anything?"

"I now rule how I should have all those years ago," Grayheart smiled. "You of all people should know that."

"You think that the only way to rule effectively is to make them fear you?"

"If someone fears you, then you control that person," Grayheart answered. "Fear means control. They may have their kings, but even they bow to me. In the end you will bow to me as well."

"I will be smote dead before I bow to what you have become," Shadowlark spat. "You are a tyrant and a monster. The kind of man that Nate Grayman would have killed. You are a heartless wretch and the only way I can stand the sight of you is to remember the man that you used to be."

"All the same, you're coming with me," Grayheart shrugged as if Shadowlark's words meant nothing at all to him. "It's been a while since you've been home and Rossaletta has just been dying to see you."

"Then let her die," Shadowlark said. "It'd save me some trouble."

"The Dragon's Empress," I whispered.

"Yes, my dear." He rubbed my cheek, but I jerked away from him. "You will get to meet my lovely Rossaletta. I'm sure she would love to see you as well."

"Enough of your talk," Shadowlark snapped. "I'll go with you, but the girls stay here."

"What?" Me and Grayheart asked at the same time.

"I'm not leaving them here," Grayheart told him. "They know too much for me to leave them behind, but then again I could just take Billy and not worry about Clara. You know Billy's importance in all of this, if you know nothing else about it."

Shadowlark clenched his jaw and gave Grayheart a cold stare. I wasn't sure what he had meant by that comment, but it seemed that he had hit Shadowlark where it hurt.

"If you take Billy then you'll have to take me," Clara crossed her arms across her chest. "I'll just follow you if you don't."

"I advise you missy, it's not wise to get strong willed with me," Grayheart told her.

212

"Call me 'missy' one more time and you'll see the meaning of the term 'strong willed'."

"I'm not a very patient man. I'll take you along, but not because you asked to be taken. You may be of some use."

They bound our hands and led us and our horses through the woods. We were led to a place with a small dock that was off by itself.

I could not help but stop and stare at what was lying in wait for us. A ship loomed ahead in the darkness. Its masts reached toward the starry sky as if they were trying to unveil something that the night sky wanted to keep concealed. All was silent except for the waves breaking on the shore and the wind blowing eerily through the riggings of the *Dragon's Empress*.

I was forced forward, none too gently. A feeling of dread crept into my heart as I stepped onto the deck. It was as if I had left one world and stepped into a completely different one.

Grayheart came up behind me. He was close enough that I could feel his breath on the back of my neck. "Welcome," he whispered into my ear. "Aboard the *Dragon's Empress*."

Chapter

Nine

The three of us sat in the brig of the cursed *Dragon's Empress*. I had been in worse places before, but I could not remember when. The floor and walls creaked and groaned as if it was protesting the idea of simply being anywhere at all. It seemed tired and weary, like it needed rest, but could see no such thing anywhere in the near future.

I tried to calm myself down. I just listened to the sound of the waves hitting the side of the ship. In a way it was quite peaceful.

"Is he going to kill us?" I asked Shadowlark.

He didn't answer directly, he just asked, "Are you afraid?"

I leaned against the side of the ship, closed my eyes and sighed deeply as if I could breathe in the sound of the waves. "No," I whispered.

"No," he shook his head. "He's not going to kill us. Not yet anyway."

I looked over at him. He was sitting right across from me with his back against the bars of our cell.

I just sighed. I knew I had made a vow not to look back, but at that moment I wanted to be back at the orphanage with Clara and Davy. I wanted to sit and listen to Mr. McHale tell his stories. I wanted to go around the church and pick up eggs. Heck, I would've settled for being thrown in the room, or to be at my mother's house, I just didn't want to be on that ship. It was then that I remembered the wish that I had made about having an adventure like Mr. McHale. That had been a completely different Billy that made that wish. At the time I had figured that none of my other wishes had come true, so there would be no harm in making one more. Little did I know that later I would wish that I could have my old life back, but I knew that I would never be able to go back. All of that was gone. The church was gone, Mr. McHale was gone and I wasn't sure if I would ever see Davy again. At least I still had Clara and now I had Shadowlark.

I looked up at the ceiling and decided that it was best to focus on what I was doing at the moment. There was no use wishing for something that would never happen. I would only succeed in torturing myself if I kept on thinking about other places that I could be.

Just then, came in and a man came in and unlocked our cell.

"The captain requests to see Billy Scarlet," the man said.

I walked up to the door. "I'm here," I told him.

"Come with me," the man said.

"Be careful," I heard Shadowlark say as we walked out.

Walking across the deck gave me a chill in my bones. There didn't seem to be a friendly face on the whole ship. I caught sight of some odd little creature flying around in the riggings. It was barely starting to get light outside, but I still couldn't tell what it was and I didn't dare ask.

The man pushed me forward very roughly. I tried to keep my footing, but it was hard. The man stopped at the door of the cabin and motioned for me to go in.

I walked in. Grayheart was standing at the far end of the room, staring out the window.

"It's been quite an odd night, don't you agree?" He turned and faced me. There was something different about him. He seemed very confused and uncertain about what he was saying.

"Yes," I nodded. "What do you want with me?"

"Me, you and Shadowlark are all of the same race," he said. "It was a race of people that could talk to wind, water and fire. Yes, they sound rather fascinating, but they were stupid and barbaric. They would not embrace the rule of mortal men as they should have," With every sentence he sounded more and more uncertain. "They allowed our race to crumble into dust. They thought that Shadowlark would make a better ruler, but that was their choice and now they have to pay for it. I should have ruled and now I do. Between me and Rossaletta our world is how it always should have been. Even the kings bow to me."

"I'm not going to bow to you if that's what you want," I told him.

He clenched his jaw as if he was thinking really hard. The way that he was acting was very distracting. I would have rather had him act like his normal, horrible self instead of being as confused as he was.

"You have a very strong will," he said. "Tell me, is it your will that keeps pushing me away or is it something else?"

"It's not just my will. I despise you with my entire being."

He looked at me as if he had no idea why I would say such a thing, then he smiled. "Why is that? Because Shadowlark told you I was bad? Have I ever harmed you in any way?"

He had a point, but I wasn't going to fall for his mind and word games. "It doesn't matter why I don't like you the point is that I don't. I'm not interested in your word games either."

"I think that you are," he said. "You long to know where you come in with all of this and you know that I'll tell you things that Shadowlark won't. I can and will tell you."

"With what condition? I really don't care what you could tell me. Shadowlark would tell me about it if I asked him."

"He would not and you know it. He won't tell you no matter how much

216

you ask. No matter how much he loves you."

"I don't know what you're talking about," I said, quite surprised at him saying that Shadowlark loved me.

"I think you do," he smiled.

"I don't know what has gotten into your head, but you need to get over it. Just because you have lost all of your honor and dignity doesn't mean that Shadowlark has done the same."

At that moment sun light poured in through the window and the second it touched his face, he began to change. He stopped and looked at me as if he was seeing me for the first time. "Shadowlark?" he asked. "You mean Jameson, right?"

"Jameson?" I asked.

"Yes," he nodded. "That's his real name. Billy," He grabbed my arm and to my surprise, he held me very gently. "I have to tell you something."

I jerked away from him. "Leave me alone. You..........." I stopped. I felt all strange inside. I felt like I was falling asleep.

"Billy." He sounded very concerned. "Are you all right?"

"I feel strange," I answered.

Just then Newheart burst through the door.

"Captain," he said. "She must return to her cell."

"Rafe?" I looked at him and I felt like I knew who he was.

"Damn," Newheart huffed. He then came over to me, and the last thing I remembered was getting hit in the head really hard.

   ***

I slowly began to come around, but when I did, I was not where I expected to be. I was chained to a column in a court yard. My head was aching, but for some reason, I felt like I was dreaming.

"Billy, are you alright?"

I looked to my right and saw that Grayheart was chained to the column next to me. He was different. He did not seem as dangerous and hostile as he had before. I wasn't sure how, but somehow I knew that I was not in the same place or time that I had been in before.

"Billy?" he asked again. He looked at me with more concern than I thought him capable of showing. "Are you alright?"

"I'm fine," I blinked hard in the light.

I was suddenly aware of a sharp pain in my right side. I looked down and saw that there wasn't any blood, so I figured I could not be too badly hurt. It was the same kind of pain that I had gotten when Averrit had kicked me in the ribs.

"Where are we?" My voice was tired and hoarse. I wasn't sure what exactly I had been through, but it was obviously a very bad ordeal.

Before he could answer my question, a woman in a deep purple, velvet dress came walking across the courtyard. Her footsteps were loud and hollow on the polished stone. She was followed by a man who was dressed in dressed all in black, from his shirt to his boots.

Right away I was sure of two things. One, this was the woman, Rossaletta that I had been told of; and two; I was not in the same time that I had been in before. I wasn't sure how that was possible, but I knew I was in the world that I had so often seen in my dreams. I was in the place that gave me the feelings that I would get when I looked at certain people, like my father and Shadowlark.

The man strode out in front of Rossaletta and stopped about twelve paces in front of us. He rubbed his hands together, as if he was immensely satisfied with himself. "The great king Nate Grayman and the legendarily beautiful Sabilla Scarlet. I must say, neither of you live up to what I've been told."

"Sirus Morton, you're not as large and fierce a man as I was led to believe," Nate jested.

Sirus made no comment, he just scoffed loudly. "I'm sure you know why you're here."

"Because you're a sick bastard with no regard for human life," I spat as if I knew everything about this man and the situation at hand, when truly, I knew nothing about either, but somehow I did know.

He laughed and walked over to me. "I wonder why a girl who is as sweet as you would speak to me so venomously."

"Is the answer to that question not obvious?" I shook the chains as a way to make my point clear.

He gave me a vile grin and stepped entirely too close to me. His chest was almost touching mine. He put his hands on the wall just above my shoulders. "I would love to let you lose."

"Sirus," Nate's voice was like a hammer hitting iron. "Your dealings are with me and me only, leave her out of it."

"You are my prisoners." I could feel his breath on my face. "I can deal with you how I wish."

"Well, deal with Nate first." I could tell by the tone in her voice that Rossaletta was getting annoyed with Sirus' behavior.

He stepped back from me and glanced at Nate. He took a deep breath, examined his fingernails, then looked back at Nate. "Tell me Nate, what do you know of the Jade Eye and the Dragon's Heart?"

"More than you," Nate smiled.

Sirus grimaced. "Tell me what you know and I will let the two of you go safe and sound."

"Until you know what I am, you will never be able to fathom what I know, much less be able to hear it yourself."

"You dare tease me like this, Grayman?" he snarled.

"I'll be the judge of what I do or do not dare do."

This answer did not please Sirus in the least bit. He sneered and glanced at me. "Perhaps you'll tell when you're under a little bit of pressure," He pulled a dagger from his belt and stalked over to me. He rubbed the blade across my cheek.

"Leave her alone, Sirus." Nate's words were so harsh that Sirus flinched, but he did not get away from me.

He rubbed the flat of the blade across my throat, then ran it along my shoulder, this time, cutting me.

I cried out in pain. "Get away from me, you evil snake."

"Tell me what I want to know, Grayman," He ran the knife down my arm, cutting my shirt sleeve. The blade was unnaturally sharp. He must have sharpened it for days in anticipation of this event.

I tried to pull away from him, but there was nowhere for me to go. I looked over at Nate, pleading for his help, but I knew there was nothing he could do either.

All the same, he nodded to me. "Leave her alone, or I swear I will break these chains and kill you, Sirus."

The words sent a chill through me. I wasn't sure how it was possible, but I knew that Nate would follow through on what he was saying.

"Tell me what I want to know, Grayman!" This time his voice was far more threatening. Nate had not even had a moment to speak when Sirus reached around my back and cut me through my shirt.

Though I tried with all my might to hold back, I couldn't help but scream. The way that the cut burned made me suspect that the blade had poison or something of the like on it.

Suddenly, the room was filled with the sound of chain links breaking.

"Sirus, stop!" Rossaletta yelled in a panic. "He meant what he said!"

Sirus turned around just in time for Nate to break himself loose. He pulled the sword from Sirus' belt and ran him through with it.

"No!" Rossaletta screamed as Sirus fell to the floor, lifeless.

I couldn't say a word or move, but somehow, I managed to look over at Nate. He had this odd glowing coming from his chest.

Rossaletta, then threw him against the wall with some unseen force, causing him to drop the sword. She stalked over to him and tore his shirt open, but it was painfully obvious that she was not prepared for what she saw. She stumbled backwards and just started for a long moment.

There on Nate's chest was an angel with its face turned upward. Beneath it in fine gold script was the word *Promise*.

She gasped. "Elpine Daza." She slowly backed away from him, releasing him as she did. Her eyes strayed down to Sirus' body lying motionless on the floor. Her eyes filled with tears, but it was soon replaced with rage. "Why?!" She demanded to no one in particular. She kicked the sword that Nate had used, across the room, causing it to clatter against the wall on the far side of the courtyard. "Why did you not listen, you witless bastard?!"

I wasn't sure if she was demanding this of Nate or Sirus.

She then ran out of the room.

Nate came over to me and broke the chains off my wrists. He pulled me to him, but when touched my back I flinched. The cut on my back was obviously very deep.

"Let me see that," he said.

I turned around. "Is it bad?"

"It will scar, but it will heal up just fine."

I turned back to him and looked at the angel that was still burning bright on his chest. I whispered, "Promise, fearless, see." In my heart, I knew what I was talking about, but in my mind, I had no idea.

He took my hand. "Promise."

I then heard the sound of beating wings and something picked me up.

Before I could see what was going on, I started to wake up. I felt the wooden deck beneath me as well as the sway of the ship. I opened my eyes and I was back in my cell. I was more than relieved to see Clara and Shadowlark.

I looked around for a moment. I got the feeling that what had just happened, while at present it may have been a dream, there was a point in time that it had not been.

"What happened?" I asked.

"I was hoping that you could tell us," Clara said.

"I was talking to Grayheart," I told them. "I felt really tired, then Newheart came in and hit me in the head. I don't really remember much about why Newheart was there. How long have I been knocked out?"

"About an hour or so," Shadowlark answered. "You said that you felt very tired. What happened before you got tired?"

"What do you mean?" I asked.

"Was he acting strange or anything?" he asked.

"Yes," I nodded. "He was acting all confused, like he wasn't sure what he was supposed to do or say."

"Did he give you anything to drink or eat or anything like that?"

"No," I stood up. I was still shaken up from my dream and I was having trouble remembering what had happened while I was in the room with Grayheart. "He touched my arm. It was weird. He was very gentle and that's very unlike him. He..... he said that he wanted to tell me something," I thought really hard. I tried to remember more. "Newheart came in and it was like I knew him. He told Grayheart that I needed to go back to my cell. I called him Rafe then he cussed and hit me."

"Something here doesn't seem quite right," Shadowlark rubbed his chin. "You started feeling tired after he touched you? That's all? Nothing else went on?"

"No," I shook my head, wishing they would not ask me so many questions. "Not that I can remember. We talked for a little while before that and that was all just his, 'I want to rule the world speech'," I thought some more. "He called you Jameson. He was talking something about the part that I play in all of this and he said that you wouldn't tell me."

"He called me Jameson?" he asked. "Are you sure?"

"Yes," I answered. "Why?"

"Jameson is my real name," he told me. "He hasn't called me that in years." He shook his head as if he couldn't believe it. "He hasn't called me that since........." his voice trailed off and he sat there quietly. He looked very distance and I didn't know what to say or if I should say anything so I just sat down next to him.

"Are you all right?" I asked.

He nodded.

"While I was knocked out, I had an odd dream."

"It must not have been a nice one," Clara sat down next to me. "You were tossing around a good bit. We tried to wake you up, but we couldn't, so we just decided to wait until you came around."

"Just tell me one thing," I lifted the back of my shirt up. "Do I have a scar on my back?"

"Yes," Clara nodded. "You've always had that scar."

I just nodded.

"What did you dream about?" Shadowlark looked at me, thoughtfully.

Before I could tell him anything, Grayheart walked in. He seemed like a completely different person than who I had talked to earlier, or than I had seen in my dream. He unlocked the cell and motioned to us. "Come with me."

We, reluctantly, followed him. He led us up on deck.

The first thing that I noticed was that we were surrounded by large canyons that reached way up into the blue sky above us. Ahead all I could see was seemingly endless canyon. There was maybe twenty feet in between us and the canyon on either side of us. The water looked black and mysterious. It seemed to be a very dangerous, as well as peculiar, place. If the ship were to stray off course for even a brief moment, it would ram into the canyon walls and end the entire voyage.

Grayheart walked over to the rail of the ship. "Come here," he said.

He did not seem as demanding or harsh as usual, but that did not mean that any of us trusted him in least bit. All the same, something in his voice made us curious of what he was doing, so we followed him.

"What are you doing?" Shadowlark asked.

"Watch the water," Grayheart pulled a small stone out of his pocket.

"Quit playing your games, Grayheart," Shadowlark huffed. "I don't know what you're trying to do, but I don't like it."

"And you think I care what you like or not?" Grayheart laughed a little then looked at me and Clara. "Shadowlark knows this, but I don't believe that you do, so I will go ahead and tell the two of you that we are in the death rocks," he smiled. "I'm certain that the two of you will soon find out why they bear that name," With that he dropped the stone in the water like a child playing some sort of game.

I looked over the edge just as the stone hit the water. The small splash that it made seemed to break some sort of silence that was beyond what we could hear. The water rippled out in circles just as it normally does when something gets dropped in, but then, just beneath the surface, the water began to swirl. I wanted to look away, but something inside me made me keep staring at the water as if my life depended on it. Slowly a creature began to come to the surface. It had a long dark colored body, like that of a snake. It had black and gold scales that sparkled when it got closer to the surface. It stuck its head up, out of the water. It had orange glowing eyes that stared at me with great hatred as if I was the one who disturbed it. It then let out a loud, horrible shriek.

I turned away and cover my ears until it was gone. It was not that the creature had frightened me, but that it was so loud that I could hardly stand it. It's piercing cry echoed down the canyons and bounced off the walls like it was a heavy object tied to a rope and was swinging back and forth, hitting the walls as it went.

Grayheart laughed.

"What are you trying to prove here?" Shadowlark asked.

"I just want the three of you to be able to enjoy all of the sights to be seen here," he said. "And I also would like for you to meet all of the inhabitants that you can. What a pity it would be for you to pass through and not see who calls this place home."

"If you are referring to the ghosts, then you are greatly mistaking about the home part of it," Shadowlark scoffed. "Nothing calls this place home. Not one of the creatures that live in this cursed place is here by choice. Even the ghosts are trapped here against their will."

My heart jumped into my throat at the thought of ghosts. I had already been slightly disturbed by Grayheart's strange behavior, had a dream that was completely unexplainable as far as I could tell, and screamed at by a sea snake then the thought of seeing ghosts was just more than I really wanted to think about at the moment.

"And does it really matter right now?" Grayheart laughed.

"So what now?" Shadowlark asked. "Do you have any further plan other than showing us an angry sea snake? Because so far your attempts to makes us fear you, have come across as quite weak."

"This is only the beginning," Grayheart told him.

"Oh is it?" Shadowlark asked in a sarcastic tone. "I look forward to what you have planned next. Pray, tell us before I die of suspense."

"Trust me brother, you will regret taunting me like this," Grayheart huffed.

"Go ahead then," Shadowlark smiled. "Try and make me regret it. I have all day. As a matter of fact, I have the rest of my life, however long it may be. Of all the things that have happened to me in my lifetime, the only one that I'll regret will be taunting you."

"Look, brother."

"I have a name."

"Shadowlark," Grayheart scoffed.

"Not quite, but you're getting there."

Grayheart stared at him for a moment, looking far more annoyed than angry, and I could never be sure, but it seemed that for a small second, he got a glint of true amusement in his eye. It was not to last long, though. "As I have said before, I'm not very patient with your antics, brother."

"You didn't say that, you said you were disgusted with them."

At that moment, I was certain that Grayheart was going to throw a fit and stomp off.

"Just say what you have to say and be done with it," Shadowlark huffed.

It seemed slightly strange how Shadowlark could really get to Grayheart in ways that no one else could. He seemed to know everything that would get under his brothers skin and annoy the daylights out of him.

"Very well," Grayheart looked as if he was keeping a secret that only he knew and he was fixing break the news to hundreds of people. "Because I know that you like this place so much," He examined his fingernails as he was very bored with the situation. "I'm going to let you and our two dear friends spend your night up here on the deck, so that you may meet more of the inhabitants of the death rocks."

"Very well," Shadowlark shrugged as if he didn't care what Grayheart was saying. "And is that supposed to bother us in any way? Is that supposed to scare us?"

"We'll see," Grayheart nodded. "Take them back below and don't bring them back up here until just before sun set."

With that, the three of us were escorted, none to gently I might add, back to the brig. We were shoved back into the cell then the men left us alone.

"What happens at night fall?" Clara asked. "Why would he want to leave us out there?"

"The ghosts come out when the sun sets," Shadowlark answered.

***

The day passed by faster than I wanted it to, but in a way it didn't go very quick either. Soon they came down below and led us back up on deck. To my surprise, Grayheart wasn't there. Only Newheart and a few of the other men were on deck.

"Where's Grayheart?" Shadowlark asked. "Did he not wish to watch as we were made subject to all of this?"

"He has business to tend to." Newheart had an odd look in his eye when he said this and he cast me a strange glance as if to tell me to keep my mouth shut, but for what reason, I had no idea.

"So are any lookouts to be posted?" One of the men asked.

"Not this night," Newheart answered. "Maybe tomorrow, but tonight I want them to be truly alone." With that, he signaled to all of the men and they followed him down below deck.

Pretty soon we were all by ourselves. Just as the sun disappeared behind the canyons there came an odd humming sound. I looked around and slowly, figures began appearing out of thin air. They seemed to be forming out of, yet into, some sort of fog.

My whole body tensed and I just stood there, not wanting to move. Not only did I not want to move, I didn't want to make a noise at all. I felt like if I moved, something terrible might happen. The ghosts began wandering around the deck as if they were trying to find something. They looked like clouds of mist with faces and if they moved right I could see the rest of their form.

One of them stopped in front of me and just stared. It had a pleading look in its eyes as if it wanted to tell me something, but it didn't know how to say it to me. It began to reach out to me.

I felt like I was going to scream. I just wanted to be somewhere else, anywhere else. I would have settled for being at my mother's house with her yelling at me that she didn't want me, than to be on this ship in the Death Rocks.

I started to back away when I felt something touch my back. I turned around and saw that it was Shadowlark.

"Don't be afraid," he told me. "Newheart and the rest of the crew will be watching us. Don't give them the satisfaction of seeing you act scared. That is the point of this whole thing. They want to arouse a fear in us. They want us to beg them to not put us out here anymore. If we do that, they will put us back up here just because we're afraid of it. If you fear what they can do to you, then they control you. Don't give them that."

We all went to the bow of the ship and sat down.

"I just want to go home," I said. Even as the words came out of my mouth I realized that I didn't have a home. The closest thing that I had to a home was the *Victory* and even that wasn't my home. It was as if I had been thrown into the world to be an aimless wanderer.

"As do they," Shadowlark motioned toward one of the ghosts. "They were lost here after the curse was put on this place. They will wander here until the curse is broken. Until then they have no home. It's the same with all of the creatures that live here. They have been forced to live here. Since Rossaletta has started to take over, a shroud of darkness has fallen over this whole world."

"Is there anything beautiful here?" I asked.

He looked at me and nodded slowly. "Yes, miss Sabilla." He rubbed my cheek. "There is beauty in this world." He looked off into the distance as if in deep thought. "Have either of you ever seen a mountain or desert?"

"No," I answered.

Clara shook her head.

"They are in your world," he told us. "I'm sure that you've heard of them before. Here, there are mountains that reach all the way up into the clouds. They are so tall and majestic that when you stand next to the you feel as if the mountain it's self has a heart beating somewhere deep within the earth. I believe that God put mountains on the earth so that if we ever begin to feel like we are mighty, large and powerful all we have to do is go stand beside one of them and we will feel our own size once again."

"And what about deserts?" Clara asked.

"The first time you look at a desert you will truly believe that you're dreaming," he told us. "It looks like a sea of golden sand. At night the wind blows the sand and the dunes shift like the sea. Very rarely do you come across trees and water, but the places that you do find them, the water is crystal clear and it is said to have healing powers. People say that it's the water fairies that give it its healing properties. They are small creatures that dance on top of the water. They are some of the most beautiful things that you will ever see. They dance around and sing wonderful songs in a language that only they can understand."

As the night went on, he told us of forests that were so thick and dark that even in the day time it looked like night; and of castles that were on islands in the middle of the bottomless sea. His stories went on, of creatures great and small, of battles between the mortal men and immortals. He told us of the beautiful lady Jazzlyne, queen of the immortals and of the evil *Dragon's Empress,* Rossaletta who was born only half immortal and by way of magic became so powerful that no one could touch her.

I could picture every bit of it in my head. His words painted pictures and scenes right before my eyes. I could hear and see all of it as if I was right there when it happened. Slowly, between the stories and the sound of his voice, I drifted off into a peaceful sleep. The next morning I awoke to see the sun barely peeking over the top of the colorless canyons that rose out of the water on either side of us.

I stood up and walked over to the edge of the ship and stared at the canyon wall. It looked so cold and forbidding. It was almost as if I could see the faces of the people that were cursed to wander in this place, in the rock. I felt a hand on my shoulder. I turned around and saw that it was only Shadowlark.

"Do not stare at them for too long," he told me. "They will call you to them."

"I have no home, just as them," I said. "But as soon as I can find a way to break this curse, I will. They will not wander for eternity."

He smiled.

"Those places that you told us about last night," I said. "They sounded too beautiful to be real. I wish that I could see all of it."

"Someday you will," he smiled. "Someday I'll take you there."

Just then, the ship began to come to life. Men poured out of the cabins and got to work all around us. They paid us no mind. As a matter of fact they seemed to pretend that we weren't even there. About ten minutes after all the others came out Grayheart came out of his cabin. Unlike all the other men, he came right over to us.

"I trust you enjoyed your night," he laughed. Upon seeing no expression on Shadowlark's face, he turned to me.

"Oh, we thoroughly enjoyed it," Clara joined us.

"Ah, miss Honeycut," he said. "At least I see that the night has not robbed you of your voice. It seems that the other two no longer have the ability to speak."

"You will find that I, in fact, have not lost my voice, but only find that I have no reason to waste the capacity there in upon the likes of one such as you," Shadowlark smiled.

Grayheart shook his head. "I'm glad to see the night didn't change you," he said in a slightly annoyed tone.

"Yes," I nodded. "As a matter of fact, all of us are quite fine, thank you."

"I'm glad," he smiled.

"Oh, I'm sure you are," Clara said.

"I knew another Miss Honeycut once," Grayheart looked at Clara. "She was a lady of the night. She was quite wonderful, if I might say so myself. You looked just like her except for one thing," He looked at her as if he was thinking really hard. "She was right when she said that you had my eyes," With that he walked away.

Clara just stood there looking like someone had just slapped her for no reason.

"That can't be true," she whispered. "He can't be my father. He's no more than maybe thirty years old. He couldn't be my father." She turned to Shadowlark. "Could he?"

"Our race has been given long life," he told her. "We're not immortals neither are we mortal. It's hard to know exactly how old he is. I cannot say whether he is your father or not, but..." He stopped as if he had simply run out of words, but there was a look in his eyes that said things were suddenly starting to make sense to him. "I just don't know."

***

We sailed through the death rocks for the next three days. Every night, they made us sleep on the deck and each night was worse than the one before it. On the third night the whole ship was enveloped in a mist. It was all around us, but it didn't come on the deck. There were all sorts of strange and eerie noises coming from within the mist.

That night, Grayheart had posted two men to be guards on deck. As if we would even think of jumping off the ship in such a place.

Both of the guards seemed very uneasy and I could not blame them for that. I didn't know of any person who would have been comfortable in such a place.

The guards kept walking back and forth and it started to get slightly annoying, but I continued to watch them. One of the men looked to be in his mid-thirties though with these men you could never really tell. He had long, mousy brown hair and a stern face. He paced along the starboard rail of the ship with his hand always on the hilt of his sword.

The other man looked like he was about nineteen. He had jet black hair and a very sharp jaw. He had a pleasant face and for some reason, he didn't look like he belonged on the *Dragon's Empress*. He was about as peculiar as my father when it came to not seeming like he belonged. He apparently knew Shadowlark because he came over and sat on a barrel next to us. He looked me in the eye and it sort of surprised me to see that his eyes were gold.

"Hello, Autimun," Shadowlark nodded.

"So this is Billy Scarlet's daughter?" Autimun looked at me. "I should have guessed as much. She has that same how would you say?" He paused for a moment. "Differentness, about her."

"Oh, thank you," I nodded. "I love it when people compliment me in such a way."

Autimun laughed. I could tell right away that he was very arrogant, but I had found that was just how some men were, but then again there were plenty of women who were the same way they just had different ways of going about it.

"Very nice to meet you and I guess that I should just call you Autimun," I liked the way that his name rolled off my tongue. "And you can call me Billy."

"That should be easy to remember," he nodded then turned to Clara. "And I'm guessing that you're the one that's supposed to be Grayheart's daughter. You do have his eyes, or at least ones that look a lot like his."

I could tell that Clara was not liking any of this and I couldn't blame her. My father was a pirate, but at least I had known that all my life. To have just found out that your father was a man like Nate Grayheart was quite overwhelming, I'm sure.

"I still don't get any of this," she said. "He's supposed to be very old, but he doesn't look a day over thirty five."

"Is that so?" Autimun asked. "Well, tell me something. How old do you think I am Miss Grayheart?"

"You can call me Clara," she told him. "And I would guess that you're nineteen."

"No, I'm not, Clara," he smiled. "I'll give you one hint and no more. I'm ten or so, years younger than Shadowlark."

"Okay," Clara turned to Shadowlark. "How old are you?"

"Younger than Grayheart," he told her.

"Oh, come on," Clara urged.

"Fine." Shadowlark sighed. "He's forty."

"You're fifty?" I asked.

He nodded. "Give or take a few years here and there."

"And how old are the two of you?" Autimun asked.

I got an odd feeling in my stomach. I wasn't sure if I wanted them to know my age because the two of them were so much older than me, but then I figured that they were going to find out soon enough so I might as well tell them.

"I'm twenty," I answered.

"Me too," Clara added. "How come neither of you have red eyes like Billy? The three of you are supposed to be of the same race aren't you?"

"It just depends on who your parent are," Shadowlark told her. "My father was of our race, but my mother wasn't so I got brown eyes like her. Autimun's parents were both halfblooded so, he got gold eyes. Children with half-blood parents could get eyes that are anywhere from red to mother of pearl. If you ask me, I think that it's quite complicated."

Just then, there was a loud cracking noise and the ship began to move.

"Damn it," Autimun swore and ran to the helm.

We caught up with him in time to see him call to Grayheart through the listening tube that led down to the captain's quarters.

"Captain," he called. "Something broke the anchor rope and the ship is moving fast," He then took the helm. "We weren't prepared for this yet."

"For what?" I asked.

"To go through the void." He pointed ahead of us.

I looked up ahead and saw what looked like a deep black cave.

Men came pouring out on deck.

Autimun yelled orders as if he was the captain. "Secure all lines! Everyone get your life lines! Full sails! Light every lamp! Everybody hold on!"

The current began to pick up. The ship moved faster and faster with every passing second. The deck swayed hard beneath my feet. Me, Clara and Shadowlark held tight to the rail.

I looked up at Autimun. He held so tight to the wheel that his knuckles were white. I could only imagine how hard it was to keep the ship from hitting the canyon walls.

"What's happening?" I asked.

"Just hold on," Shadowlark told us. "If something goes wrong we could be sent spiraling through the void, then, God only knows where we would end up if we ended up anywhere at all."

"Everybody hang on!" Autimun yelled. "We're going too fast!"

The ship lurched forward, then jolted really hard and was thrown into a hard spiral.

I felt my feet lift up off the deck and all I could see was darkness. I squinched my eyes shut. For a moment I felt like this was my end. I would spend my last moments floating away in nothing, but darkness, or either I would go back to join all of the inhabitants of the death rocks.

Suddenly I felt a hand around my wrist. I looked up. The entire ship was glowing, but even with how beautiful and amazing it looked, the ship was not what I was looking at. I couldn't take my eyes off of Shadowlark, whose grip was so strong that I was sure that he could have snapped my arm like a twig if he had wanted to.

"It's okay," he told me. "I've got you. I'm not going to let you go." He pulled me up so effortlessly that it surprised me.

The second that my feet hit the deck, Grayheart burst out of his cabin and stormed up to the helm with such fury that it scared me. Had I been standing at the helm, I would have been terrified. He grabbed Autimun by the collar.

"I would like for you explain to me why we entered this void in such a manner that we could have lost members of our crew in the process," Grayheart hissed. "We have to enter this void at the right time or there's no telling where we'll end up. Because of your brilliance, we could end up God only knows where. How do you explain that?"

"Sir, the anchor rope broke," Autimun told him. "There was nothing else that I could do. We had no time to drop the other anchor. I tried my best to keep the ship as steady as possible."

"You *tried* your best?" Grayheart scoffed. "Well, I'll see to it that from now on you will *do* your best instead of just trying. Boson, tie him to the grating and give him five lashings," Grayheart shoved Autimun so hard that he fell to his knees. "Your back will remind you about *trying* your best."

Autimun got back to his feet. His eyes blazed with so much hatred that instead of looking gold, they looked like fire.

They set up the grating then two men tied him to it and tore his shirt off of his back.

The boson, a tall man with dark hair and a vile grin, who obviously enjoyed his job entirely too much, took the cat-o-nine whip, from his belt. He caressed the weapon as if it was his pet. Grayheart gave him a nod and the man beat Autimun so badly that he was unable to stand afterwards. When they untied him, he fell to his knees.

I ran over to him.

"Don't help me," he whispered. He had such pain and hatred in his eyes that I was sure that if he had've had the strength he would have killed Grayheart on the spot.

"Would you look at that?" Grayheart mused. "It seems that Miss Scarlet has taken a fancy to our golden eyed boy. Isn't that sweet?"

I felt anger begin to boil inside of me. I had already taken more of Grayheart's taunting than I could really stand, and was ready to hurt him. Hearing his laughter only made me madder. It was almost as if Autimun had passed on his anger to me. The anger grew so strong that I felt like I was going to explode. I stood up and punched Grayheart across the jaw with all my might.

He stumbled backward with a shocked expression on his face. I had not even known that I could hit him that hard. It even shocked me to see how he stumbled back.

He got his footing back and then he looked at me as if he was shocked that I was the one that hit him. I could tell that he was mad, but I was ready for anything that he would try to do to me. I was even sure that if he had taken a swing at me, I could very well have beaten him.

"What was that all about?" he stammered.

"Do you really need me to answer that question for you?" I asked.

"Very well," he huffed. "Tie her up and give her five lashings as well."

"No," Shadowlark said.

Grayheart smiled. "And how are you going to stop me?"

The wind began to pick up and Shadowlark disappeared.

Grayhearts angry expression mingled with that of panic. "Find him!" he yelled.

I looked over at Clara. She had my sea bag over her shoulder and was slowly making her way to the life boat that was hanging over the side of the ship.

"Get Autimun up and the two of you go to the life boat," I heard Shadowlark whisper.

I looked around and saw that no one was paying me any attention. I knelt down next to Autimun. "I guess you heard that," I said.

He nodded.

"Come on," I helped him up and the two of us went to the life boat.

"You want me?" Shadowlark laughed. "Come and get me."

"You think you're terribly clever," Grayheart looked around with a look of disgust on his face. "You may be able to escape me now, but where will you go? You can't go back through the death rocks. You know that there's nowhere in our world that you can hide from me. You may try to hide the truth from the girls, but they will find out sooner than you want," He looked around, but still could not find any sign of Shadowlark. "You may be able to hide from me now, but you won't be able to in our world."

"I don't mean to." Just as Shadowlark said it, Grayheart looked as if he had been tripped.

The next thing that I knew, Shadowlark was in the boat with us. He cut it loose, we let up the sail, he called on the wind, and we flew quickly through the void.

I looked back at the *Empress*. It was all lit up. It looked like a ghost ship floating eerily through a starless night sky. Grayheart, himself, had taken the wheel. He turned the ship to follow us.

When I looked ahead I saw a light. It was brighter than the *Empress* and we were heading straight toward it.

"What now?" Autimun asked. "I've never done this in a life boat before and neither have you."

"Just hang on," Shadowlark told him. "And let's hope that our entry here isn't as bumpy as yours was back there."

I looked back at the *Empress*. It was getting a lot closer, but that didn't worry me half as bad as the fact that it now looked the same way that Mr. McHale had described it in his book.

"It's in our world now," Shadowlark said as if he could read my thoughts. "You can now see it as it truly is."

The light grew so bright that it was hard to keep my eyes open. Just as we were about to go into the light everything around us changed and we were floating in the ocean with land not very far off from us.

"What just happened?" Clara asked bewildered.

"We just entered our world," Autimun told her.

The wind gently propelled us toward the island

I kept looking around, expecting the *Empress* to just appear out of nowhere, but it never did.

As we got closer to the land, all of it began to seem very familiar. It was as though I had seen all of it, but not in real life, only in a dream. The land, the wind, the water, all of it seemed so familiar to me and it seemed to be whispering some form of greeting. It was then that something appeared in my mind's eye. It was almost as if it were a memory. A picture of me sailing these waters on a ship called the *Sleeping Fury*.

"The *Sleeping Fury*," I whispered.

Shadowlark looked at me with a surprised look on his face.

"I was on a ship with that name on these waters once," I said. "But I don't see how that's possible. I've never been here before."

Autimun and Shadowlark exchanged an odd look that I didn't understand, but neither of them said anything.

I looked over at Clara. She looked about as confused as I was.

"This place," Clara whispered, as if talking loud would make the world disappear. "It seems so familiar. I feel like I've been here before."

"Is it possible for either of us to have been here?" I asked.

Shadowlark sighed deeply. "Quite."

No one said anything else until we got to land.

"Where are we?" I asked as we pulled the boat onto the shore.

"Martinia," Autimun answered. "There's a city on the other side of that forest."

The forest that was before us was very dense and spooky looking. The trees were very large with dark, rough looking bark and all manner of vines and moss growing on and around them. The leaves were so large and thick that they could have very well been used as a tent.

'That must be one of the forests that Shadowlark told us about,' I thought.

"It'll take us at least a day's walk to get across the forest," Autimun continued. "But it would be a lot longer if we tried to bypass it."

I grabbed my sea bag and threw it over my shoulder. It amazed me that through everything, I had still managed to keep my sea bag.

"Let's go," Shadowlark said.

We followed him through the woods. Once we were under the trees, things got pretty dark. The air felt heavy and damp and it smelled strongly of rotting leaves. The ground was wet and very soft and muddy in some places. There were pools of dark murky water, here and there. It was as if something was lurking just below the surface waiting for someone to be brave and get a little too close.

We followed an old path that looked as if it hadn't been used in many years. We walked until it was too dark to see the ground in front of us, then we stopped and made camp.

Shadowlark built a fire and Clara immediately got to work on Autimun's back. It had quit bleeding, but it still looked pretty bad.

I lay down and stared into the blackness of the trees. I just laid there listening to the sounds of the night; the fire crackling, Clara and Autimun talking in quiet voices, the sound of bugs and animals that I could not name singing and howling. I slowly drifted off to sleep, but I awoke only a few hours later. The fire was still burning, but it had burned down a good bit. Clara was sleeping not too far from me, and Autimun was sleeping on the other side of the fire. I looked around and didn't see Shadowlark. I sat up and looked towards the woods. He was standing a little ways away from us, propped against a tree. He

Savannah J. Parker and Zeke Parker

just stared into the seemingly endless woods.

I got up and walked over to him. When he turned and looked at me, he looked very tired as if the events of the day had drained all the energy out of him.

I was going to ask him if he was okay, but for reason I could not explain I asked, "How did you know that my name was Sabilla? Only my parents and the people closest to me knew what my real name was so how did you?"

He closed his eyes and sighed as if the very thought of it was painful. It broke my heart to see such pain in his eyes. For a while I was afraid that he wasn't going to answer, but he finally did.

"The same way that I know that dandelions are your favorite flower and that you wish on them any chance you get, and that your favorite color is the blue of the sky on a day in mid-autumn and that your favorite way for me to touch you is like this." He gently caressed the side of my neck.

I then took his hand and held it in both of mine. I loved his hands. They were more beautiful than any other hands that I had ever seen. It's odd of me to say so, but I had always paid attention to hands.

"Please," I whispered. "Please tell me how you know all of this."

"It's harder to explain then you think," he sighed.

I let go of his hand and looked away. Grayheart had been right. Shadowlark wasn't going to tell me anything. I felt tears in my eyes, but I wasn't going to let myself cry in front of him.

He rubbed my shoulders and sighed. "I don't want to be the only man that can make you cry," He turned me around to face him. "I suppose it's only right for me to tell you, though I'm not sure you'll believe me."

"Okay," I nodded. "Go on."

He smiled. "I knew the three of you," he began. "You, Clara and Davy. We fought together in a battle when you were seventeen. You and Clara dressed up as men so that you could fight. The only ones that knew about it were me and

240

Davy. The four of us would watch out for each other during that time. You always acted like you didn't care much of anything about me except when we were in battle. Things kept on that way. It was like we had an understanding, you and Clara fought, me and Davy kept your secret and we all watched out for one another. I slowly fell in love with you and I just felt so strange about it. I felt as if loving you was forbidden and in a sense it was." He paused for a long moment before continuing. "I didn't know what to do or say, all I knew is that I felt very awkward when I would try to talk to you. One day you just asked me why I was acting so weird and I just flat out told you. I expected you to laugh at me or something, but instead, you said that you were hoping I was going to say that.

"Once we were older we decided to get married. That was when the world turned dark. Grayheart and Rossaletta made their first attack on our people and you, Clara and Davy were taken by the immortals in the realm of age. When I asked them why, they told me that it was because Grayheart had struck a bargain with them to make him immortal. Now when you're dealing with realm rats, they name the price and in this case the price was you three. I then struck a bargain of my own with them. I asked them to give you back. They said they would, but of course they set the price and their deal was that they would wait twelve years to give you back and when you came back the three of you would be children, but not in this one, in the other one. When I found you in Florida it had been thirty two years since I had last seen you. They told me that you wouldn't remember me, but I guess I just didn't believe them." He stopped there and just stared at me like a man who had just bared his soul. "Do you have any kind of reaction to this?"

"Why would Grayheart trade us?" I asked. "What were we to him?"

Before he could answer we saw torches coming our way in the woods. He drew his sword and we ducked behind a hollow log.

"Who is that?" I asked.

"I don't know." He handed me a pistol. "Soldiers maybe, but they wouldn't be here unless...." He paused.

"Unless what?" I asked.

"Unless they know we're here."

We watched the light get closer and closer. There were at least five men on horse, clad in silver armor. On their breast plates there was the symbol of the jade eye.

Shadowlark looked back at the fire. "Autimun," he whispered, but Autimun didn't stir. "Autimun, get up," He still laid there. Shadowlark picked up a stick and threw it over toward the fire, waking both Clara and Autimun. He then motioned for the two of them to join us.

"What's wrong?" Autimun asked, drowsily.

"Shhhh. Get down," Shadowlark told them. "Soldiers."

They ducked down with us.

"I think they're on our side," Autimun said. "They may not know me. I'll go see what they want."

"Wait," I said suddenly remembering where Autimun had come from. "Who are you anyway? Okay, we meet you on the *Empress* and we automatically trust you?"

"It's a fine time for you to ask such a question," Autimun laughed. "You really are great with your timing aren't you?"

"I've known Autimun for years," Shadowlark told me. "He's a kind of spy. Good grief. Now is not the time."

Autimun got up and went over to where the men could see him. He waved to them.

They rode over to him.

"Who are you?" One of the men asked.

"You may call me Caranova for the time being," Autimun answered. "Are you lost or are you looking for someone?"

"We got a message from the Linthrids that one of our own has returned," the man, who asked his name, spoke again. "His name is Shadowlark and they said that he has brought three friends with him."

"You seem familiar," Autimun said. "What's your name?"

"You may call me Gator for the time being," the man answered. "If you happen to see Shadowlark, tell him that Firedrake wants to see him."

"Wait," Shadowlark stood up and beckoned for me and Clara to follow.

"So it's true," Gator dismounted. "They really are back, but where's Davy? Did the realm rats go back on their deal?"

"He's still back in the other world."

"What are they talking about?" Clara asked.

"It's quite a long story," Shadowlark answered.

Gator smiled. "And I believe that you will have time to tell it."

Chapter
Ten

Shadowlark explained to Clara, who she was, which only seemed to surprise her a little bit. It was almost as if she had been expecting this the whole time or that she had known for years. Needless to say, she was a lot less surprised than I, or most others would have been in such a situation. As he explained, we rode through the forest on horseback. It was a dense forest with trees that looked to be hundreds of years old. The path that we travelled was only wide enough for two people to ride side by side. One may not have even been able to notice it if they had been walking twenty feet away.

I reached down and rubbed my horse's neck. After doing this I wondered what had become of Elizabeth back on the *Empress*. She had always been a really good horse and I hoped that if Grayheart sold her, that she would at least be sold to a nice caring person.

I listened to the low murmur of conversation between Shadowlark and Gator. Gator and his men had a different kind of accent than Shadowlark. All of them spoke with a Spanish sounding accent. For a moment I wondered why they had a different accent than Shadowlark, but then I just figured that they must have come from different places, just like in our world.

I liked to hear them talking. It was the only noise besides the sound of the horses hooves hitting the ground and it kept me from feeling to strange after hearing about my newly discovered, past life. I couldn't hear what they were saying, but just to hear their voices was soothing to me. It was as if silence would have been entirely too much for me.

My thoughts were interrupted by us coming into a village. Well, not so much of a village, it was more of a camp site. There were at least four large tents scattered about the landscape. I couldn't tell much in the dark, but by what I could see, we were in a clearing that was surrounded by a dense thicket, then layers and layers of dark looking trees. There were only a few torches lit, but as we got closer, I could tell that there were at least ten or more tents.

I saw a woman standing in front of one of the tents. She had long dark hair with a nice, pleasant face. She looked rather young, but I couldn't really tell. Even if I had been close enough to her I wouldn't have been able to guess her age, with the way people in this world aged.

Her eyes scanned the soldiers for a moment then her face brightened.

"Shadowlark!" she exclaimed and ran over toward us.

Shadowlark quickly dismounted, ran over and hugged her.

Suddenly, I felt like I had been stabbed in the heart. Who was this woman?

"Why have you been gone so long?" she asked.

"It's a long story and I'm sure I'll be able to tell it sometime, or it may just speak for itself." He seemed overjoyed to see her. "Anyway, how's Marshall?"

"Oh, you won't believe how much he's grown," she told him.

My heart sunk so deep inside of me that I felt like it had hit the ground and sunk twelve feet. What had I expected? Yes, me and Shadowlark had been in love with me, but that was in another life for me. I did love him though. If I had not realized it before, I realized at that moment, but he obviously loved this woman and Marshall, who I guessed would be their son. What could I do? It had been thirty two years. I wouldn't hold it against him for moving on with his life. I was the past. I felt bad because I loved him, but I felt guilty for thinking that he should have waited for me all of those years.

"Come with me," he took her hand and led her over to where me and Clara had dismounted.

"Billy, Clara, it's so good to see the two of you again," she looked at us expectantly.

'Oh this makes it even better for both her and myself,' I thought. 'We knew each other. This is just lovely I wonder who she was back then. Maybe we only knew each other in passing. I would hate for him to be married to someone like my sister or best friend.'

"Who are you?" Clara asked, trying not to sound rude.

I looked at Shadowlark, who whispered something to the woman. She nodded, but the smile had faded from her face.

"Billy, Clara, this is Nellie," he told us. "She's my sister."

I smiled, suddenly feeling quite foolish to have panicked in such a way. "It's good to meet you," I told her. "I guess you already know who I am."

"Yes, I do," she nodded.

"As a matter of fact I'll bet that you know me better than I do."

She laughed. "I suppose that you can say that, but only in a manner of speaking. I only knew you a very long time ago."

"And I'm glad of that," I said. "Because I want someone to help me remember who I am, or at least to tell me who I was."

***

Me and Clara went to the tent with Nellie, while Shadowlark went to speak with the man named Firedrake. I had wanted to go with him, but he told me that it was best that I waited to meet him until the morning and I didn't protest. I wanted to get some sleep anyway. I'd had a very long day and as much as I didn't want him to leave me, I wanted to get some restful sleep, the kind of which I had not had in weeks. Yes, I had slept peacefully the one night on the

Empress, but I had not slept the whole night and that certainly did not make up for all the nights that I had not slept at all.

Marshall, as it turns out, was Nellie's son. The boy's father was gone to the north for battle training, but was said to be back in two days. Marshall was a very cute little boy. He was almost four and had fair skin, feathery, blond hair, with amber colored eyes that were slightly red right around the pupil. He had been asleep, but he woke up when all of us came inside.

"I caught a frog today," he told his mother as we came inside.

"I know," she smiled. "You showed him to me."

"Who are they?" He looked at us curiously.

"Marshall, this is Clara Honeycut and Billy Scarlet," she told him. "They are going to be staying with us for a little while."

"In the morning I can show you my frog," he told me.

"That's good," I smiled. "I look forward to seeing him."

"Okay, little man," Nellie laughed. "Time for you to get back to bed."

Nellie got Marshall back to bed then fixed me and Clara each a straw mat and a blanket. She was just about to blow out our lamp when Clara stopped her.

"Wait a minute," Clara whispered.

"What is it?" Nellie asked.

"I just want to know something," Clara said. "Is Grayheart really my father?"

Nellie closed her eyes and sighed. When she opened them again, she nodded. "Yes Clara, I'm afraid he is."

"Why didn't Shadowlark tell me then?" Clara asked.

"Because he doesn't know. He never did. Very few people did, because Grayheart wasn't married to your mother and he was a future king. He did help raise you, but he had to give you to a family that he knew would be able to take care of you. With all the wars that were breaking out, he wanted you to be safe. That was back when he was a good man and cared about people besides himself. Not even our parents knew that you had been born, Clara. He said that he felt that it would be selfish of him to keep you from the good kind of life that you should have. It's odd enough to think that in the end he did just what he never wanted to do," Nellie answered. "There's a lot that the two of you don't remember. You must understand that you've forgotten your entire lives and then started new ones."

"Do we have the same parents that we did before?" I asked.

"Yes," Nellie nodded. "I guess. Obviously you do because your name is Billy Scarlet and Grayheart is still Clara's father and I guess your mothers are still the same."

"Did I have a twin sister before?" I asked.

"No you didn't. At least not that any of us knew," she said. "That's odd."

"Do you mind us asking these questions?" I asked.

She smiled. "Not at all. I want to help and if there's anything you want to know, then ask me."

"Shadowlark said that he struck a deal with the realm rats," I said.

She just sat down next to my bed. "Yes he did and that was very hard for him."

"He also said that there was always a price to be paid when you're dealing with them."

"That's true," she nodded. "They love to cheat people, but Laquendor, their leader, tries not to let that happen very often, but no matter what, the prices are always steep."

"And what did Shadowlark pay?" I asked. "I know he said that the price was that we would come back in twelve years, but that doesn't seem like something that these people would do. There must have been more."

"The price for him was the same price that Grayheart paid for his immortality," she answered. "I just supposed that Laquendor figured that he had suffered enough by losing you in the first place that he wouldn't make the price so high that he would have to give anything else up. If there was any more to the deal then I have never heard of it."

I was heartbroken for Shadowlark. He had searched for me for thirty-two years and finally when he found me, I had not known who he was. "What did he do?"

"What could he do?" she shook her head. "He focused all of his strength on fighting Rossaletta's army, but soon even that proved to be no use. Grayheart was too powerful and though Shadowlark was a great leader our people had lost faith after they lost Nate. He still had his people to take care of. He told me that he may have failed you, but he wasn't going to fail his people. He tried as hard as he could, but he was hardly able to unite the people of our race, but he did get help from men and immortals. He fought for the greater part of thirty years, but he couldn't keep Rossaletta's forces at bay, so we laid low for a while, building our own strength. In ways this was a good thing, but it has proved to be more costly than we thought. In those times Rossaletta and Grayheart have become almost too powerful for us to handle. The war that we face now is far worse than any that we have faced yet."

"He didn't fail me," I said. "As far as I can tell, there was nothing he, or anyone could have done. Why did he think that?"

"I don't know. I tried to tell him that it wasn't his fault, but he blamed himself for years, even after it was said that you might would be back."

"Did anyone know when we came back?" I asked.

"Yes," she nodded. "I knew and your father knew."

"Shadowlark didn't?"

She shook her head. "He didn't. Not at first anyway."

"Why?" I asked. "If he had been through so much to find me and to bring me back?"

"It was a hard situation for all of us and no one even knew where you were. So it was a hard call. It would have been like searching for a needle in a haystack, looking for you in that world."

"So, who told him?" I asked.

"No one," she answered. "One day about ten years ago, he came to me and said that he had a feeling that you were back. He couldn't explain it, he just knew. By this point the wars had started back, but he would go to your world off and on to see if he could find you."

"Ten years ago?" Clara asked. "But you made it sound like you knew exactly when we came back and her father definitely would have. So how come neither of you told him?"

"I found out by accident," she sighed. "I have known William Scarlet since we were children and I had gone to see him, but when I got to his house I heard him speak of you being back. Neither of us had the heart to tell him what was going on. It would have torn him up even more to see the three of you, especially Billy, as children and to see how much all of you had changed. That you wouldn't know him after all that he had been through."

I nodded. I could understand the reasoning behind it, but that didn't make it any less painful. I wanted to change things, but there was no way for me to go back and do that.

"Well, you need to get some sleep. We'll talk some more in the morning." With that she blew out the lamp and went over to where her bed was.

I rolled over and pulled my covers around me tight. I wanted so badly to be back on the *Victory* with Davy and Apollo. The thought of either of them made me feel very homesick which wasn't a feeling that I was used to.

I stayed awake until Shadowlark came in. He slept on the far side of the tent. Before laying down he just sat there as if he was lost and confused. He put his face in his hands and sighed, helplessly. I wondered what Firedrake had told him. I wanted to go over to him and comfort him and to tell him that I had heard of all he had been through to find me, that I was here now and I would never leave him again and that none of what had happened was his fault, but something stopped me from doing so.

He laid back and stared at the ceiling for a long moment. He then looked in my direction. I knew it was too dark for him to see that I was awake, but I could feel his eyes on mine. I knew that he was thinking about all that we had talked to Nellie about, even though he had not been there while we had talked about it. Finally, he rolled over and pulled the covers over him, but I wasn't sure that he was sleeping.

For a long time, I just laid in my bed listening to the odd noises that were coming from the forest outside. Some of them I could tell were animals much like ones in my own world, but others sounded like banshees who were seeking to frighten any soul who dared enter the woods at night. I closed my eyes tight. There was something dark and sort of sinister about this world. It was a strange place filled with strange people, but weirdest thing about it was that just about everybody knew who I was and I didn't know any of them. Some of the names sounded familiar, but other than that I knew nothing about anything.

   ***

That next morning we woke up pretty early. We had a breakfast of biscuits and bacon.

Marshall came over to me holding a rather large frog. I had seem frogs before, never any that big. Its size was almost alarming. He was almost the size of a cat. "This is Mergy. I told you I'd show him to you."

"Mergy?" I asked, curious of the name. "He's a big boy, isn't he?"

He nodded then went over to tell Shadowlark about the frog.

"Mergy, is it?" Shadowlark nodded. "Why did you name him that?"

"Cause mama said that he was livin' in a mergy pond when I found him so I guess he's the Mergy of the pond."

"Ah," Shadowlark smiled. He held up a piece of bacon. "Do mergy's eat bacon?"

Marshall looked at him as if that was the most ridiculous thing that he had ever heard. "He's a mergy pond frog and mergy pond frogs eat mergy pond bugs. Bacon makes mergy frogs sick."

"Oh," Shadowlark nodded. "Forgive me. I'd hate to make him sick."

Just then Nellie saw what Marshall was doing. "Marshall, go wash your hands and put that frog away. You don't need to get him near the food. That's gross. You'll get everybody sick."

"Yes, ma'am," he nodded and went outside.

Shadowlark looked at me and smiled.

"It seems you have some experience with children and mergy frogs," I said.

"Children yes, mergy frogs, I've never heard of one, but obviously they can't eat bacon," he laughed.

Just then Gator came in.

"Firedrake wants to see Billy and Clara," he said.

"When?" Shadowlark asked.

"As soon as possible," Gator answered and walked out.

"Are you coming with us?" I asked Shadowlark.

"Yes," he nodded. "If you want me to."

"Yes," I nodded. "Please come."

"Okay." He stood up and beckoned us to follow him.

I sat my plate down, stood up, and the three of us headed outside. It was a nice brisk morning. Dew still hung on the leaves and grass. The camp did not seem so strange in the daylight. It actually seemed quite nice. With so many soldiers around I had expected it to be a war camp, but in the light of the morning I saw that it was more of a family camp, a place where they kept and protected the women and children.

Many of the tents had fires burning in front of them. Women tended the fires and cooked breakfast. Some of them had older children helping them while others had very young children and babies with them.

"Who is this man named Firedrake?" Clara asked. "Is he your brother?"

"No, he's an immortal prince," Shadowlark answered. "He's lady Jazzlyne's only brother and unlike a lot of the immortals, he sided with us. You see, I'm not always here to lead our people, so he helps me out. He's also a dragon tamer and he's been my friend for many years."

"Shadowlark?" Clara said. "Did you know that Grayheart is my father?"

"Back on the *Empress* was the first time I had heard of it," he answered.

"Last night Nellie told me that he really was," she told him. "I guess that would make you my uncle."

"I'd suppose so," he said. "If I had've known I would have told you sooner, but you must understand that I'm not sure of all of Grayheart's doings."

We walked in silence for a while. I wanted to talk to him about what Nellie had told me about him, but I knew that I shouldn't. We were back, so how we left and what he went through to get us back didn't matter so much anymore.

It was then that we arrived in front of a large greenish colored tent. It looked like it was made to blend into its surroundings. It also looked like it was made to be moved around very easily. Shadowlark was just about to open the tent flap when someone called to us from behind.

"Now that is a sight I have not seen in a long time. Too long as a matter of fact."

We turned around and saw a man. He had long, dark, curly hair, brown eyes, a beard that only grew right on his chin, and a mustache. He was a little bit taller than Shadowlark and he had a thin scar across his left cheek. All in all, he was a quite charming man and the scar just seemed to add to his charm.

"Good morning, Firedrake," Shadowlark said.

"Good morning," Firedrake nodded.

"Hello, sir," I smiled. "I'd guess that you know who I am. Everyone here seems to know that, whether I know them or not. Why did you call for us?"

"Well," he said. "I heard that you were back and even if you don't remember me, I had to see you. The thought of you being back is almost too good to be true."

My eyes were drawn to his right arm. He was wearing a sleeveless shirt so I couldn't help but notice that he had a very detailed tattoo of a dragon. It didn't look much like I would have guessed a dragon from this world would look like. Somehow, this dragon looked majestic. Its wings were spread as if it were flying and it had a different kind of look in its eyes. It didn't look angry or evil, but somehow very distant as if it were trying to remember something. I was sure that whoever the artist was that drew this picture was very skilled at their craft. It was the most detailed tattoo that I had ever seen. I wasn't sure, but I guessed that he had it because he was a dragon tamer.

"So you like my dragon?" he asked.

I blushed a little because I didn't think that he noticed me looking at it. "Is it because you're a dragon tamer?"

He nodded. "It's custom to get a tattoo to identify your occupation. I have a dragon; Shadowlark has a crossed sword and torch. I see that you have a tattoo as well, but I'm not sure what a naked mermaid means."

"It means we're sailors," Clara told him.

He just nodded and laughed a little. He then turned to Shadowlark and they started talking, but instead of listening to what they were saying, my attention was drawn to a torch that was still burning from the night before. The only thing that seemed unusual about it was the fact that the fire seemed to be trying to tell me something.

"Come on," it seemed to whisper. "Let's play."

Its giddy voice startled me a little, but all the same, it sparked a longing within me that felt strange yet very familiar.

One spark broke free of the rest of the torch and floated over to me. It went from a small spark, to a good sized flame. It danced around me and circled my arms like vines. I felt almost as if I was playing with an old friend that I had not seen in years. As it moved around me, its color changed from orange, to red, then blue and green. It was amazing. While it was doing its little dance, I heard music that was similar to what I heard when Shadowlark had first shown me how to speak to the wind. I watched it fly around. It then flared up really big and startled me. When I jumped back it shrunk back down to a mere spark as if I had offended it.

"I'm sorry," I whispered. "I didn't mean it," But it didn't listen. It floated back over to join the rest of the torch.

"Well, I see that fire is still your friend," Firedrake said.

"I didn't know that it ever was," I looked from Firedrake to Shadowlark to Clara. The three of them looked sort of confused. "What?" I asked.

"Oh nothing," Clara shrugged. "You just have a bird made of blue fire perched on your shoulder. You know no big deal."

I looked on my shoulder and sure enough there was a bird perched there. It looked like a blue jay, but it was roughly the size of a hawk. Pulses of color ran down its body causing it to change colors. It went from blue to green, then purple and orange. I reached out to it and it started to fly around. It winked then flew in a very tight circle, turned into a large butterfly that flew around slowly for a moment, and then flew back into the torch.

"How did that happen?" I asked.

"You spoke to it," Shadowlark told me. "It was one of the languages that you were born with. You see each of us has something like that it just happens to be fire that you were born knowing to speak to. You may not remember, but it was you, Billy Scarlet, who taught me to speak to fire."

"I don't understand," I said.

"You don't have to," Firedrake answered. "It's what you were born to do, so you do it whether you realize it or not." He looked over on the other side of the tent. "Oh yes, there's one more person here that would like to see you."

"Who?" I asked. "Will I remember this one?"

"I believe you will," he smiled. "Lord Scarlet!" Firedrake called and to my surprise, Billy Scarlet, my father, came over to us.

I went over and threw my arms around him. "What are you doing here?"

"Well, I may sail in your world, but when I want to rest for a while I come here, to my home land," He told me. "Though right now it doesn't seem like a very peaceful place. I was called here to help fight the war. As a lord, I've been appointed as general of the northern army."

"A lord?" I smiled.

"Well, I'm not here just to be anyone's shadow, now am I?" he laughed.

I laughed a little as well. "It's so good to see you."

"There's one person I want you to meet," he told me. "Well, you've already met him, but I want you to know who he is. Jase, come here."

Jase, the Spanish man from his crew, came over to us.

"Billy, this is Jase," he said. "And Jase is your brother. He was born in this world which is why he sounds Spanish, but either way, he's your brother."

I smiled, but I wasn't sure what to think. "Well," I said. "Maybe you'll like me better than my sister did."

"Sister?" Billy asked. "You have a sister?"

It was then that I remembered him telling me that he only had two children that he knew of and I realized that me must have meant me and Jase and that Gabriella must have never told him about Emmaline.

"A twin sister," I answered. "Actually."

"Oh." He looked at me for a moment, then shrugged. "What's done is done. I can't change anything now. All it means is that I have three children. Good heavens I hope that's all."

***

Later that day I was walking around by myself. I had to see more of this world that was supposed to be my own. I walked to a small stream and sat down next to it.

I watched some of the creatures. They were all somewhat similar to the ones in our world. A spider was sitting on a bush next to me weaving a web. Instead of looking like a normal spider, it looked more like a fairy with long arms and legs. The webs came out of its long slender fingers. It looked more like it was knitting than spinning a web.

I looked down at the water just in time to see a turtle come onto the shore. It startled me slightly to see that it had teeth, but it startled me even more when it took off flying the same way that a beetle would.

A bee was buzzing around a flower and watching me intently. It looked like any normal bee only slightly bigger. Just before it flew off it winked at me.

I sighed. So many things here seemed very friendly, but more things seemed dark and mean.

"I figured you would be here," came the unmistakable voice of Nate Grayheart.

I looked behind me and there he stood. Nate Grayheart. I stood up and reached for my sword, but I noticed he wasn't making a move to fight or even to argue. He had his shirt off and he looked like he must have been swimming. Water droplets streaked his muscled chest and back. He walked to the edge of the water and knelt down to get a drink of water from the stream. I watched him very carefully. I wasn't sure what he was planning to do, but I wasn't sure whether I should try to get away or stay with him. My first thought was to run, but I didn't know how many men he'd have waiting for me in the woods.

I stepped a little closer to him and he turned back around to face me. When he did, I was shocked and surprised to see the same tattoo on his chest that I had seen in my dream. It wasn't as bright as it had been in my dream, but it was the same one. The angel had its face turned upward and underneath it, in fine gold script was the word *Promise*.

He stood up and pulled his shirt on, but he did it slowly as if he wanted to make sure that I had seen the tattoo.

"What does that mean?" I asked.

"What does what mean?"

"Your tattoo," I said. "What does it mean?"

He stared at me for a long moment and he looked like he was fixing to answer when I heard the sound of a pistol being cocked behind me.

I turned around. Newheart stood holding a cocked pistol aimed at my head. A few more of their men were with him.

I didn't say a word I just stared straight into his eyes.

Newheart stepped closer to me so that the pistol would be right parallel with my forehead, but I didn't even flinch. "Go ahead," he smiled. "Call for help."

I just gave him a mocking smile. "You'd like that wouldn't you?"

His expression turned grim, but I stood my ground.

"You can kill me if you like, but I will not call for anyone," I told him.

Grayheart walked over, snatched the pistol from Newheart, and scoffed. "I don't know why I even keep you around." He then turned to me. "I don't believe you know what I'm capable of, Billy."

"Is that the only threat you can come up with?" I asked. "So far it seems that you have no actions to back up your words."

"Don't taunt me, Billy," he huffed. "You may find out what I can do sooner than you ever wished."

"I don't give a damn what you can or can't do," I told him. "And I'm not afraid of you either."

"Very well," he said and hit me in the back of the head.

Just before everything got dark I called to Shadowlark through the wind. "Grayheart's got me. Don't come...... yet."

***

When I awoke, I was lying in a court yard that was paved with black stones. There were large columns with torches burning on them, because night had already fallen. I sat up and saw that there was a fountain in the middle of the court yard. Grayheart was sitting on the edge of the fountain. I stood up and started to walk toward him.

The way that the torch light shone on his face made him look very young and innocent and almost childlike. He truly was the most handsome man that I had ever seen.

I stopped just before I got to him.

"Come closer, Sabilla," he said so quietly that I could hardly hear him. "I have something to tell you."

I walked over and sat down next to him.

"Good girl," he smiled in a way that made me glad to know that I had a knife in each of my boots.

"What do you want?" I asked.

"I have two things to tell you," he said.

"And what is that?" I asked.

"First I will tell you of your past, then of your future. By now, I'm sure that you've been told of who you are, but I know that there are a few things that have been left out, because you have been told of all of this by people that don't know the whole story."

"What are you talking about?" I asked.

"I'm sure that Shadowlark hasn't told you of your connection to me." He stroked the water as if it was a living thing, which made me even more cautious. "You see, back many years ago I was good friends with your father. We fought together many times and when I saved his life for the first time, he promised me your hand in marriage. You were sort of young at the time, but you had no objections. At the time I was on my way to becoming something that our people would call great. It was then that I met Rossaletta. She opened my eyes to all the faults of our people. At first I didn't believe her. I was as ignorant and foolish as my brother. Soon I realized that you were too far out of my reach and I had nothing left with our people. I joined Rossaletta and became the head of her army. Shadowlark was then appointed ruler of our people and you and him fell in love. My heart was shattered and Rossaletta was the only one that I could turn to. She loved me more than you ever did," His face was very close to mine at this point and I wasn't sure why he was doing this. "You broke my heart," he whispered. "After you told me that you would follow me to the ends of the earth."

"And what do you think my reasons were, Grayheart?" I asked, my voice as cold as possible. I had very little sympathy for this man.

He sighed and leaned back on his elbows. "I suppose the answer is in the question then," He gave me a relaxed look of annoyance.

"And what of my future?"

He motioned to the water. "See for yourself."

I looked in the water and saw a lady in a crimson dress, on the back of a dragon. The wind blew hard across her. As the scenery moved I saw that she was leading a large army; an army of thousands. I wasn't sure how big Shadowlark's army was, but I was sure that this was the largest concentration of men that I had ever seen in one place at one time.

"My army is already on the move," he said. "They'll be to your friends before daybreak."

"Shadowlark," I said to the wind. "His army is coming," I hoped that he could hear me and Grayheart would not.

I stood up and glared at Grayheart. "I don't care who I was before or why you hate your brother. You are a horrible man. Rossaletta has corrupted you and you don't even see it."

He stood up and slapped me so hard that I fell flat on my back.

"At least you knew the fate of your friends, but all I can see of your future is death." He put his foot on my throat. "Now it's time for you to go away and stay gone."

I gasped for air and punched his ankle.

He smiled. "That's right, scream. No one's going to hear you."

I reached into my boot, pulled out my knife and buried the blade as deep as it would go, in his ankle. He screamed and stumbled backward.

I got to my feet and held my knife at the ready.

The sight of him in pain sent a picture to my mind. It was of me and him in a battle. He was on the ground wounded and I fought to save his life. I shook my head to get the picture out of my mind.

He came at me, but I rolled out of the way.

"What does your tattoo mean?" I wasn't sure why I asked it. The words just seemed to come out without me thinking.

I could tell that he had not expected me to ask such a question. "It's something that is no longer a part a me, Sabilla." He pulled his sword and swung it at me.

I dodged his blow and the sword hit the side of the fountain.

"It's still there and it is as much a part of you as anything else."

I noticed that my sword was sitting on the edge of the fountain. I grabbed and swung it upward just in time to block a hard blow from Grayheart. He took out a dagger and held it in his left hand, then took on a stance that I had never seen anyone use in a sword fight before. He held the dagger in a way that almost looked backward and he stood in a way that looked like he would pounce at any moment.

I held my sword at the ready, but I knew that when he decided to strike I would not be ready for it. I had no idea what he was going to do or when he was going to do it. All I knew was the minute I put my guard down he was going to strike.

He then leapt at me, swinging his sword at such a speed that almost killed me just to keep up. He was twirling the dagger in a clockwise motion which would not have been hard to deal with had he not been using a sword as well. I could not block both of them at the same time. He locked his sword onto mine and spun it around in circles until I could no longer hold onto it. My hands slipped from my sword and he knocked it away. I heard it hit on the paving stones a few feet away, but I didn't dare look to see where it had landed.

He backed me against the fountain and was fixing to deliver the death blow. I quickly rolled out of the way and called the fire from the torches to stand between me and him and there was a wall of fire formed.

I stood there for a moment trying to catch my breath. While we stared at each other through the fire, for a brief moment his face showed the same innocence as it had when he was sitting alone on the fountain.

He took a step toward me and the fire flared up.

"Go ahead and do it. I dare you," I said, just above a whisper. "I suppose that our lives were a small price to pay for your immortality. Though, I still don't see how Davy fits into all of this. Our lives were small and insignificant, but what about yours? Did you know that you would be trading Nathaniel Grayman for Nate Grayheart or were you already Grayheart by then? Your immortality is a curse. Who's turned you into such a monster?" In my life as a sailor, I had killed men before, but even hurting Nate Grayheart made me feel a sharp pain, like a hot knife in my heart and I didn't know why. "Why did you let Rossaletta do this to you? How could you have let all of this happen? Do you have no feeling at all?"

He pulled out his pistol, pointed it at me, and cocked it. "That's not who I am anymore."

I let the fire wall down and walked over to him.

"Go ahead and shoot," I told him and put my knife away. "At least I know that God will tell me the rest of the story when I see him."

He had a white knuckle grip on the gun, but instead of shooting, he just stood there. His hand began shaking. I knew he wanted to shoot me, but something was keeping him from doing it. He started to lower the pistol.

Suddenly, there came the sound of beating wings. I looked up and saw a large lizard looking creature. It was gray and it had a rounded off nose. It swooped down and caught me with its feet, then took back to the sky.

I had a feeling that it was some sort of dragon and I hoped that it was one of Firedrake's tame ones and not some mother dragon that was taking me away to feed me to her hungry children. That would have just been a terrible end to a horrible day.

As we flew, I grew angry with myself. I could have kicked myself for acting the way I had and not fighting Grayheart harder than I did. I felt very strange inside when I thought of how I felt when I hurt him. Then something else came to my mind. Why had I asked what his tattoo meant? There was also one more thing to question. Why had he not shot me when he had the chance? I didn't know what it was, but something had stopped him from pulling that trigger.

I tried to push all of those thoughts from my mind and concentrate on what we would do when Grayheart's men attacked. I hoped that Shadowlark had gotten both of the messages that I had sent him on the wind. If he had not, things were going to be chaotic in a few minutes.

The dragon began to slow down and I could see the camp in the distance. The creature landed and gently set me down. Firedrake and Shadowlark were standing there waiting to meet me.

"Are you all right?" Shadowlark asked.

"I'm fine," I nodded. "Thank you, Firedrake, for sending your dragon to get me."

"That's not a dragon, Billy," he told me. "That's a simple lizard."

"Well, thank you anyway," I said.

"You're welcome." he nodded. It was then that someone called him and he walked away.

I hugged Shadowlark really tight.

"What all did he tell you?" He gently put his arms around me.

"He said that you wouldn't know any of it," I told him. "He said that I was supposed to get married to him back then."

"That part I did know," he answered.

"Why didn't you tell me?" I asked.

"I was going to," he said. "I didn't think that he was going to get the chance first. The two of you had broken off the engagement a year before I even met you."

I nodded and stepped back from him. "I couldn't fight him. Not straight up."

"Don't feel bad about that," he told me. "Very few can. I probably don't have to tell you that he is a very complex kind of fighter. Don't worry, if the time comes that you have to fight him you will find your strength. He obviously couldn't find the strength to fight you either otherwise you probably wouldn't be here."

I smiled and looked at his full set of armor. "I have to get ready for the battle. They'll be here before morning."

"You don't have to fight," he told me.

"Yes I do," I nodded. "I'd feel left out if I didn't."

Chapter

Eleven

I stood in one of the tents, getting on all of my armor. Clara had gotten hers on before I had gotten back, so I was alone, but I didn't mind. I had so much on my mind that it would not do for me to be around other people. I put on the thick mail shirt and the breast and back plate.

Just as I got my sword strapped on, I heard someone behind me. I turned around to see who it was and found myself staring into the dark green eyes of Domonic O'Reilly. He was standing too close for comfort, but not for long. He grabbed a helmet that was sitting on a box that was right next to me, then he stepped back.

"Hello, Mr. O'Reilly," I said.

"Hello, Scarlet," he smiled. "I thought I'd find ya here. You seemed like the kind o' girl that would fight in a battle whether she was allowed to er not." He paused. "So, been in any drinkin' games as of late?"

"No, I haven't, thank you very much," I laughed. "Have you?"

"None since you darlin'," he shook his head. "None since you."

"So you're fighting too?" I asked.

"Yes, I am, Scarlet," he nodded. "We all are, an' I don't expect fer things ta look good fer us. Far as I hear the enemy 'as an army of one thousand, at most we have five hundred, but that does not determine the outcome of such things I don't suppose."

Just then someone called him.

"Well, I'll be seeing you, Scarlet." With that he left and once again, I was alone.

I sat down on a crate and put my face in my hands. I was scared. I was not very close with Domonic, but just to hear him say 'I'll be seeing you' made me want to cry. I hoped that I would see him again. I didn't want to be in a war, but if I was to stay behind and some of my friends were to get hurt I would blame myself forever. So, the truth was that I was more afraid for my friends than I was for myself. I felt one small tear fall down my cheek. It always felt very strange to cry. I also wondered why water came out of people's eyes when they were sad. One tear was all that I let fall. It ran down my cheek and I watched it hit the ground in front of me.

"Billy," I heard Shadowlark's voice. "Are you okay?"

I stood up and looked at him. "I'm fine," I lied, but I knew if I had told him that I was truly terrified out of my wits then he would have made me stay behind even though everyone else that was going to be fighting was scared as well.

"Are you ready?" he asked.

"Not yet," I took off my medallion and put it on him.

"I can't take this," he whispered.

I put my finger over his lips. "I need you to have this. I need to know that if something was to happen to me that at least you would have something more than memories of me. I don't want to leave you all alone again."

He didn't say anything. He just nodded.

"There's one more thing." Before he could say anything, I kissed him. I kissed him in a way that I had never kissed any other man. It was then that I realized that I loved him more than I ever thought I could love anyone.

266

"I love you, Billy," he whispered.

"I'll never stop loving you." I laughed a little at the way it sounded to say that, but it was more than true.

We stood there for a long moment in each other's arms. I did not want to let go. I wanted to hold onto him forever and let him know that he would never lose me again.

"I..." Before he could say anything else there was a loud horn blast. "It's time," he whispered.

I went and got my helmet and the two of us went outside. All of the men were mounting their horses. I took my mount so that Shadowlark and Clara were on my right and Billy and Jase were on my left.

Firedrake rode out in front of us. "We're going to meet them in the valley of Armandere. We have close to five hundred men and I don't really have to tell all of you that they have more. No matter what the outcome, we will be victorious. Now we ride to what may be our last battle. May God help us," With that, we headed to the battle field.

"You're really good with morale aren't you Firedrake?" Shadowlark laughed a little.

"I'll let you do the big speech then," Firedrake said.

The rest of the ride was silent except for the sounds of armor clanking together and hooves hitting the ground.

The valley of Armandere was a very gloomy place. It may have been more pleasant in the day time, but that night, I had never seen such a dreadful and empty place in all my life. There was the hill that we were on and the hill that Grayheart's men were on and the valley below. The only thing besides that was ground and sky. A cold and bleak wind blew across us. It chilled me all the way to the bone. It was as if all the battles that had been fought here, were still lingering, refusing to be forgotten.

Grayheart's men were assembled in ranks, across from us. They had a lot of torches lit, making it impossible to tell how many of them there was. All that we could see was light reflecting off their armor. I could tell that they had done this on purpose, just to see if we would get nervous and back down.

The torch light then illuminated something else that was hovering above the men. There, with his scales reflecting the torch light was the dragon that Mr. McHale had written about in his book. It had blue, green, red and gray scales. It had wings that looked as thin as canvas, and feet that were like the talons of a hawk. Its fiery eyes scanned the crowds of men before him, in anticipation of the coming battle. It was an amazing, yet terrifying creature. It was nothing like Firedrake's dragon tattoo. This dragon's gaze was set and very focused. It was horrible. It was Morogol. I said a silent prayer for strength to be able to fight this creature. I took a deep breath and I knew that I would be alright.

Shadowlark rode out in front of us. "Men do not waver," he said. "They may have dragons and they may have more men, but we have God on our side and that means we have a power that is much greater than theirs. We have a reason to fight. We fight for our families and our people, but what is their reason? They fight for their own hate and greed. They're for hate and we're for love. They think they are much more powerful than us, but I don't think that there's a man here that believes that. Do you think that their hatred for you can destroy your love for someone else? I don't think so. Power does not come in numbers my friends. Power comes in your will to beat them. Power comes from your ability to keep moving forward. Power comes from what you are given by your Creator. Now men, are you ready?"

Only a few men yelled.

"Gentlemen," he said. "Are you ready to go fight for everything that you believe in?!"

That was met with a thunderous battle cry.

Grayheart's men began to charge, as did we. The thundering of hooves made the earth beneath us shake. The sound of the battle cries from either side hung in the air like a thick heavy mist. The two armies got closer and closer until they finally met at the bottom of the valley. The sounds of metal on metal and cries of pain filled the air. The world around me moved so fast that it was hard to tell what was going on. I just struck at anyone who struck at me.

Morogol flew around above swooping down like a hawk on its prey. His wings caused a stir that was more or less a gale force wind. His screeching cry was enough to scare the wits out of a strong man.

It wasn't long before I was separated from any of my own people. I fought as hard as I could. My hands soon began to shake and my breathing grew ragged. All I saw in this battle was death and for what, I did not know. Power, maybe, but whatever the reason I found that war was pointless, but I couldn't stop fighting or I would die as would everyone that I loved.

I looked over to where Shadowlark was. He was fighting against Newheart. Newheart leapt through the air to kick him, but Shadowlark was faster and kicked him across the side of his face. Newheart rolled and got back to his feet just in time for Morogol to fly over. Rossaletta looked down at the two men. Newheart looked up at her. There was an odd look in his eyes. The glance that the two of them exchanged was something that I had not expected. She had ordered him to kill Shadowlark, I could have guessed that much, and Newheart felt such a need to please her that it made him seem desperate and scared, but there was more to it. There was something in the way that they looked at each other that was odd in a way that I could not quite put my finger on.

While Newheart was looking away, Shadowlark swung his sword and hit him across the side of the face with the flat of it. This sent him to the ground.

A look of anger that mingled with fear crossed Rossaletta's face. She quickly pulled Morogol hard to the right. I had expected her to go after Shadowlark, but instead, she came after me.

Everyone cleared out from around me as the dragon came closer. He landed on the ground right in front of me causing a small earth quake in the process. My horse shied and threw me off. I rolled over and got back to my feet, but by then the horse was already long gone. I guessed it was a good thing though. Morogol would only have killed it had it stayed.

'Elizabeth would never have done that to me,' I thought, but deep inside, I was glad that Elizabeth was not with me at the time and I hoped that wherever she was that she was safe.

I looked back behind me in hopes that someone was coming to my aid, but all I saw was the battle. Everyone was fighting everyone else and no one wanted to deal with a dragon.

I felt hot breath on my back. I knew the dragon was still there. It was like a nightmare that I could not wake up from no matter how hard I tried. I turned around and faced Morogol who stood there, towering above me. He was at least fifteen feet of armored beast, with one thing in mind.

"Kill her Morogol," she said to the dragon. "Slowly."

"You will not defeat me, you vile beast," the words were directed at both Rossaletta and Morogol.

Morogol drew back and blew fire at me. I rolled out of the way just in time to keep from getting roasted. I felt the heat from the flames as they passed me and left and charred streak on the ground. He blew fire again, but this time I stopped it.

"I may not be so good at this and you may not know me well, but you will listen," I spoke to the fire. I then threw it back at them. The look of surprise on their faces was enough to make me want to laugh.

I held my sword at the ready and looked her straight in the eye. "Why don't you get down and fight me like you're brave you mad ass, bitch."

She laughed. "You were always the one to start trouble. Trust me you don't want me to come down there. You would be dead in seconds."

"I don't think so," I said.

Morogol swung at me, trying to slash me with his claws. I ducked out of the way and swung my sword at him, catching him across the bottom of his foot. He screeched with pain and flew up out of my reach.

"God keep me strong," I whispered.

I stood there waiting for him to fly back down. I was in a bit of a clearing in the battle no one else really seemed to want to come near the dragon any more now than they had when he had first come over to me, and I could not blame them. I really didn't want to be near him either; it just seemed that I had no say in the matter.

Suddenly, I heard a really loud crashing noise and looked up. Billy and Jase were not too far off from me, fighting back to back. I hadn't seen where their horses had gone, but the crashing sound was them, with the help of a few others, knocking over some form of war machine.

When I turned back to face Rossaletta, something from the fallen machine flew up and hit me, knocking me to the ground. Morogol then swooped down and tried once again to catch his claws in my back, but Clara came out of nowhere and hit him across the side of his face with her sword. The sword shattered like glass, but Morogol screeched and flew back out of her reach.

Shadowlark came over and helped me up. I saw that my father had also come to my aid and I could not have been more thankful or happy to see any one of them.

The dragon stopped and seemed to ask Rossaletta something.

"No Morogol," she purred. "I want to have a little bit of fun with them first. After I'm done, you can have them." She then turned to us. "Look at this. A king, a pirate, and two vagabond girls, it's funny how at this moment I hold the fate of all of them in my hands."

"You can't win, Rossaletta," Billy said. "In the end, you know that you'll lose."

"Oh really?" she smiled.

"How could you do what you've done to Grayheart?" I asked. "Why him? Why can't you just leave him alone?"

"Why should I do that?" she asked mockingly. "I could never give up my greatest masterpiece until his time is up."

"Quit it with your games," Shadowlark huffed. "If you're going to fight, then fight, but it's like Billy said, you won't win and you know it."

"One thing I've learned about life is that only few things are certain," she laughed. "And one of those things is that when I fight, I win. Now as for you two." She turned to me and Clara. "You really need to learn your place, but I have no time for that now. It's time for you to go."

Suddenly, the world around me began to fade.

"Billy! Clara!" The names were yelled by, both my father and Shadowlark, but I could hardly hear them. It was as if they were calling me from far away.

I couldn't make a sound. I couldn't do anything. It seemed that all my focus was pulled to where Newheart was, getting back to his feet. He pulled a gun from his belt, cocked it, and aimed it right at Shadowlark's head.

"No!" I screamed.

Shadowlark looked back. I heard a loud gun shot, then the world was gone and all was dark.

Chapter

Twelve

At first I thought I was dead. I felt like I had when I had been thrown off the *Empress* and was floating through the void. I tried to open my eyes, but I saw nothing but darkness. Had I gone blind? I took a deep breath, then I began to come around. I felt sunlight on my skin. The wind blew across my face and I smelled the salt air. It was a welcome smell. I could hear the sound of wind blowing through ship's riggings. It was something I had not heard in quite a while and despite the fact that I liked the sound and had been longing to hear it for quite some time, it was somewhat alarming.

"I really must be dead," I thought. "She really killed me this time. I hope all the others are okay. Maybe they'll win the battle."

"Billy?" came a voice that I had not heard in what seemed like ages, nor did I expect to hear it in this situation. I had been so sure that I was dead, but it seemed that I may have been greatly mistaken in the matter. "Clara?"

I opened my eyes and found myself staring into the dark, yet familiar eyes of one seaman Davy Mitchems.

"Davy?" I could hardly believe what I was seeing.

"Yes, it's me." He helped us up.

I looked around and realized that I wasn't dead, but instead I was on the deck of my old home, the *H.M.S. Victory.*

Apollo walked over to us and smiled. "Well, Miss Scarlet," he said. "I guess my grandfather was right about you."